The Adventures of
Team Murphy

The Adventures of
Team Murphy

Carol Doose

THE ADVENTURES OF TEAM MURPHY

iUniverse books may be ordered through booksellers or by contacting:

iUniverse
1663 Liberty Drive
Bloomington, IN 47403
www.iuniverse.com
844-349-9409

ISBN: 978-1-6632-4094-1 (sc)
ISBN: 978-1-6632-4095-8 (e)

Library of Congress Control Number: 2022910648

Print information available on the last page.

iUniverse rev. date: 06/02/2022

Contents

Book Five: Inspiration Day Celebration

Book Six: Camping at Rainbow Falls

Book Seven: Growing Up Sasquatch

Book Eight: In the Game

Acknowledgments

Like many other authors, I have to give my supportive family my gratitude for helping me through this process of bringing my ideas to print. They were not only my inspiration but often were the raw materials I built upon.

BOOK ONE

The Magician's Cape

Chapter 1

Growing Bored

Off the eastern shore of the continent of Bodenia, there lies an island called St. Delus. Asterville is one of the many nurturing villages on this little-known island and the place called home for Ardan and Isabel, along with their parents Mitch and Angela Murphy.

The twins will soon be turning five and are looking forward to attending kindergarten in the fall. Until then, they have this painfully long, very painfully long, summer ahead. How can they fill so much time with interesting activities?

Since they had outgrown naps, Mother, in her desire to help, was spending afternoons *playing school* with them. This was also her way of transitioning the twins to the structure that would be expected of them as students in the fall—"structure" being the operative word here for her overactive duet. The twins lived for excitement. Mother knew settling down would be difficult for them.

As luck would have it, Isabel and Ardan were naturals in this academic adventure. They loved the mind-searching activities hidden within the pages of ordinary books and, as imaginative youngsters, they found this fed into their investigative minds perfectly.

However, this was morning, and Mother was busy with her household chores. What could they do to fill the monotonous hours ahead on this warm, sunny day?

The real bummer handicapping their energetic nature was that Mother made them stay in their own yard to play. Why, pray tell? Had she forgotten what it was like to be four—*almost five*? They were sure the real

1

adventure was just on the other side of that picket fence. Confinement to the rambunctious pair had become more problematic with each succeeding day. Maybe actually turning five would earn them the freedom to explore the ever-beckoning call of the world beyond that white-washed barrier of entrapment.

By now, they'd overused and abused their swings and slide. They'd built every style of castle and object imaginable in the sandbox. Not a toad or squirrel lived within these boundaries that didn't boast its very own name—especially little Snickerdoodle, the newly born bunny to Dippsydoodle and Wackydoodle.

The whole quirky rabbit family was a little off center of gravity. Even within their own wacked-up world, they were unusual. From day one, Snickerdoodle decided it was his job—no it was his birthright—to entertain the twins. Should he poke his head out or not? Yes—no? Ooopsy daisy. No, no … no, no-*no*. His first venture out of the nest left him tumbling head over heels into the enchanted fairyland the twins had spent countless hours erecting for their miniature friends—friends who were so tiny, they were invisible to the naked eye. But not to the twins.

The magical nymphs allowed the children into their world of mystical activities. These immortal deities sensed that Isabel and Ardan had the ability to understand the scope of life that existed outside the range of what might be called "normal" to most people. The children's belief was unshakable as to their reality. After all, they'd been interacting with these delicate, winged fairies on a regular basis. The procedure used in communicating with them was all through thought transference. Eventually, the twins would learn that this was a rare process very few humans possessed. Maybe no one else could do it; at least the youngsters had not found it to be so. Perhaps they would learn more about this ability once they were in school. That was their hope anyway.

The tiny fairies understood Snickerdoodle's lack of coordination even to the point of enjoying his antics—destructive as they were. The twins attitude was that they'd built the fairyland once; they would simply rebuild it. This time, they'd add extra features to afford their friends new experiences. The pint-sized creatures enjoyed a lifestyle of uncomplicated activity. Their innate ability to sense danger had kept them safe and undisturbed for untold centuries.

Despite the absurd boundary restrictions, the bored twins were determined to make the most of this, their last summer as *children*. Most of their whole lives had been spent in this very yard, and they knew every dull, monotonous inch of it. Oh, how they wished that something new and exciting would come their way.

"What shall we do today?" Ardan asked Isabel. She was the "go-to" partner in the duo. Ardan could usually count on her for a new, brilliant idea.

Sitting on the porch step, Isabel searched the depths of her innermost imagination. "We've done it all, Ardan. I do not think there is anything new for us to do—ever! Nothing new ever!" she exclaimed in sheer desperation. Pacing to and fro she announced, "I have *brain freeze!*"

"Impossible, *Lizzy.*" By using the nickname she detested the most, Ardan was hoping to jolt her enterprising brain into action. "Come up with an idea, any idea. You never fail us. Think, Izzy. Think. I'm begging you."

"Not working, *little brother*," she mocked him back. She was, after all, a whole eight minutes older, a point of which she took every advantage. "I'm in serious crises! My brain is *dead.*" Isabel drew her wrist to her forehead and crumpled to the ground for emphasis. "*Dead!*"

Chapter 2

A Welcome Gift

As luck would have it, their father brought home an oddly shaped box that very night. It wasn't outlandishly huge you understand, but big enough to be intriguing. Father, who owned a hardware/general store with Grandpa Murphy, had been given the carton from their favorite traveling salesman, Hank Henderson.

"Uncle Hank stopped in today on his monthly routine and brought in this very interesting package," Father said as he placed the box on the floor in the living room.

Hank was from the mainland of Bodenia and took supply orders from the Murphys to restock the hardware store. More importantly, he keeps the Murphys abreast of the latest trends available in the marketplace. Over the years, Hank had become a welcome guest in the Murphy household, partaking in many family dinners. A man in his early forties with a wife and four children of his own, Hank was the life of the party, entertaining everyone with his many true-to-life tales of happenings in his travels. Maybe it was a trait all salesmen had—this ability to engage others. "Uncle" Hank (not by actual relationship) had known the twins from their birth and had been acutely attuned to their unique personalities. Because of this opportunity of watching the precocious duo grow, Hank believed the twins would find the contents of this particular box more than a little interesting.

"Hank said he thought of you kids immediately when he came across this box in an antique store in Bodenia," Father said as he mysteriously related the "find" to Ardan and Isabel. "He was sorry he couldn't give it to you himself, but he was on a tight schedule and will visit with you at a later time. Meanwhile, he hopes you'll enjoy it."

Mitch and Angela laughed as their children shook the boxes' contents. The twins each took turns trying to figure out what might be inside. Guessing what might be in a gift was something the twins enjoyed doing, especially at Christmas when packages were so beautifully wrapped and decorated—packages that had just been lying there … under the tree … for such a long time. Unopened gifts were a brain-teasing exercise of sheer torture.

"Sounds like pieces of Grandpa's old mustache cup mixed up with Granny's wig." Ardan giggled thinking of Grandpa's *crumb duster*.

"Are you kidding me?" Isabel chimed in. "Be serious. Sounds more like an ancient Peruvian rain stick or maybe the shrunken head of a pygmy Indian."

"*What?* Where did that come from? You be serious, Bubblehead," Ardan said with amusement. He couldn't help but marvel at his sister's resourceful imagination. Where did she come up with this stuff? She was smart to the point of being dumb about it. She knew so much that it just tumbled out at the strangest of times.

"Be careful," Father warned. "I don't know that some of the items might possibly be breakable. You can open the box right after supper. Now, go wash your hands and come into the dining room. Mother's serving her famous lasagna tonight."

After supper? Are you kidding? Giving each other a disappointed look, the twins dutifully scuffled off.

Dinner dragged on. It seemed to the children that Mother and Father were drawing out the family meal on purpose. They talked about the weather, the neighbor, whether or not they should get a new refrigerator. Would, could parents be so devious as to keep their dearest and only children in this state of deep suspense?

Ardan kicked Isabel under the table, trying to get her attention. What could they do to bring this whole meal thing to an end? When Isabel gave him "the look," he darted his eyes back and forth between their parents. She took the hint. As twins, they could almost read each other's minds. This ability was becoming an art form, and they were not beneath perfecting it. In fact, they were learning there were certain advantages to their mind coordination—advantages that would come in handy over the years through their many exploits.

Isabel stretched her arms out full length and then drew them in for an exaggerated tummy rub. "Guess I must have eaten too much. I am totally stuffed! That was a really, really great supper, Mom. Best ever! You outdid yourself. Yes, sir, a really great meal!"

A little schmoozing could go a long way. And hopefully, it would end this boring supper talk. Looking at Ardan's expression, Isabel had to struggle to contain the smile that begged across her lips. She wiped her face with her napkin to disguise this blatant pandering of their mother's cooking. She hoped one of her giggle fits wouldn't happen. They often consumed her at the most inappropriate times.

Ardan, on the other hand, was far more obvious, nearly falling out of his chair as he fought to stifle a laugh. Isabel was great, he had to admit.

Father caught on to their less-than-subtle attempt at getting to the mysterious box in the living room. The box had been like a magnet pulling at the twins throughout the entire meal. With an understanding smile, he said, "All right young'uns, bring your plates to the kitchen while Mother and I clear the rest of the supper dishes."

With the elongated supper over (no matter how tasty it truly was), Father put the box back in the middle of the living room floor. Carefully, the twins opened the first flap of the package and then another and started pulling out the contents one by one. There was a deck of cards, coins, a scarf. This was not living up to what they were expecting. In fact, it was utterly disappointing—hardly worthy of good old Uncle Hank. They already had all this stuff. But, they were not ones to give up too easily, and something is better than nothing at all. Right?

Ah, what's this? A wand, a magician's cape with secret pockets, and a black top hat with a false bottom. Now this had promise. The children's faces went from mild interest to high excitement in one single heartbeat. With renewed gusto, they dove into the cardboard container.

"*Wow*! This is cool!" Ardan said while donning the newly acquired articles. The hat was a little big, as well as the cape, but that simply made it more dramatic. He whipped the cape over his face in a fake Dracula pose.

Best of all, buried in the very bottom of the carton, almost completely hidden, was a book of magic tricks and mysterious spells. "Ardan, look at this! This has to be absolutely ancient," Isabel declared flamboyantly as she exhibited her discovery. Uncle Hank had come through after all.

Without hesitation, both Isabel and Ardan opened the book. They could hardly control their excitement as this newly found opportunity virtually opened up before them. The chance to explore the unknown was now at their fingertips. Imagine the possibilities of a real magic spell.

The amused twins exchanged quizzical looks between themselves as they turned the yellowed pages of the leather-bound *Masterpiece of Mystical Powers*. Page one showed secrets of making items disappear. A few pages later, you could learn about doubling, even quadrupling objects. Learning how to read minds (or at least give the appearance of it) was just a partnership between magician and assistant.

All too soon, the bewitching hour of bedtime rolled around. Mitch and Angela gave their children warm hugs before sending them up to bed. "We'll be up in a minute to tuck you in," Father said. "I found a great story about Houdini to read to you tonight. I think you'll like it."

The children put everything back into the box and took it to their playroom upstairs.

The twins had the whole upper level of the house. They each had a bedroom at opposite ends of the floor. In the middle, they shared a large activity center / playroom /(and currently) mock classroom. Isabel and Ardan were fortunate to have parents who introduced them to a wide variety of subjects. Unwittingly, this also fed into the twins' overactive imaginations. They could conjure up the most outlandish ideas. What if? Could this happen? Maybe if not this, then that. But how? Life was an endless bank of possibilities. No more brain freeze for the Murphy twins. No, sir! Life had suddenly taken on a new perspective.

Ardan and Isabel found it hard to tuck away the box that held so much wonderment. But it had to be. Mother and Father were strict about bedtime, especially since they no longer took naps. Still, sleep did not always come easily to active minds that simply could not rest on command.

After story time on their comfy, worn-out couch, Mother and Father wished their overly inspired youngsters a good night. "Love you and like you," Father finished with the family salutation that was carried over from Grandpa's mother. She always wanted her children to know that, along with her unconditional love, she truly liked them. She liked the people they had become and was proud of them in the way they chose to live their lives. It wasn't that she didn't recognize their shortcomings, but that was a part of growing up and making the right choices.

"Where are we to begin?" Isabel asked Ardan while she twirled about in a fairylike fashion. "There is almost too, too much crammed into that one tiny, little box!"

There she goes again, Ardan thought. Isabel certainly had a flare for the dramatic. "We'll sort it out tomorrow, Mini-mite." He smiled as he tipped his new hat and bowed in an extravagant gesture of his own. "Good night, fair damsel."

At what had become a ritual, Ardan soaked in the vastness of the sky while he closed his curtains for the night. The sky and its occupants had intrigued Ardan for as long as he could remember, even in his very short life. The universe seemed to hold so much unexplained mystery.

As Ardan turned, he could have sworn the stars were twinkling in a mischievous way. *It's my imagination*, he thought, *too much excitement.*

Long after story time, Ardan finally fell into a deep and blissful sleep.

Chapter 3

Practicing for the Show

The next day, the Murphy twins worked as a team. How do you turn one coin into two, or three even? Can the secret pocket in the cape store the extra coins? How does the hat work? And just how do you use a spell?

Because they were just learning to read simple words, the versatile youngsters drew upon the well-illustrated tricks to aid their discovery into this new world of "prestidigitation" (magic). Occasionally, they had to ask their mother or father to read a portion of the text to them, but they kept that to a minimum so as not to give away too much of the surprise when they put on a magic show that was already forming in their minds.

This odd little box kept Isabel and Ardan busy the rest of the summer. They worked on developing tricks to perform for their family. The twins had already targeted Grandpa to become an audience participant. He always enjoyed interaction with the twins. In fact, he could be downright silly at times, getting down on his hands and knees, acting like a third child. For a sixty-six-year-old, Grandpa had an energy level that was envied by his peers. He still worked every day in the family hardware store and enjoyed networking with the large variety of customers who often came in just to "shoot the breeze."

And they would use Uncle Hank (since he'd found the treasure to begin with) as witness to their magically turning the coin under one cup into three under a totally different one.

Ardan would be the designated magician, with Isabel as his proficient assistant. Her job was to distract the audience with grandiose gestures as she pranced about. All the while, Ardan would be pulling off a switcheroo with the props—resulting in jaw-dropping stunts. At least that was the expected result.

They needed a grand finale—something to *wow* the audience, something that would leave them totally bewildered.

"Hey, how about *me* sawing *you* in half?" Ardan suggested laughingly. "You know—*something awesome.* You could squeal like a pig while I make two of you. Ew. Not two of *you.* We could call you Izzy and Lizzy."

"Stop it, Ardan. You can just forget that bit of nonsense. You're not about to cut me in half!" She stomped her foot for emphasis. "Not a chance, bro!"

"What would that make us," he continued despite her protest, "*triplets?* Oh my gosh, we could be triplets. Think what we could do with another cohort! The possibilities are endless."

Isabel was not amused. "Let's just get back to the show and figure out our big ending. Maybe you could turn me into a puppet, and I could dance around with strings hanging everywhere," she positioned her feet one in front of the other to form a T, drew her rounded arms over her head, and after a simple plié, she opened up to a full spin. "Oops," she giggled as she lost her balance and stumbled over her own clumsy feet.

With a loud, exaggerated sigh, Ardan shook his head. "No, definitely not that," he responded, his eyes rolling to the top of his head.

They also gave up on the idea of sawing Isabel in half (thank goodness) and decided instead on making her disappear. Yes, that would work. Isabel would simply disappear.

Ardan had been using a folding table for some of his tricks. If they covered the table with a sheet, Isabel could hide under it and no one would see her. His cape wasn't big enough to conceal Isabel's escape, so Ardan used a second sheet to toss around while she slid under the table.

"*Sorry!*" Isabel had become entangled in the table sheet and nearly pulled everything to the floor.

Then Ardan whisked the cover sheet away so quickly he knocked over a lamp.

Day after day they worked, trying to perfect the concept of her disappearing. This proved to be harder than they'd originally thought it would be.

Then on a Friday the thirteenth, it happened. Isabel was behind the cover sheet. Ardan shouted out the magic spell in the most eerie voice he could muster. "Wacki-Wooki!" He fluttered the sheet and flipped it into the air.

When he looked around, Isabel was gone. "Hey! We've got it! That was super," he exclaimed excitedly. "Now we have a real show! Boy, oh boy, will we surprise the folks."

After a confused moment, Ardan said, "Isabel, you can come out now. You were so good! No, you were more than good. You were great!" *Imagine that. It worked*, he thought again to himself.

Ardan waited, and yet Isabel did not come out. He looked under the table. She wasn't there. "Hey. Where did you decide to hide?" he asked.

No answer.

"Ha. Ha. You had your laugh, Houdini. Show me what you did. I said I like it. OK already, where are you?" He was becoming more than a little impatient with his sister.

Still there was no Isabel. What kind of game was she playing—trick the trickster? This wasn't at all funny anymore. Ardan looked in the closets, under the desks and behind the bookcase. She wasn't anywhere. Now, he was beginning to worry. What could have happened? What had gone wrong? Fear replaced the anger he had built against her little game of hide-and-seek.

Ardan shook his head, hoping to jar his brain. Did magic really work? Could he have cast a spell? No! They were just playing. It was all just a game. Magic wasn't real. *OK then, where's Isabel?* he thought while pacing about. *What kind of hocus-pocus did I use? Abracadabra? Open sesame? Shazam? What was it?*

"I made it up!" he realized, shouting out loud. Ardan knew he was talking to himself. But under the circumstances, it seemed justified. "What was it? How can I reverse this magic?" He walked back and forth, racking his brain, trying to remember.

"Wacki-Wooki! That's what I said. Wacki-Wooki. Wacki-Wooki!" he shouted. It wasn't working. He tried it again and again. Still nothing. "I know. I'll say the actual words themselves backwards to reverse what I did. Oh, I hope this works." Ardan closed his eyes tightly. Using the same haunting voice, Ardan chanted, "Ikoow-Ikcaw! Please, please bring my Isabel back!"

Poof! There she was under the table, where she was supposed to be in the first place.

Isabel shook her head. "What happened?" she asked, looking bewildered.

"Don't you know? Where did you go?" Ardan inquired, hoping for some logic to explain this very puzzling situation.

"What are you talking about? I'm here … right?" she queried. "But, Ardan, I have to say, I feel *sooo* … weird. I'm like totally—I mean like totally—confused."

Ardan asked Isabel to retrace her steps while they tried to figure out what had just happened.

"Well, I was hiding under the table just like we practiced," she stammered. "Then, well then, I feel like I took a nap and had a ghostly, supernatural dream or something. Did I nap? I don't remember details of any dream either, but, Ardan, none of this feels real to me."

"Goofus, you were just gone. I looked everywhere for you. And then you reappeared in the first place I looked." Ardan was of no help at all.

"I think," Ardan admitted, "I used some magic words. That can't be it, can it? But, Isabel, you were totally gone. I simply couldn't find you anywhere until I reversed the magic words."

The twins decided not to say anything more about the disappearance until they could figure it out for themselves. They had never heard of anyone having such an experience as this. Was this crazy talk? Were they crazy? Would other people think they were crazy, maybe had bats in the belfry if they knew about Isabel truly disappearing? Without question, the twins knew that Isabel had actually disappeared!

"Remember the looks we got when we told people about our wood nymphs?" Ardan recalled with horror. "Nobody believed us. In fact, I felt like they made fun of us—not openly but smiling and treating us like it was just cute childish play. Imaginary friends, my eye. Is that what happens when you become an adult? You lose the ability to connect with things outside the everyday usual? And who makes the decision on what's accepted as normal? Isabel, I think it's best if we don't talk about this."

Ardan was right. They could not chance asking about it. This was to remain their secret—at least for the time being.

෧ᙡᙡᙙ෨

They were both quiet at supper that night—so quiet that Father declared, "What's up with you kids? You're quieter than church mice." In truth, silence was very unlike these precocious youngsters.

"Ugh," Ardan groaned under his breath. Dad always had some dumb, old-timer saying like that. Yet, it felt good to know at least some things were back to normal. *Yeah, like we're a normal family. When did that happen?*

"You're not sick, are you?" Mother chimed in. She reached over to Isabel, "Your head doesn't feel warm. Are you OK, sweetheart?" She suddenly worried.

"Yes, I mean no, Mom. I'm fine." Isabel felt the need to reassure her parents. "We're both fine. I think we just got too carried away today, and we're just a little tired. But we're fine."

"Must just be that Friday the thirteenth curse," Father mysteriously uttered while laughing at his own attempt at humor.

෧ᙡᙡᙙ෨

Before Ardan shut the curtains on that ominous Friday the thirteenth night, he looked directly at the stars and said in hushed words:

Twinkle, twinkle if you must,
I will be more careful
Of that you can trust!

As Ardan turned to move away, he could have sworn the Man in the Moon winked at him.

13

Chapter 4

Show Time

The twins would do their magic show—just not with the disappearing act. That went the way of sawing Isabel in half.

The audience consisted of Grandpa and Grandma Murphy, Uncle Randy and Aunt Cheryl, their parents, family friend Humphrey Moore, and especially Uncle Hank.

This was the twin's magical debut, and they were understandably nervous. Their confidence was quickly giving way to stage fright. The last rehearsal had gone off without a hitch. They told themselves they only needed to rely on those skills now.

Once they started, the twins flawlessly ran through a series of tricks. Grandpa was perplexed when he saw his pocket watch get smashed under a black scarf only to have it reappear—*intact*—in the hat perched on the table. They miraculously separated connected rings, coins multiplied, and Ardan found a quarter in Grandma's ear. All in all, their hard work practicing was paying off with an amused audience.

Prior to the performance, Isabel had used an eraser to write cryptic forecasts, like "a big gift," or "money 4 U," and other simple prophecies. The twins had been practicing printing their letters, and the first reader books provided them with words. They drew from those resources as a guide for their fortune-telling predictions. Ardan carefully brushed the eraser crumbs off the paper and stacked the sheets on the table. When the proper time in the act arrived, Ardan announced he would forecast the future for each person in the audience. Isabel sprinkled "magic dust" across the seemingly plain paper. As the dust (ashes from the fireplace) adhered to the eraser residue, the messages slowly began to reveal themselves. Everyone was amused at their cleverness.

The twins still had one more trick up their sleeves. As a climax, Ardan and Isabel would show off their mind reading skills.

"I will leave the room now and have one of you pick out an item. When my trusty assistant beckons me, I shall return and correctly identify the object," Ardan professed with great certainty. Bowing gracefully, he retreated a respectable distance, fully out of earshot from the audience.

Isabel took over and asked Ol' Humphrey Moore to choose the first article. "How about that table lamp?" he whispered to Isabel.

"That should do it. Ardan, you can come back in now," she called loudly.

Isabel began the routine. "Is it this picture?"

"No," was Ardan's reply.

"Is the chosen article the stuffed bear on the shelf?" Isabel asked.

"No indeed," he replied with confidence.

"This red pillow?"

"No," Ardan answered.

"Is it this table lamp?" she asked.

"Yes."

Everyone was intrigued but believed that, if they continued to play, this would be the one trick they could figure out.

After many attempts, Uncle Randy didn't say a word and only pointed to the stuffed bear Ardan had rejected one other time.

"You may return." Isabel cued her brother's return. "Is it the yellow flower?" she began.

"No."

"The green box?" Isabel turned her back to her brother to show she was not giving him any facial directions.

"No."

"The picture on the wall?"

"No."

"How about that clock?" Isabel pointed to the red clock on the wall.

"No," he responded.

"Is it the stuffed bear?"

"Yes, it is the bear," Ardan answered with complete assurance.

The audience tackled the trick from every angle. Was it the fifth item? Did Isabel raise her voice? Did she wink? They knew Ardan hadn't overheard them. What then?

Always leave your audience guessing. True to the magician's code of ethics of never revealing how a trick is executed, the twins did not explain. And no one figured out that it was always the next item after Isabel pointed to an item that was *red*. If the item picked by the participant was also red, red still applied. The chosen article would simply be the second red item pointed to.

At bedtime that night, the youngsters talked of their perceived magical powers used to amuse the family. Exhausted from the stress of giving an almost flawless performance, the twins willingly made their way to their beds.

As Ardan shut his curtains, he looked again to his imaginary friend in the moon.

Friend of mine,
Forever in time,
We will always be
What no others can see
Completely entwined.

This time, it was Ardan who winked at the moon.

BOOK TWO

The Birthday Wish

Chapter 5

The Twins Turn Five

The day could not have been more beautiful. The weather was not too hot or humid as was usual for August in Asterville. Last night's rain left the grass a lush, bright green. The fall asters were already in bloom framing the Murphy home in colorful shades of gold, red, and orange. Because of their great beauty, the aster flower had become the namesake of the town when it was settled a mere 140 years ago.

This day was special. You see, Ardan and Isabel would be turning five, and a big celebration was planned with family and friends. Yesterday, Father had hoisted a huge tent in the backyard. Today, the tables were to be covered with red-and-white checkered cloths.

"It's a little breezy. I think we should tape the corners. What do you think?" Aunt Cheryl asked of her favorite niece as they spread the plastic coverings.

"Oh yes, I agree," Isabel replied, always glad when she could do things with her mother's sister. "Do you think Uncle Hank will be able to make it? He said he'd try."

"If he can be here, I'm sure he will," Aunt Cheryl assured her. "It'll be interesting to see what kind of gift he comes up with. He always finds the most unique things, but I doubt he could ever top that magic kit. By the way, you kids did an awesome job with your performance. Uncle Randy and I still haven't figured out how you can read minds. You can't really do that—can you?"

They both got a chuckle out of such an absurd idea.

"Thanks. We had a lot of fun doing that. But never say never. Maybe we can read minds," she teased in a singsong voice. "We've done two other magic shows for our friends since the one we did for you. Everyone seems to like things that hold a touch of mystery, and Ardan's really good with his hand tricks. He says, 'It's all in the wrist.'"

On a more serious note, Isabel asked, "Do you think we'll have enough cake and ice cream? You know how Grandpa likes dessert." With a laugh Isabel added, "I'll bet he asks for a piece of each of our cakes. And that isn't so he doesn't favor one of us over the other either. He just likes dessert." Grandpa was one of the good guys, always leaving a warm smile in her heart.

"I imagine that's exactly what he'll do. He does love his sweets. Probably not a good idea to let him overdo, but what can you do with someone his age? He's fully set in his ways," with a slight shaking of her head, Aunt Cheryl simply smiled. "Now, *you* young lady, we still have time to teach you healthier habits."

"Bummer," Isabel muttered under her breath. When did all this healthy eating stuff come up? Certainly not in Grandpa's time. Had this been sprung on her generation as some sort of punishment? Were children part of some experimental testing group? A sudden realization struck her. Isabel became worried about her loveable sidekick. "Grandpa's OK, isn't he? I mean he's healthy, right?"

"Oh, of course he's healthy. I didn't mean to imply that he wasn't." Her aunt realized she might have carried this sugar thing a bit too far for a five-year-old to grasp. "Come on," she said, changing the subject and encouraging her niece along. "Let's see if your mom needs help in the kitchen."

Meanwhile, Ardan was glued to his favorite uncle. Projects were a lot more fun when Uncle Randy was involved. The two "buds" started hanging streamers and balloons all over the backyard. The effect was turning the landscape into a vibrant carnival. "I like the multicolor balloons the best," Ardan said while admiring their handiwork. "I'm sure glad you have that air pump. I couldn't blow well enough to help you."

"It's always wise to take shortcuts whenever you can." Uncle Randy winked. "This way, I get to save my breath for talking—and picking on you!" With that, he chased Ardan around the tent.

Caught off guard, Ardan was an easy catch. Uncle Randy gave him a quick toss in the air before getting back to business.

"We have enough balloons for everyone to take some home with them. That way they can keep enjoying the fun long after the party's over," Uncle Randy added as the two got back to the job at hand. "Well now, birthday boy, we just have the games to set up and then *we are ready!*" he said, emphasizing the final phrase while rubbing Ardan's bristly crew cut. The kid in Uncle Randy was beginning to rear its mischievous head. He was just as excited as Ardan was to get the show on the road.

Mother was putting the last touches on the cakes when Aunt Cheryl and Isabel entered the kitchen. "They're beautiful, Mom," Isabel complimented her very capable mother. There wasn't much her mother couldn't accomplish in the kitchen. She was an exceptional cook. Everyone looked for Angela Murphy's dishes at potlucks. She made sure she added a special decorative touch on her dish. Presentation she called it. Modestly, she said that she wasn't that good a cook—it just looked pretty so it went down better.

Anticipation was over the edge for the young, highly excited twins. Now that all the finishing touches were in play, the waiting became unbearable. Busy hands were definitely an advantage over idle ones.

The family hardware store closed at noon on Saturdays, so Father would be home soon. That meant their guests would be along shortly thereafter.

As expected, Grandpa and Grandma were the first to arrive. "Bless your little, pea-pickin' hearts—five years old already." Gramps shook his head in disbelief. "How time does fly. Happy birthday, young'uns." He struggled with hugs while at the same time trying to balance a stack of wrapped presents.

"Hi, Grandpa, Grandma," Isabel gleefully greeted her grandparents. "Can we help you carry something?" She was eyeing the gifts and not the food.

Fortunately, Uncle Randy arrived just in time to help relieve the older folks of their awkward bundles. He grabbed the food and headed to the kitchen. The twins each took a grandparent (with their bedazzled gifts) and headed directly to the setup in the garden.

So far, Isabel and Ardan were their only grandchildren, and the senior Murphys took advantage of it by spoiling them.

Grandma's hair was a silvery white with soft natural waves. *Why didn't I get waves instead of kinky curls?* Isabel lamented to herself. Ardan and Isabel couldn't remember a time when her blue eyes (that sometimes turned greenish depending on what she wore) were not twinkling behind that bright smile. Aging had actually enhanced her deepening dimples, adding to the sweetness she carried in her bright smile.

Once when Isabel fell and scraped her knee falling off her bike, Grandma cleaned it up with gentle, loving care. Isabel hardly felt a thing because Grandma distracted her with a tell-all tale about how Isabel's own father had fallen from a tree while trying to hang a bird feeder. "Your father was afraid to tell us what happened. He knew he shouldn't have been up there. Luckily, he couldn't hide the cut, and I was able to clean it out before it got infected. There," she had said, "when your scrape heals, you'll never know it happened." That was the way Grandma applied "painless medicine"—just take your mind off it.

Before long, other people started to arrive. It wasn't so much about receiving presents (which Ardan and Isabel were anticipating) as it was about having fun with everyone who would be there. The twins loved a large gathering and all the activity that came along with it.

Uncle Randy started the activities among the younger set. He tended to generate a lot of horseplay, and the children were eager to get started. When Dad joined in, it became utter chaos! Games rotated from tag to hide-and-seek to red rover and general hi-jinks. And of course, everyone had to try to pin the tail on the proverbial donkey, who, this year, was a pirate who needed a ponytail. Old and young alike joined in the outlandish activities. Ol' Humphrey Moore gave everyone a giggle when a stray ball bounced off his head.

"OK, who did it?" Ol' Humphrey bellowed, professing great indignation as he targeted the perpetrator in return. Game on. You would have totally miscalculated him, if you thought Humphrey Moore couldn't run because of his waning years. Well think again, because Ol' Humphrey proved he was still quick on his feet. Ol' Humphrey, as he was always referred to, was a favorite among the youngsters due mainly to his *stupendous* tales. He was a virtual Santa Clause in absentia if you will, spreading joy and goodwill to one and all. Needless to say, he was beloved by everyone—young and old alike.

Finally, Mother and Aunt Cheryl brought out the birthday cakes. Isabel had a pink princess cake and Ardan's had Star Wars characters. Each cake had the customary five candles representing the five years of their lives. In family tradition, the twins were each given a large individual candle to hold. This was the one to grow on and, most importantly, the one to make that special birthday *wish* on. As expected, the Happy Birthday song was loud and way, way off tune.

Grateful to have the serenade over, the twins each drew in a deep breath ... and ... blew.

Chapter 6

Wishes Can Come True

"Where are we?" Ardan asked his sister.

"I don't have any idea!" Isabel replied, wonder struck. "The last thing I remember is blowing out my wishing candle."

The streets were full of cars, buses, and taxi cabs, the likes of which Ardan and Isabel had never seen before. Impatient people were hustling about their busy day. Cars were honking. Lights were flashing from red to yellow to green. People acted as if they had tunnel vision in a predetermined program with one singular objective in mind, all of which was encapsulated in a barrier of tall buildings. Feeling the stress and tension of the situation, they both wanted out of there. The two small children cowered against one of the glassed-in stores to continue their discussion.

"Me too. Blowing out my candle is the last thing I remember doing," Ardan responded. "That and making a wish," he added. After a moment of reflection, Ardan asked, "Do you think? Could it be?" His mind was spinning. Were his thoughts playing tricks on him? "Isabel? What did you wish for?"

"Oh, golly." She tried to think back to the party. "Maybe to visit Bodenia. I've always wanted to see what life was like on the mainland. Uncle Hank tells so many stories about life there. I thought it would be fun if we could visit—just once. You know, curiosity."

"Why, I wished for that too!" he declared, shocked by the possibility. "Twins really do think alike. Do you think wishes can come true? Are we on the mainland?"

Ardan and Isabel felt very uncomfortable amid the hubbub. Still uncertain what was happening to them and, worse, what lay ahead for them, the two worked their way out of the business district into the less crowded residential area.

"This is better. It feels more like home," Isabel said. "But what are we to do? And just how can we get back to Asterville?"

"I can hear Grandpa now: 'Be careful what you wish for,'" Ardan said while thinking back to the birthday party. "What have we done, Isabel? More importantly, *how, how did this happen?* It doesn't make any sense."

Just then, an anxious boy approached them. Ardan and Isabel set their own problems aside.

"Have you seen my dog? He's missing, and I've been looking everywhere for him. He's my best buddy, and now he's gone." By now, the boy was near tears. His voice was quivering as he handed over a piece of paper. "Here," he said, giving them a flyer. "I've been posting these all over town."

The twins could not overlook the obvious suffering the boy was going through. Looking at the picture, Isabel saw a happy-go-lucky puppy. He was a small, frisky furball. Giving him a comical appearance was the long patch of black across his eyes, mimicking a canine masked Zorro.

The third grader's name was Jeff Swanson. He had lived his whole life here in Freemont. Bandit, as the dog was appropriately named, had been found by Jeff a few months ago. At about six weeks old, the puppy had been abandoned and near death. Immediately, Jeff had wrapped the fragile pup in his shirt and run to the family veterinarian. With the doctors' help, Jeff was able to nurse the puppy back to health. Because of Jeff's heartfelt devotion while caring for Bandit, the critter and boy were uniquely bonded for life.

Touched by the story, the twins joined forces with Jeff to hunt for little Bandit. Returning to Asterville would have to wait. Fortified with the companionship of new friends, Jeff's mission became more bearable. Jeff amused the twins with funny tales of Bandit's antics as the threesome continued on their quest.

After searching block by block, the children wandered into a desolate area overgrown with brush and ivy. Only a few boarded-up houses and businesses were left intact in an otherwise vacated block. Without anyone around, there was an eerie quiet to the place. Undaunted, the children kept calling for Bandit. He might be caught up in these tangled weeds previously called yards. If he was entrapped in some twisted vines, he was surely tired and hungry. With new urgency, the children called out for Bandit as loudly as they could.

Chapter 7

Perpetrators of Crime

"You numbskulls! Watch what you're doing!" The boss man was highly irate with Willy and Charlie. "You bums could screw up a one-car funeral. Do you realize you almost got caught? You could have blown the whole operation with your carelessness. Idiots! Confound it anyway!"

Ben Krookston had a sweet, little racket going for himself and was afraid he'd aligned himself with the wrong accomplices. The plan was a simple little moneymaker that literally bore no expense. Steal the best dogs and sell them to a distributor. The distributor took the bigger risk because he held the pets longer while looking for people who would pay handsomely for quality animals. Krookston was just the middleman and had limited contact with the "mangy mutts," as he referred to them. The way he saw it, this was all profit. But considering the cops might be getting closer, the time to move on had come. Things were becoming too hot here in Freemont.

"We was jest doin' like ya told us, boss. We followed da guy home when he left da groomers, waited till he put da dog out, den snatched 'em. How was we ta know da neighbor would choose den ta make a visit?" Willy tried to explain away the issue of nearly being caught.

As instructed, the thugs were to stake out local pet grooming businesses, make sure the pet was perky and not old, follow the owner and pet home, and then snatch the dog as soon as possible. People who took special care of their dogs had usually paid a healthy purchase price to procure the animal in the first place.

"How many dogs do you have this time?" Krookston barked.

"I think we got eleven. No old ones this time, boss. They should all fetch a tidy sum," Charlie chimed in, trying to smooth things over with the boss. "We ditched the car right away in case the neighbor got a description. It wasn't any good anyway. Then we copped a cargo van. That should be better for hauling that many mutts anyway."

If Charlie was looking for any sign of approval from Krookston, he was dead wrong.

"I'll call the distributor and see if we can move them tomorrow. Then we'll set up a new operation far away from here." Krookston could feel the cops bearing down on him. He already had a police record for forgery and couldn't risk being nabbed again in the same town.

Chapter 8

The Hunt Turns Dangerous

In an abandoned shed were about a dozen dogs of various breeds. Some were big; some were small. All of the precious pets were chained to the walls and shaking with fright in this dank, captive environment.

"Arf!" Bandit barked. He believed he heard Jeff's voice. *Yes, it is. It is Jeff,* Bandit thought. "Arf, arf, arf!" He barked as loudly as he could.

Soon the other dogs chimed in. The mismatched band of canines made an unearthly racket.

Their commotion caught the attention of the youngsters. "I think the noise is coming from over there." Ardan pointed to a shed a few hundred yards away. The building was overgrown with weeds that were all knotted and twisted together. Peeling paint from rotting wood added to its spooky appearance.

Nervously, the newly formed friends approached the dilapidated structure. Glancing from side to side, they cautiously moved closer. A heavy chain and lock secured the door. The only window was covered over from the inside. In the back of the shed, Jeff was able to move a loose piece of siding just enough to peer inside. The holes in the roof offered minimal lighting, but as Jeff's eyes adjusted to the dark interior, he was able to make out forms.

"It appears there are a lot of dogs in there. And they look like they're tied up," Jeff said as he shared what he was seeing to the twins. "*Bandit!* Bandit, is that you?"

"Arf, arf, arf," was the excited response. Bandit's heart took a leap. He was saved. Jeff was here.

"That *is* Bandit. I know it is. But how can we get him out?" Jeff started hopping up and down with excitement. Bandit was so close. How could they break into this shed?

The trio went round and round the building but found no way to get into the forbidden structure.

"We're going to need help. Let's look for the constable. He'll help us," Jeff assured them.

As they rounded the corner of the shed, the boys ran smack-dab into two men who had just exited a van. In their excitement, the trio had not heard a vehicle approach. Startled, they quickly tried to scurry out of harm's way.

"Hey, come back 'ere!" Willie yelled. He grabbed Jeff by the arm and pulled him back. "What da ya tink yer doin'?" he demanded.

Just as quickly, Charlie got a firm hold on Ardan, who had turned back to help Jeff. "What er you kids doin' around here?" he snapped, reiterating Willie's demand in slightly better English.

"We didn't do anything wrong, mister, honest," a frightened Jeff replied. Who were these people?

"Well, ya was trespassin', and dat's breakin' da law," Willie threatened. "What er we gonna do wit' 'em, Charlie?"

Realizing the boys were in deep trouble, Isabel came out of hiding. Luckily, she had chosen to go around the other side of the shed and, when she'd heard the commotion, had ducked behind a pile of trash.

Charlie caught a glimpse of her out of the corner of his eye. "Hey, get over here. How many more of you little rug rats are there?" he demanded.

Isabel approached the group with a sweetness only she could achieve. "Just me, sir. I'm the only other one." She took a deep breath for courage and continued. "Sir, we didn't mean to trespass. We were just playing catch. And you see, Ardan here"—she pointed to her brother—"well, he's a bit clumsy and ... he missed. The ball bounced into your yard. We were just chasing it." Isabel displayed a ball she'd found in the junk pile as proof. "We're sorry, mister." She continued making her case. "Honest. We'll just be on our way and promise not to bother you again."

"What da ya tink, Charlie?" Willy had no idea how to handle this. Charlie was the brains. Had the children discovered the dogs? he wondered.

The mutts were quiet now, clearly afraid of the thieves upon hearing their voices.

Since that episode with that neighbor, who'd nearly caught them snatching the last dog, Charlie dreaded admitting another snafu to Krookston. One more slip, and Krookston would have their hides. The gang would be closing the operation tomorrow anyway. And who would listen to a bunch of snot-nosed brats. "We'll let ya go dis time. *But* I'm warnin' ya, if I ketch ya round 'ere agin, I'll turn ya in ta da cops, and ya'll all do time in da slammer. *Get it? Now scram*! And don't let us ketch ya 'ere agin!"

The trio didn't need a second warning to scram. They were out of there in a flash.

Once out of earshot, Ardan smiled at his sister. "I was so proud of you coming up with that story. You really are a lifesaver. I've always known I can count on you, partner." He gave Isabel a big squeeze. Although hugging was like—well, totally out of character for Ardan—he could not deny the pride he felt for Isabel's on-the-spot excuse. Jeff, too, was amazed how cool Isabel had been in an emergency.

While the kids looked for an officer, Jeff recounted to Ardan and Isabel how he'd overheard his parents talking about a possible ring of dognappers working in the area. "My folks didn't tell me directly about it, so I didn't get the full story. I guess they didn't want to worry me with Bandit being missing and all."

"Do you think all of those dogs with Bandit were stolen too?" Isabel asked.

"I don't know. Maybe. Probably," Jeff said.

"As we were leaving, I heard the taller one saying something about 'closing down the operation tomorrow.' What do you think he meant?" Isabel asked.

To Jeff's dismay, he could only assume the scoundrels would be leaving and taking the dogs with them. The very thought only added urgency to their mission of saving Bandit.

"Hey, there's Constable Ned. He's the best," Jeff said as he raced to the officer.

The kindly officer had walked this same beat for a dozen or more years. He knew his people and their offspring. "Well, hello there young

31

Jeffery. What seems to be the trouble?" he politely asked. Over the years, the kindly constable had been familiar with Jeff and his many fanciful tales. Jeff was another of those kids blessed with an active imagination.

The enlivened trio all started talking at once. The policeman could not understand a thing they said. "Slow down now. How about just one of you tell me what's going on?"

Jeff took the lead and told his wild story of dogs barking, chains, and an obscure structure in the middle of nowhere. As he told the constable about their encounter with the thieves, he tried to remember every detail, hoping it would show the urgency in retrieving Bandit. Officer Ned looked skeptical as he listened. When finished, the amused officer couldn't help smiling.

In a calming voice, he said, "Well done. That was quite a story, master Jeffery. One of your best, I must say so myself. Now run along and don't be scaring your new friends," he cautioned.

"No, truly!" Isabel jumped in. "We were there, too. We can show you. It isn't that far from here. Please, *please!*" she begged in her most dramatic performance on record.

Ardan knew it would be hard for the officer to resist Isabel. Her charm could endear the most hardened soul. Isabel was their ace in the hole.

This new girl appeared to be sincere. Since he did not know her, Officer Ned could not judge her reliability. "OK," the officer gave in to her pleading. "My squad car is over there. We'll take it."

Ned didn't really think the children were lying, but he did think their imaginations might be getting the better of them. After all, a tale as ridiculous as that couldn't possibly be true. And Jeff, well, he was a creative genius and was just hoping to get his dog back.

Approaching the older sector in Freemont, Officer Ned didn't see the van parked by the shed that the kids pointed out. But just in case, he pulled the squad car around the corner and out of sight.

The stranded dogs had stopped their useless barking. They were heartbroken to have been abandoned by Jeff and what seemed to have been their only hope of rescue. The one-time family pets did not know what fate had in store for them.

Because things were quiet when they arrived, the officer was again doubting the children. If he was questioning their elaborate story before, this was nearing confirmation of it. He yanked at the door. It did not budge. The dogs were still silent, fearing the mean men were back. The stillness made the officer even more hesitant. His right eyebrow raised as his head tilted to one side. "Jeff-er-ey? Is this your idea of a joke?"

Jeff ran forward. What if the dogs had been moved? Maybe they were too late. "Bandit! Bandit, are you still in there?" he yelled.

Upon hearing the familiar voice, Bandit howled! Again the other dogs chimed in with renewed vigor. What a joyous ruckus they made.

"Well, now, let's get a better look," Constable Ned said. When he pulled back the loose board as Jeff showed him, he was astounded. The children had been right all along. Constable Ned could only believe they were also right about the run-in with the thieves.

Without further ado, the officer called headquarters, giving the details of his find. An unmarked police car quietly rolled up to join them. Officer Ned was given permission to retrieve Bandit and bring the children home. Entering from the rear, the officers checked to be sure the other dogs were in good condition, fed, and watered. The front door would be left intact so as not to raise suspicion with the culprits.

Meanwhile, the police captain formulated a plan to catch the perps red-handed when they came back for their cache of canine. The two detectives would conceal themselves and remain on stakeout. When the culprits physically had the pets in tow, they would be arrested for stolen property, and the town's citizens could finally be at ease. Pet owners all across town had been on edge, never knowing if their own beloved pet might be targeted next. Breaking the case would be a big relief to the entire community. Once the police placed the thieves in custody, the department could go about the task of returning the animals to their rightful owners.

Jeff received a hero's welcome when he returned home. Officer Ned explained the situation to Jeff's parents and praised the trio for their heroics. The Swansons were grateful no one was hurt while dealing with loathsome crooks. Just the thought of the children interacting with criminals made them cringe. The possibilities of how dangerous this could have been left his parents unnerved. They felt terrible at not having better protected Jeff and these two sweet companions. What bravery. How fortunate things turned out this way.

Ardan and Isabel enjoyed sharing in Bandit's reunion with Jeff's family. As it turned out, Jeff was part of a large family, who lovingly embraced the twins as if they were their own. Reluctantly, Ardan and Isabel needed to take their leave, saying they weren't from here and were only visiting relatives in the area as a way of explaining their presence. Jeff's parents told the twins they should visit anytime they were back in Freemont.

Jeff, too, felt saddened to say goodbye. The bravery of the twins touched him deeply, and to think they'd jumped right in to help a complete stranger—him. Well, he would never forget them, ever. "Promise we'll see each other again," Jeff begged when they parted. The three had shared in a unique event. He hated the thought that they might never see each other again. Although their time together was brief, Jeff and the twins felt a special bond that day.

"Indeed we will. Promise," Isabel said intuitively.

The cops' sting caught the whole unscrupulous gang. While under interrogation, Krookston turned on the others and even gave up the distributor, hoping to get a reduced sentence for himself. His lack of loyalty was clearly to save his own unworthy skin.

Young Jeffery would eventually receive an award for his tenacity in solving the mystery of the disappearing dogs. Unwittingly, his future was being molded by this event. Jeff's interest in animals would, in time, become his career.

Chapter 9

Facing Their Dilemma

Isabel and Arden found a spot under a maple tree to rest while contemplating their own personal dilemma. Just how would they get back to Asterville?

"Ardan," Isabel said in a small, sad voice. "Will we ever see our own family again? I miss Mom and Dad." She wasn't acting now. Her sadness was real and seemingly impossible to rectify. Tears began to stream down her reddened cheeks.

"Remember how much fun it was at our birthday party? Especially when Grandpa put a bow on his head and pretended he was our present," Ardan said, attempting to bring a smile to his sister's face. After all, they were *a team*! They would figure out this problem of theirs together.

Isabel did get a giggle just thinking about their silly grandpa and their whole funny family. You never know how lucky you are to have such a loving family—that is, until you've lost it.

"Isabel," Ardan said, "do you still have that big candle in your pocket?"

"I think so. Why?" she asked.

"Well, do you think, if we wish on it again, we might go home?" he hopefully offered.

"We can try. Let's do it. Ready?" she said excitedly, not wanting to waste a minute more.

With a nod, the twins made the same wish at the same time—to be back home again, home in Asterville, home with friends and, most of all, with family.

Chapter 10

Makes No Sense

It worked! They were home. Apparently no one had missed them. Seemingly, nothing unusual had happened. The party continued. The cakes were being cut. And Grandpa, well he was in the process of getting a slice of each cake with two scoops of ice cream. Uncle Hank surprised them with a chemistry set—watch out world. Aunt Cheryl, with her interest in reading, hoped the twins would be stimulated by books she'd picked out about space and the universe.

"Readers are leaders," Uncle Randy stated. As a technical adviser to a research firm in Asterville, he knew the importance of an education. "The ability of being able to read is the foundation of each and every subject taught. There's no way around it."

When the afternoon drew to a close, no one wanted to see the party end. Everyone went home loaded up with party favors, balloons, and candy from the pirate piñata. Ol' Humphrey told the youngsters tales of when the pirates actually landed on St. Delus and clashed with the original settlers.

Exciting as that was, evening was fast approaching, and children need their sleep.

<hr />

Weird. How come they weren't missed? Isabel and Ardan knew Jeff and Bandit were real. They knew Constable Ned existed. But how could this experience be explained? Were they the only ones to have an excursion like this? Why had no one ever spoken of these things?

Because the twins were afraid people would think they were "nuts" if they talked about these unusual events, they again felt they had to keep the secret to themselves. Luckily, they had each other to confide in. These unique experiences just made them closer as brother and sister.

That night as they headed off to bed, Ardan told Isabel about the conversation he overheard between Grandpa Murphy and their father. (Children learn a lot from simply *overhearing* conversations when adults think they're safely out of earshot.) Ardan couldn't understand it all, but the adults had spoken of a fourth dimension, where two different things could happen independently at the same time—even in the same space. "How strange is that?" he stated. "Dad and Gramps didn't seem to believe it, of course. But what if?"

"I think you're right. That is a strange, a very strange, idea. But I can't think about it now, Ardan. It's been a big day, and I'm tired. Good night. Sleep tight," she said, heading off to bed. Almost as an afterthought, Isabel added, "Do you think this event has anything to do with that thing that happened to me when we were doing our magic show? You know, when I disappeared and we couldn't figure where I was?"

"Wow, there's a thought! What could it mean? Are you scared, Wonder Nut?" Ardan thoughtfully asked. *Should they be worried?* he wondered.

"No, not scared. Bad things could have happened, I guess. But when we were involved in the middle of it, I didn't have time to be scared," she replied. In an attempt to defuse the seriousness of a possible fourth dimension, she simply giggled. "But I'm glad you're my brother and that we're in this together. If I'm nuts, well then, so are you. My crazy, mixed-up little brother."

"We're a *team*, Stumble Bum." He gave her another unordinary but comforting hug. "Good night. And I'm glad, too, that you're my sister."

As what had become his usual routine, Ardan went to close the curtains. This night as he spoke to the moon, he said,

Hey diddle, diddle
The cat and the fiddle.
The cow jumped over the moon.
All the dogs laughed

To see how the cops
Did away with the goons.

The moon was a mere sliver of itself but shown just as proudly as it always did.

As Mitch and Angela tucked their exhausted children in, they were granted only the weakest response.

"Good night, my birthday pair." Mother smiled.

"Love you and like you. Pleasant dreams," Father added.

Proudly, they stepped back, remembering the moment of the twins' births a mere five years ago.

BOOK THREE

The First Day of School

Chapter 11

Finally

A once-in-a-lifetime event was on the horizon for Ardan and Isabel. Just like you only have once chance at making a first impression, well there is just one time to experience your very first day at school. And the twins had anticipated this for a very long time. In just one more day, they would be full-fledged kindergarteners, and they wanted it to be memorable. Imagine seeing your friends every day without having to schedule a playdate. Friends not only afforded a new perspective to the impulsive twins' own way of playing, they also offered a fresh, lively interaction to everyday conversations. Funny how each person looked at the very same thing differently. But to Ardan and Isabel, those different viewpoints were inspiring. The twins were naturally outgoing and planned to get to know their new classmates quickly—since they never knew a stranger, so to speak. This opportunity of meeting more kids their own age was mind-boggling.

"Ardan, I was wonder how many kids we might already know that could be in our class. I'm think there might be Gwendolyn Kramer, Jay Reynolds, and is that new girl from church, Nancy something, our age? I don't know if she'll be in kindergarten or first grade." Isabel was already trying to figure out the whole cast of characters in the classroom. What would/could each of them bring to the table? This could be quite interesting.

"I think she's in first grade, but Frankie Morgan is our age. He could be in our class," Ardan said thoughtfully. "Ah, so, my little Viener Schnitzel, me thinks school holds promise. We should fit right in."

To help transition the twins to the new routine of the classroom, Mother had started playing school with them at home a few months ago when they outgrew taking naps. As important as naps were, Mother also realized that her twins were growing up. Once they were in school, naps would be replaced with downtime anyway. She would be remiss not to realize that discipline was badly needed to keep her overactive youngsters "on task." They had a tendency to "mind wander" if a particular topic didn't interest them. Mother hoped that introducing them to the routine of school activities would prove useful in the long scheme of things. She hoped the teacher would appreciate her intent, even if she wasn't able to perfect it.

Their reading vocabulary was growing, adding more sight words each day. When they'd planned the magic show, Mom's teachings had come in handy. Learning to the twins was like pouring chocolate over ice cream—never enough. Then there was cake—was there some kind of underlying rule on how much frosting is too much? Not in their world. That was how learning was, limitless. Isabel and Ardan simply couldn't get enough of it. Uncle Randy's words boosted them along. "Readers are leaders," he'd say. He forgot to add how much fun it could be, and Mother had a gift for choosing the most inspiring books that reenforced the theory.

The children were certain that, once they were in school, they would learn about the many exciting, new adventures this wide world had to offer. As sure as they knew pigs couldn't fly (they can't, right?), they knew that this island of St. Delus was but a small part of a humungous world. Now they would get to learn, not just about other continents, but about *what, when, and how* other people lived.

"Hey, Bubblehead, wanna get the flash cards out?" Ardan asked Isabel.

"Love to, *baby brother*. I hope you're not going to call me all those names in front of our new friends at school. Or are you?" she protested. "You'll have everyone doing it. I'll be bullied."

"They wouldn't dare!" Ardan was suddenly offended to think someone would actually pick on his sister. "You know, I don't do it to hurt you. Gosh, I don't even know why I like to tease you, but it's not out of meanness—that's for sure." He looked her in the eye. "You know that, don't you?"

The truth of it was that Ardan (as with most young boys) found it hard to express his admiration and, yes, affection for another person. Doing crazy, off-the-wall, weird things was just an awkward, boyish way of trying to show that he really did care. After all, Isabel was Ardan's wingman. He depended on her for practically everything. They were a team!

"You know, I've learned it's just your way. But I live for the day you outgrow that boyish goofiness of yours." With a quirky smile while still trying to hold back the giggles that often consumed her at the most awkward of times, Isabel pulled out the cards with pictures of items on one side and the spelling of it on the back. The competitive twins braced for a spell down.

"You first," she taunted him. "I'll bet I can stump you in just five turns of the cards.

"Bring it on." Ardan was eager now to show off.

"Not to change the subject, but do you think we'll learn about this fourth dimension thingamajig in school? Wouldn't it be great to find out it's a normal thing and that it happens to other people, too? Then maybe we can talk about it and not be laughed at. That's what I worry about the most—that we'll be laughed at and that everyone will think we're crazy. I don't feel any different than the other kids. But I'd like the freedom to talk about our outside adventures."

"Remember when I told you about Grandpa and Dad talking about the fourth dimension? They also mentioned other big words like *telepathy, thought transference, time travel, clairvoy* … something or other. You know, big words that sound scary. Are they all the same thing? Or are there many different kinds of these experiences? If I thought our folks would believe us, I'd feel better about talking to them. But, you know how they reacted to our wood nymphs as just being imaginary friends. I don't want that to happen again."

Isabel had to agree. Better off keeping the secret until they had more information on the subject.

"I thought once about bringing it up when Dad was telling stories about his grandmother. He was saying how spending the weekend on the farm with her and his grandpa was like having a new experience every visit. They even nicknamed her 'Crazy Grandma.'"

"Crazy in a good, funny way but definitely not like other grandmas." Isabel laughed. Isabel had seen pictures of her father's grandma in her goofy getups—of which there were many.

"The story I like best is when Grandpa, our grandpa I mean, tells how that, just out of the blue, she'd short-sheet their beds." Ardan laughed. "'Just keeping you on your toes,' she'd say."

"Sounds like, since they didn't have TV and video games back then, she invented entertainment for them. Grandpa said he liked the treasure hunts she sent him on, just to find his birthday present, and her wild stories to explain a simple act of nature."

"Yeah," Ardan laughed, "and Grandpa said that, since they didn't have many books to read at bedtime, she'd relate tales that almost sounded like they were her own personal adventures. And best of all, as she tucked them in, she always let them know she loved them and liked them even more. I'm glad our folks still keep that up. It's nice to know they like us too, not just because we're their kids. You kinda have to love your own kids, right? But to know they like us, really like us—well that feels special."

"Hey, do you think she had these episodes like us?" Isabel asked with a whisper of hope.

"I wish she were alive today. I'd bet my rock collection she at least would have listened to us without judging us. And," he continued, "I'd bet she would have understood."

The twins occupied most of the day practicing their printing of numbers and letters. Although their hands were occupied, their thoughts still fell back to the possibility of hearing someone else talk about the *fourth dimension*.

Chapter 12

Rise and Shine

No one had to wake them. Not this morning. The twins were up and dressed quicker than a pitcher can throw a fast ball across home plate. They were down the stairs faster than a player rounding third base. One might say they were anxious, if one were to put a name on it. The two rambunctious twins were getting to go to school—today!

Isabel was cursed with a mop of extra curly red hair that was a bear to brush out. To keep it out of the way, she usually wet it down and pulled it off her face into a ponytail. No matter how hard she tried, wisps of the unruly strands still worked their way out, framing her face in kinky ringlets. She felt like a Brillo pad. Today, she was too busy to care about such incidentals. Looking in the mirror, she saw a set of sparkling blue eyes looking back at her—eyes so full of color, they were a clear giveaway to her expectations.

Ardan, on the other hand, had thick, straight red hair. Since his hair too had a mind of its own with a variety of cowlicks, Father had the barber keep it trimmed short. In the summer, he would get it "pruned" down to a full crew cut. One quick rub with a washcloth over his "dome," and Ardan was on his way.

Mother fixed a nutritious breakfast of orange juice, milk, scrambled eggs, and banana nut bread. She didn't want growling tummies distracting them from listening to the teacher. The twins each had a brand-new backpack with a full variety of school supplies and with plenty of room left over for a good healthy lunch.

After giving his mother a tight squeeze, Ardan slid into his chair at the kitchen table. "Thanks, Mom, you are the best cook I know." With a twinge of mischief he added, "I don't care *what* Isabel says."

"*Ardan,*" Isabel shouted. "I never say anything bad about your cooking, Mom. Don't listen to him. You know I tell everyone you're the best cook. *And* you're the very best cook in all of Asterville—the whole world even!" Isabel glared at her rabble-rousing brother as she took her place at the table. Humph.

Meals were always special for the Murphy family. The time was used to share each other's dreams and experiences. This morning, however, Father found it necessary to warn the dynamic duo to behave themselves. His parting words were, "I know you're excited about your first day, kids. But I want you on your best behavior. Go easy on the teacher. She's a very nice lady and a good friend. Do not, I say do *not* turn everything cattywampus for her on your first day. Try giving her a break-in period." As much as he loved his children, Mitch was aware that they were a mite … overzealous, to say the least.

Since this was their first day, Mother drove the twins to school. After that, they would be allowed to walk with the other neighbor children. The walk would take no more than ten to twelve minutes, providing they didn't dawdle along the way. Their next-door neighbor, Margie McClain, was the crossing guard. Although her primary duty was to ensure the children's safety crossing the street, she also chose to start their day with a cheery send-off. She was ever so much like the doting grandmother of everyone's dream. Asterville was blessed to have her among so many other good-hearted people living there.

Mother led the children through the school doors. Isabel and Ardan had been to the school many times before. But today, the brick building felt like a huge museum—cold and a bit intimidating. When Mother had registered the twins last month, an aide had given them a tour of the rooms they would be using. This helped familiarize Isabel and Ardan with the building, but the difference this time was that they would now be on their own. There was comfort, however, in having a sibling at your side. On your own was different for them compared to the other new students—with them being twins and all. Isabel and Ardan were each a significant part of a *team*, each the sidekick of the other.

Mother gave both of her youngsters an embarrassing hug goodbye and watched as they walked down the hall hand in hand. The hallway was full of proud parents turning over the care of their children to someone else, albeit a trained educator. These same parents wondered who would miss the other more—child or parent.

Chapter 13

On Their Own

"Good morning, boys and girls," the teacher said. "My name is Mrs. Peterson. I am here to teach you the basic steps you will need in all avenues of learning. I hope you will find education as exciting as I do. For the next few days, I want to learn more about each of you. I want to see how much you already know about numbers, the alphabet, shapes, and colors. You are all special, and I'll be working with you, not only as a class, but individually too. But especially, I want each of you to learn about each other. Friendships are a firm cornerstone in having a happy life. And each one of you has your own unique personality to explore and share."

She seemed nice and friendly, and she smiled a lot. They guessed her to be in her thirties or forties, but then everyone looks old to a five-year-old. Mrs. Peterson told them that she had two children of her own, in high school already, and that her husband was a plumber. In the future, she promised to share some of the interesting things he found on the job.

After roll call, Mrs. Peterson had the students sit on a round, colorful carpet that was edged with the letters of the alphabet. She chose a clever story about meddlesome farm animals to read to the class. The story was cute and very funny. That put everyone at ease. When the donkey kicked over the water trough, the piglets started to play in it, mixing the dirt and water until it turned to mud. The prissy hen got her tail feathers dirty, making the goat fall down laughing, landing on the bunny rabbit, who jumped over the—well it went on and on like Old McDonald's farm. Mrs. Peterson was a good storyteller. She read with a lot of feeling and excitement, and the numerous illustrations added to the story's infectious humor in their own way.

Isabel and Ardan were assigned seats across the room from one another, which was different, since they generally did everything together. After all they were a *team*—didn't Mrs. Peterson realize that? How were they to coordinate their ideas? All good ones, of course. Most of their antics were formulated through eye contact and facial expressions. That was their usual method of reading each other's thoughts.

The morning went by quickly. They did a craft with egg cartons, yarn, and lots of sticky glue. They sang a few songs and marched around the room following different directives from various students. Maybe they were airplanes or robots or even eerie ghosts. Mrs. Peterson did manage to skillfully introduce some actual learning issues, but on the whole, her focus was on having the students interact with each other in fun ways while getting acquainted.

Archie McNabb shared a desk in Ardan's quad unit. Jay Reynolds and Gwendolyn Kramer completed the square arrangement. It didn't take long for Archie to establish himself as the class cutup. Archie's egg carton was the creepy, crawly centipede with red eyes and strings of vomit coming from its mouth. Archie was the marching leader who chose everyone to be weird aliens when his turn came up as leader, and Archie himself was an intimidating, hysterical creature. It might take longer to learn the names of the other classmates, but everyone knew who Archie was—immediately.

Archie was not only funny but also showed how kind he was when a homesick Margaret Willis started to cry. Archie was the one who made her laugh when he put corn curls up his nose and crossed his eyes in a totally disarming way. And it was Archie who watched out for her the rest of the day.

Soon, the bell rang, indicating recess. Outside was a vast array of playground equipment in a large open field. The colorful equipment was bright and inviting. Children squealed as they raced in different directions. Archie watched as Margaret joined a girl with a jump rope. When he felt she was at ease, Archie grabbed a ball and started a game of catch with a few of the other kindergarten boys.

Luckily, Isabel and Ardan found swings next to each other. These swings were much bigger than the ones at home. They held great potential.

Noting the heaviness of the chains holding the yellow plastic seats, Ardan remarked, "Even Paul Bunyan couldn't break this down. I've never seen anything this huge before. Hey, Cuckoo Bird, I bet I can swing higher that you can," Ardan challenged his sister.

"I'll take that bet *little* brother," Isabel answered emphatically. She enjoyed being a whole eight minutes older.

The twins had never swung so high before. If humans could fly, then they were flying. Soaring would be a better term—into the wild blue yonder. Birds made it look so easy, and now these petite humans were capturing the same euphoric experience. As they pumped their short little legs to get higher and higher, the wind swept around them, almost taking their breath away. The momentum of reaching the highest point of the arc and being pulled back by gravity left them with a telltale feeling in the pit of their stomachs. Fear suddenly enveloped them. Just as suddenly, the situation turned from fun to terrifying. Instinctively, they both regretted the dare. Then, *kaboom*; it happened. The two fledglings fell backward out of the safety of their swings, hitting the ground with a loud thud. Their little wings were left dangling, limp at their sides.

Everything went blank.

"Call the nurse! The Murphy twins are hurt!" the playground monitor shouted as she ran to the unmoving duo. She realized the twins never should have been allowed on this particular piece of equipment. These larger swings were meant for older students. Almost immediately, the substitute nurse was at the scene. The regular nurse was off due to an illness in the family.

Chapter 14

What Just Happened?

The twins had never experienced total silence before. The quiet was quickly broken as they heard wheels rolling down a tiled floor. Isabel and Ardan could make out a nurse at the end of the hall. Turning her cart, she entered one of the rooms. Down the corridor on the left, a doctor was having a serious conversation with a man and woman. The woman was crying.

"Isn't that Nurse Tyler?" Ardan asked Isabel. Mrs. Tyler was the school nurse. The twins had met her at registration. But she wasn't at school today. Was she working at the hospital now? How curious.

"Are we hurt?" Ardan asked, looking over his body for wounds. "I don't feel bad, but we did take quite a fall."

"I'm OK, too. No, I don't think we're hurt or anything. We're not in a bed, and I don't see any bandages on us," Isabel observed.

"You're right. We're OK. But this is *not* school. It looks more like a hospital," Ardan said, taking in his sterile surroundings. "How did we get here? And why are we here?"

"Oh, no!" Isabel cried out. Her eyes widened, and her face drained of color. "I think it's happening again. We're somewhere other than where we started. It feels like that dimension thingamajig. Let's duck into this room until we can figure this out. I don't want anyone finding us just yet. What would we tell them? Do we know why we're here? What if they ask?"

The room they chose happened to be occupied. In the hospital bed was a small boy who appeared to be asleep. No, he wasn't asleep. He was in a coma. Instinctively, Isabel reached for his hand. His fingers were burning hot. She looked at Ardan through worried brows, her face displaying the concern she felt inside. Ardan instantly read his sister's expression and lifted the boy's other hand. With youthful compassion, he held it tenderly.

The twins began to realize that this was why they had been drawn to the hospital. Somehow, this young boy needed them. Even though the twins were only five, they understood the responsibility that lay before them. But *how* could they be of any help—with them being so young and all?

"Isabel, this boy is really sick. I mean *really* sick," Ardan worried aloud. The fever made the boy restless. He was twisting and turning in his bed. Low moans were the only sounds coming from his weakened body.

Isabel and Ardan began talking to the boy in soothing tones, encouraging him to relax and take deep breaths. Although the boy could not talk, the three began communicating through thoughts.

His name was Matthew Tyler. In his coma, Matthew explained how his mind was running like a movie of his life—family, events, all flashing by in rapid succession. The movie kept playing over and over, faster and faster. His thoughts were spinning totally out of control. Visions were like a kaleidoscope of colors. Try as he might, he could not break free from this repetitive cycle. His brain was utterly exhausted from the process.

With barely any strength left, Matthew explained that he could hear voices, but they were far away, as if in a tunnel—echoing, not totally coherent. The fever not only made his head hurt but also had his whole body aching in pain. He was trying to be brave, but he really wished for some relief, no matter how little it might be.

Isabel and Ardan continued talking to Matthew. They especially worked on motivating him, encouraging him to employ all his energy to fight this wicked virus.

The twin's presence seemed to be helping him. Shortly, Matthew felt the switch being flipped off, allowing the friction in his mind to slow down its maddening pace. Isabel told him to keep taking long deep breaths. The oxygen would help his blood fight the virus and keep his brain healthy. At long last, as his anxiety lessened, Matthew appeared to relax. His small body had been through a traumatic ordeal these last few days.

Isabel gave Ardan that wicked little smile she got when about to embark on some mischief. "Matthew," she whispered, "think of a creepy centipede with big, bright red eyes. He's in your body gobbling up all those tasty, old germs. He has such a big appetite and is oh so hungry. Can you see him, Matthew? He's eating all the pain away. Can you feel him eating? He's here to make you better."

"Isabel, that's the silliest thing I've ever heard. I can't believe you'd come up with such a ridiculous idea," Ardan stammered, shocked that, at such a serious time as this, his sister would talk about something as off the wall as that. But the more he thought about it, he couldn't help but laugh at the very quirkiness of a centipede eating germs—inside someone's body. "That sounds like something Archie would say."

"Exactly. Laughter is the best medicine for all kinds of fears, and for illnesses, too, I'll bet. It helped Margaret. And look, Matthew thinks it's funny too." She ran her cool hand across his warm forehead. "Matthew, you see the centipede, don't you? He's real funny-looking, isn't he? Our classmate, Archie, created him just today, and I'm sure that creature was meant especially for you. When you get back to school, you'll meet Archie, and I know you'll like him."

As Matthew started to feel better, his thoughts turned to his parents. He expressed how very worried he was about them. He wanted his Mom and Dad to know the medicine was working. He could feel it. Would Isabel let them know—tell them he would be better?

As an afterthought, Matthew also conveyed to Isabel that the centipede didn't like the germs and threw up after eating them. How good it was to know that Matthew had a sense of humor too. And yes, Archie's centipede had indeed vomited. How could Matthew, or Archie for that matter, have known? This was all too strange.

In earnest, he pleaded again with the twins to tell his folks that everything would be all right. Isabel couldn't help but admire Matthew for his great concern for his parents while he himself was critically ill. The twins would welcome Matthew as a friend when he was well enough to join them at school.

As the twins sat with Matthew, they felt his temperature take a dramatic turn downward. Still they held his hands and continued with words of encouragement. Just in case laughter really was good for the soul, they threw in a good dose of funny trivia—mostly about Archie and his antics.

In retrospect, the twins knew the kindergarten class was full of memorable students, many of whom would surely make their mark on an unsuspecting world.

"Isabel," Ardan said softly, "why doesn't he wake up?"

"I know he wants to, Ardan," she responded. "That is the one last bridge he has to cross. I'm not sure how much more we can do."

Just then, the door behind the twins opened, allowing the doctor and Matthew's parents to enter. They looked at Ardan and Isabel with curiosity.

"I hope you don't mind that we wandered in here. The door was open." Isabel walked over to the Tylers. Minding Matthew's plea, she added, "I think Matthew is feeling better now. You shouldn't worry anymore. He's going to be just fine." Isabel was reassuring Matthew's parents, just as he'd wished her to do.

Mrs. Tyler managed a slight smile and thanked the twins. She was warmed by their comforting words, especially coming from children so young. Mrs. Tyler went to her son and spoke his name softly, "Matthew. Dearest Matthew, we need you so. Please come back to us. We love you so much more than you can know."

Upon hearing his mother's voice, Matthew stirred.

"He's waking up!" Mrs. Tyler said excitedly. She looked at the doctor for confirmation. Had he seen it, too? He had indeed and was now joining Mrs. Tyler at Matthew's bedside.

Matthew struggled, trying to open his eyes. Words would not yet form as he made a valiant effort to speak. But weak as it was, his smile was there to tell the story. Seeing his mother and father at his side was all the medicine the small child needed. His parents love was the necessary element needed to complete Matthew's recovery.

"The little lady is right," the doctor said, concurring with Isabel's diagnosis as he checked the boy's eyes for signs of activity. While lifting Matt's wrist to take his pulse, the doctor could feel that the fever was all but gone. "The fever's broken. Matthew is on the road back. He's going to recover." The doctor stressed that it was important for the parents to stop worrying; instead, he wanted them to put all their focus on Matthew getting better. It would take time, but the doctor assured the Tylers that there would be no permanent damage. All Matthew needed now was time and lots of loving care.

The doctor rang for the nurse, and soon the room was bustling with activity. The twins used this as an opportunity to leave the room unnoticed. Back in the hallway, the two marveled at Matthew's fighting spirit and his deep love for his parents.

For a change, Ardan and Isabel felt grateful to possess this unique ability of bridging the dimensional gap. Because of it, they were able to connect with Matthew and help him break that repetitive cycle whirling aimlessly in his mind. The experience showed Isabel and Ardan that modern medicine, coupled with parental love, were the real keys in his healing. The fourth dimension was no longer considered a curse. The twins could now see how the special gift could also be a blessing.

Chapter 15

Life Goes On

The nurse on duty asked the playground monitor to help her by taking one of the twins, who were left lying flat on their backs underneath the very swings that had taken them to such heights of exhilaration. First, the aides raised the Murphy twins' arms above their heads and lifted gently on their rib cages.

"Take a deep breath," the nurse was saying to them.

Just as young birds faulter in their first attempts at flying, Isabel and Ardan had experienced their own plight in winged aviation.

"You had the wind knocked out of you when you fell," the nurse explained. "Just breathe deeply. You'll be all right. That's it. Take a few deep breaths."

Just as it had worked for Matthew, deep breathing was working for Ardan and Isabel. Within minutes, the twins sparked back to reality.

At school, no one had missed the wandering duo when they made their unconventional visit to the hospital. In truth, the twins were only unconscious for a minute or so. In everybody's eyes, they were just lying on the ground with the wind knocked out of them. And as for Mrs. Tyler, well, she was so concerned about Matthew that she never took a good look at the two children who had wandered into her sick child's room. No, her focus was on her own little boy.

Life has a funny habit of going on. Things just picked up from where they'd left off. And that was a good thing.

Archie had one more bit of mischief up his sleeve when, after lunch, he mixed up all the name cards. The children, thinking the teacher had done it, shuffled into the wrong seats. Archie would make it worth coming to school every day, just to see what he would do next. He was one interesting kind of kid.

At supper that night, the twins had so much to tell their parents about their first day at school. Of course, Archie was the main topic. The one big thing they could not share was what had happened with Matthew Tyler, lest people, or even their beloved parents, thought them to be a bit weird. No, as usual, they held the experience to themselves. One day—one day, maybe—they would be able to share these unorthodox adventures. But until they themselves knew more about the fourth dimension, they could not even share this with their very loving parents.

Ardan did his nightly ritual with the universe, saying:

In your world above,
You send moonbeams of love.

That night, Ardan saw his first shooting star.
The children were asleep before their parents could tuck them in.

BOOK FOUR
The Halloween Roundup

Chapter 16

Pumpkin Creations

Here it was Halloween again and time to carve their annual pumpkins. Father brought home one of those orange, lumpy objects for each member of the family to create his or her own masterpiece.

"This is so fun!" Ardan declared, plunging his hands into the cavity of his own personal pumpkin. "What do you think, Pip-squeak? Is it gooey enough for you?" he asked Isabel. Ardan twisted his fingers around the spidery, stringy fibers and pulled out a big handful of the oozy seeds.

"I'm going in!" Isabel chuckled. She was the other partner in this awesome duo. "Icky," she cried out, examining her own mushy wad of goop. "Mercy, my patient lost his innards!"

"Worse than that. I think you've completely *lost* your patient, Dr. Sticky Fingers. He's gone—gone I tell you." Ardan dramatically placed his arm around Isabel's shoulder as a means of contrived comfort.

"Contraire, ye of little faith. 'Tis not so," she said while shaking off his feigned gesture. "I won't give up while there's still a chance. A little CPR, and she'll be as good as new."

"You know there's another medical advancement you could try," Ardan offered.

"Like what?" Isabel innocently asked.

"Just hit it up alongside the head."

"Don't you dare touch her!" Isabel did her best to spread herself over her patient. "Serves me right for asking."

Amused at his children's antics, Mitch patiently waited for Isabel's instructions, since he would be doing the actual carving of the pumpkins.

"I've been thinking about the story the teacher read about Florence Nightingale. Do you think we could give my pumpkin a happy smiling face, Dad? And, Mom, do you think we could make some yarn hair and a nurse's cap?" After visiting with Matthew Tyler when he was hospitalized a couple of years ago and hearing about nurse Nightingale, Isabel's interest in medicine was developing into more than a mere passing fancy.

Ardan's idea for his pumpkin was far less serious. But then, in certain respects, so was Ardan. He wanted his creation to be something totally off the wall. "How about a one-eyed cyclops?" Ardan tried to emulate the look for his father. All he accomplished was a portrayal of a twisted, cross-eyed, rubber-faced emoji. Ardan's inspiration for the cyclops came from a library book about the many unusual creatures in Greek mythology. Ardan chose the pumpkin with the most lumps and blemishes, and then he enhanced the creature's looks with a greenish yellow paint. *Awesome,* he thought as he went about creating his rendition of the man-beast. Father carved a single lopsided eye in the center of the elongated pumpkin, to the delight of Ardan's imaginative direction.

"I don't think that's a cyclops. It looks more like an alien—you know, one of those creatures you're always looking for in outer space," Isabel teased.

"Na. Space aliens are more handsome that that, Miss Solar Roller," he assured her.

"In your dreams," she retorted.

As Mitch carved the pumpkins, their mother washed the seeds, coated them with seasoned butter, and roasted them in the oven. While the seeds were still warm, the family would devour them. This was another of the family traditions the children would cherish forever.

Chapter 17

The Brewsters' Big Shindig

The finished pumpkins would to be judged at the big party their neighbors Fred and Louise Brewster had held every Halloween since their arrival on the island. Arden had won last year's competition with a goofy-looking monkey. He'd added stuffed arms and legs and a prehensile tail made from wire covered in brown material.

The Brewsters had migrated to the island of St. Delus from a place called Texas in a country very far away. They'd brought with them many traditions, such as the way they celebrated Halloween in America.

Each year on this occasion in Asterville, the Brewsters hosted a big country-style shindig. They served BBQ beef dinners with beans and roasted ears of corn from an authentic chuck wagon. A scrumptious apple cobbler topped off a perfect cowboy supper. The chuck wagon was a large horse-drawn wagon covered in white canvas. Traditionally, the vehicle was used on good old Texas cattle drives. At the Brewster party, everyone sat on the ground or on bales of hay encircling a huge campfire. They ate from tin plates and drank from tin cups.

Mr. Brewster amused his guests with endless tales of cattle roundups, rustlers, and rodeos. Everyone enjoyed listening to the stories, which become bigger and more grandiose with each telling. Mr. Brewster accented his tales of the Wild West with hand gestures befitting a cowboy on a rampage of roping and riding. Invariably, the audience became more enthralled as the stories dramatically developed. Some had been so wrapped up in the excitement that they'd literally jumped out of their seats when Fred reached the climax, whether it be a stampede, a clash with rustlers, or being thrown from a steer.

In his prime, Mr. Brewster had been a professional bull rider. He spoke of the thrill of hanging onto a bucking steer. Although little known in this part of the world, Fred Brewster had been inducted into the Bull Riding Hall of Fame in Fort Worth, Texas, of the United States of America. Years of hard riding and many torturous spills had taken their toll on Fred's body, and like the mounts he rode, he was put out to pasture. A yearning for adventure had led Fred and his wife, Louise, to St. Delus. He took the challenge and started a dude ranch where none had existed before.

One of the more joyous events of the night, especially for the younger generations, was a horse-drawn hayride that continued running trips around the back roads throughout the night—right up to time for the haunted roundup that is.

In the barn, country music would be playing. This particular style of music was different from the usual fare heard on the island. Children and adults alike joined in the uniqueness of square dancing and line dancing. Inhibitions were set aside as the villagers give this new concept of dancing *a whirl* (another colloquialism native to the older generation, which meant to give it "a try"). While attempting to square dance, someone or another invariably made a wrong turn and caused a pileup. Line dancing often repeated the disaster, with left steppers bumping into right steppers. After a bit of good-natured teasing of each other, people eventually got the hang of it, with each year showing a bit more improvement over the last.

But the highlight of the evening was definitely the spooky walk through the woods. You didn't know when or where something would pop out at you. Many of the townsfolk joined the antics by dressing in an array of costumes and haunting the woods. Other spooky artifacts might be triggered by a mere step or by tripping a wire. *Not knowing*—the anticipation of when something *might* happen—was almost as frightening as when it actually did occur.

Chapter 18

Haunted Halloween Roundup

This Halloween night, Ardan dressed as a cowboy—just like one of those Texas cowboys Mr. Brewster always talked about. "Howdy partner," Ardan drawled as he donned his tan Stetson hat. He pulled on a pair of boots with real spurs. "Boy, oh boy. Listen to these spurs jingle. Those cowpokes must have had a blast walking around in these things!"

Ardan couldn't help but noisily clop around as if he were wearing tap shoes. Grabbing his rope, he twirled it over his head and tried to rope a footstool.

"Missed it. Can't brand what you can't catch," Isabel teased in a singsong voice.

"Yeah, Miss I-Can-Do-Better-Than-You-Can. You show me how, if you're so good at it." He tried his hardest to goad Isabel into making herself look foolish. Lassoing wasn't the easiest thing to master, as he was finding out.

"No time," Mother chimed in. "Let's finish getting you ready, Miss Nightingale."

Isabel chose to wear a nurse's uniform, much like what her new idol, Florence Nightingale, might have worn back in 1840. "How in the world did the nurses work in these long gowns? It gets all twisty around my ankles." Isabel could always be counted on to exaggerate a situation, and she did not disappoint.

"You'll just have to behave like a little lady for a change," Mother said with a sigh. She could hope, couldn't she?

Angela and Mitch went as Raggedy Ann and Andy. What they lacked in imagination was compensated for by their antics. Mother raised her arms and let them dangle from her elbows while Father acted all limp and goofy by stumbling along with floppy arms and legs. Never fear, Isabel was at the ready with her first aid kit in hand.

With the family already in a jolly mood, they set out for an evening of adventure. "We're as happy as if we had good sense," Father declared using another of his vast supply of old, sappy sayings. "Especially when you consider the dangers awaiting us at the *Haunted Halloween Roundup!*" He spoke those words by raising his voice in a high, scary pitch, implying imminent terror awaited them.

Pumpkins in hand, they all marched off to the car.

⑥〜〜〜⑨

Ardan barely eked out the reply—his eyes widening at the very sight. The lane leading to the Brewster Farm was lined with scarecrows and mannequins dressed in various costumes. They looked almost lifelike. Perhaps that was because some actually were real people, who would later be hiding in the woods during the Haunted Halloween Roundup.

"Look at that one—the one with a white face and long, freakish fingers." Isabel cringed. "Is that one real?"

"I certainly hope not."

Secretly, the twins hoped for a fairy godmother to follow them with her protective wand. Surely someone would think she was appropriately attired under the circumstances. *Oh please, pretty please*, Ardan thought. He hated to admit he was a trifle nervous.

The evening was all anyone could have hoped for. Even Ol' Humphrey Moore was seen dancing with the widow Mason. The barn cat had a litter of black kittens, all cute and cuddly. Isabel and Ardan joined the other children in blind man's bluff, while parents reminisced with stories from years past.

Fortunately, a rare blue moon appeared that just might provide a teeny, tiny bit of light to help participants navigate the haunted trails. The time had come! It would be happening *now*.

With uncertain looks, one small group after another started picking their way through unmarked pathways. The object was to catch and keep as many "cows" as you could in twenty minutes. The cows were appropriately attired teenagers who were quick on their feet. The catching was more like trying to hold on to a greased pig. Eerie howls and frightening screams were seasoned with uncontrolled laughter as eager guests crept their way deeper into unknown territory. Mummy or skeleton. Witch or cow. Participants moved ahead at their own risk! No flashlights allowed!

Chapter 19

A New Twist to the Hunt

A small boy dressed in turn-of-the-century clothes approached the twins. "Will you help me?" he pleaded earnestly. "Please, please. Pirates are coming ashore. I need to warn the villagers, but I'm lost." It was obvious he was in a high state of anxiety. As he grew more excited, he also became more confused. "Help. Please."

"Cute." Ardan smiled at Isabel. "Pirates must be new this year." The twins thought this to be a fun deviation to the traditional cow roundup. But what were the rules? Were they to capture pirates? Was there a bounty—maybe a treasure hunt? Quickly, Isabel and Ardan raced after the young actor into a new unknown, ever so eager and ready to experience this addition to the Halloween activities. The twins followed the lad down to the waterfront.

"I was skipping stones in the ocean when I saw them anchor in the bay and get their skiffs ready to come ashore. A few years back when they landed the first time, they looted our village. They barely left us with enough food to make it through the winter. Believe me, that was hard on us, since our crops had already been harvested and were now in the hands of the pirates. The thieves took all our family treasures and heirlooms too. No good can come by their returning." The lad seemed anguished at the very thought of being invaded once again.

The boy's name was Arnold "Skip" (because he was always skipping rocks in any available amount of water) McGovern. He was little for his age of eleven years, a whole two years older than the twins and yet the same size. Skip was freckle-faced with a shock of unruly red hair—a typical

Scottish youth. Townsfolk regarded him as a bright young lad with a ready hand to help anyone who needed it. But mostly, Skip could make you smile on your very worst day. He carried with him his own brand of sunshine.

Sure enough, a ship was anchored in the bay just as Skip had said. And it appeared that small crafts were about to be lowered into the sea. On the forward mast hung a huge black flag with the traditional skull and crossbones, indicating the ship was inhabited by pirates.

"Ardan," Isabel whispered. "This seems real. I don't think this is part of the roundup anymore."

The twins had come to the realization they were now able to slip in and out of this fourth dimension with ease – and with no advanced warning. The transition was no longer a mystery to them. This current situation was leaving them with a very uneasy feeling. Unsettling or not, time did not allow for a mental adjustment period. They could hear boats splashing into the water and the captain barking orders.

"I'm lost. I must warn the town. Help me!" The frightened boy's pleading was desperate now. Time was a luxury they no longer enjoyed.

Ardan recalled visiting the ruins of an old settlement called Mt. Hope. The twins' parents had taken them to see it a few months ago. The village was now an historical feature of the island's first inhabitants. And yes, there was record of pirates having attacked the settlement in 1811 and again in 1813.

"I'll climb this tree. Maybe I can see where we are and get a clue on how to find the village," Ardan said as he quickly scaled a tall tree. Thankfully, the branches were well set to assist him in this challenge.

He saw a cliff ahead. On top, far off to the left were a variety of dwellings. The settlement looked different now, bustling with activity. People carrying lanterns gave the illusion of twinkling stars on earth. That had to be what Skip was looking for.

Ardan scurried down the tree and urged the other two to follow him. Reaching the bottom of the cliff, the children climbed the rugged terrain with sure-footed determination. Nearing the overhang at the apex, Ardan threw his rope up around a tree stump and pulled himself up to the summit. Isabel and Skip followed right behind. Carefully, they retrieved the rope so as not to leave it behind for the culprits to utilize.

Once they reached the top of the cliffs, the full jolt of adrenaline kicked in, giving Skip's short legs the speed of a Greek Olympian. As he neared the village, Skip shouted the alert as loudly as he could. Heads snapped to attention. Had they heard Skip right? Pirates, did he say?

Right behind on Skip's heels were the Murphy twins waving their arms in the air and echoing the same warning at the top of their lungs.

It must be so. The townsmen reacted.

The dreaded day had arrived, but this time the villagers were prepared for the marauders. Mayor Meade sounded the alarm and everyone went into action. Each villager knew exactly what was expected of him or her. Over the last two years, they had practiced the drills again and again. The drills served as an opportunity for these average, everyday citizens to hone their skills as warriors—defenders of their homes. Each had a specific task according to his or her individual strengths.

Ancient tactics were put in play at the crest of the mountain. This was the most vulnerable access to the village and the way the pirates had breached the village two years earlier.

Nets held rocks. Wedges were in place to loosen boulders that would then careen down the cliff. Dogs were trained to respond on command. Along with their rifles, the men grabbed axes to chop the ropes holding the nets of rocks. Young boys raided the family root cellars for lard that their mothers had rendered. The lard would be emptied into large black cauldrons already in place. Other young men hauled dry kindling. Once the lard was heated, the oily substance would be poured over the edge of the cliff. Not only would it be hot and burn the culprits, but it would also make the rocks slippery and harder to climb.

Some of the women set up a child care center in the church. Other women prepared the town hall as an infirmary to handle any casualties that might occur. This was where Isabel found herself, assisting by hauling buckets of water to be boiled for sterilization. Minerva Dawson was a trained midwife and would assist the only doctor. Makeshift cots were set up. Medical supplies were positioned for the doctor to respond quickly and efficiently.

Adolescents had trained as a support system to the adults, who would be based in the village, while the older teens prepared to fight side by side with their fathers on the mountain crest.

Chapter 20

Prepare for War

On the pirate ship, snarky Captain Devin was barking orders to his band of thieves. He was in his usual foul mood. During the first raid on the island, the captain had slipped and fallen down the cliff with his heavy load of ill-gotten goods. His leg had been injured, leaving him with a noticeable and painful limp. Devin wanted to take revenge on the islanders. He unjustly blamed them for his own clumsiness, totally ignoring that the injury was the result of his own thieving lifestyle. Them and their smug, better-than-thou ways. He determined that this time when the pirates were done looting, they would burn the place down. Over the past two years, hatred had built within his mind, festering the need to even the score of his own invention. Pure evil raged within his hardened heart. Without question, Devin was reported to be the meanest pirate on the high seas. As the last of a dying breed, he would be remembered in the history books for his sheer brutality.

Leaving only a skeleton crew on board the ship, the bulk of the henchmen landed on shore and secured their crafts. With the lure of a large treasure left behind from the first raid, the pirates' numbers had grown to over forty. The meek settlers were not expected to be a match for well-experienced, cutthroat villains. Like a coach firing up a team to win a championship ball game, Captain Devin ("Devil Devin" as he was called behind his back) took one last opportunity to whip his men into a frenzy. "Take everything! Leave nothing behind! Make them fear us!" he shouted.

With a mighty roar, the band of rebels charged ahead, wielding their swords high over their heads.

As they neared the woods, the bandits silenced their rhetoric to ensure a surprise attack on the settlement. Reaching the cliffs, each pirate was eager to be the first to get to the top. Caught off guard, the first to arrive were also the first to fall as boulders were released from their precarious perches. The second wave of ruthless thugs were met by a torrent of rocks loosened when the townsmen chopped the bindings that held the nets. Vats of hot oil were now heated well enough to be employed. And yet at the crest, should anyone make it that far, were vicious, snarling dogs sounding fair warning that they would attack when prompted. Necessity to feed their families made each farmer a marksman. These were no longer the meek settlers the pirates had encountered the first time around! This was a lesson the pirates were soon to learn.

One small group after another made the attempt to reach the top of the tall, rocky cliffs. Despite all the preparation the townsmen had in place, the most stubborn buccaneers did achieve their goal, only to be met by farmers and loggers who were in top physical condition due to the very nature of their occupations. These settlers were determined to defend their homes.

The canine soldiers did themselves proud as well. Reverting to their ancestral roots, the pets faced the pirates with fangs fully exposed behind sneering lips. Guttural snarls added to their savagery.

During one of the sieges, a boulder careened off Captain Devin's shoulder as he tried to pull himself over the top ridge, knocking him off the jagged cliff and plunging him to the rocky terrain below. As he hit the bottom, he had a flashback to the first raid that had left him with that devastating limp. Again, Devin could hear bones cracking. Worse yet, Devin's face slammed into the hard, solid rocks, knocking loose one of his front teeth, which left him with a distinctive whistle when speaking. His legacy was altered ever so slightly, making him known as "the Whistling Devil." However demeaning that might have been, he still retained his position as the most brutal pirate in history.

Racked with pain, Devin finally called off the attack and sounded the retreat. With the wind ripped from their own sails, the now less arrogant invaders limped or crawled back to the bay to make their pitiful escape.

Devil Devin himself had to be carried off the battlefield, cursing his own fate.

Still mindful of an additional attack, the villagers held fast to their positions on the mountaintop. The defenders who were injured were helped back to the compound for medical assistance.

Chapter 21

Ardan Faces His Own Peril

At the same time, two lone looters flanked the village from the remote, more dangerous side of the cliffs. Skip and Ardan were gathering additional wood for the fires when one of the pirates grabbed Ardan from behind and drew him in. Ardan reacted quickly. He raised his leg and thrust it backward as hard as he could, kicking the man in the shins with his spur. Before the culprit had a chance to recover, Ardan whirled around and kicked him again in the same injured leg. The pirate yelled out in pain as his leg gave way. It buckled and the creep went down crumpling into a puddle of self-pity. He would never live down being taken by a child.

Fiery Skip was wielding a good-sized chunk of wood at the other pirate, hitting his mark several times. Help seemed to come from nowhere, yet from everywhere at once, as other youth arrived to assist. Fired up with desire to save their friends, the youngsters piled on the marauders like bees on a bear caught stealing the hives' prized honey stash.

Realizing how futile their efforts were, the pirates made their own hasty departure.

The entire skirmish with the pirates proved to be somewhat brief. As confrontational as the incident was, the pirates left without harming the village and were not able to acquire any new loot. The history books would prove out that the pirates never returned for a third raid.

Ardan helped Skip to the infirmary. Skip incurred a cut on his forehead and several bruises from his encounter.

Isabel was relieved to see the two boys. News had not yet reached the makeshift hospital. This whole situation was foreign to the twins and their generation. Sea pirates were all but obsolete and only known about because of history books and old movies on television.

Isabel grabbed a wet cloth and immediately proceeded to wash the blood from Skip's face. Head wounds tended to bleed profusely, when in fact, the origin can sometimes be quite minor. Dr. Jenkins stepped up to relieve her. He was impressed with the work Isabel had exhibited while assisting the medical team. Her skills were remarkable and fit in well with the other assistants. During the intense activity, she had not drawn undo attention to herself, thanks in part to her Halloween costume. In the excitement, no one questioned her sudden appearance into their midst.

Isabel reached for her first aid kit and handed the doctor a Band-Aid. "Here," she said. "This is the largest one I have, but I think it will cover the wound."

Dr. Jenkins drew his head back. With furrowed brows, he viewed the article with suspicion. "What in the world is this?" he queried.

"It's just a Band-Aid," she said. But then midsentence, she realized that maybe Band-Aids hadn't been invented yet. "Here, you just pull off the protective paper and place the cloth over the wound. The adhesive on the edges will hold it in place," she explained.

The doctor applied the new contraption as Isabel suggested—all the while his mind was pondering the importance of this small wonder he held in his hands. His train of thought was interrupted when the doors of the town hall opened, and new patients arrived.

In another few minutes, hardy shouts of victory greeted the staff. Most of the front line remained to guard the perimeter of the village. Only those with injuries returned. Thankfully, nothing was of major consequence. Twisted ankles. Cuts and bruises. The hand-to-hand skirmishes had been few and brief. Isabel remained to stand shoulder to shoulder with the medical support team, completing all tasks assigned to her.

Shortly after that, the team that had stayed behind as lookouts also entered the hospital and announced that the pirates had pulled up anchor and sailed out to sea.

"Hail to the defenders!" Minerva Dawson chanted.

"Hail to the defenders," the others repeated in unison, throwing their fists high above their heads. *"To the defenders!"*

With that news, Ardan and Isabel seized the moment to slip away. The Murphy twins shared their individual experiences with each other as they headed back to the Brewster farm. Since they were still uncomfortable discussing their bizarre episodes with anyone else, the children would also keep this event to themselves. Ardan and Isabel had come to realize that this phenomenon was unique, and only they experienced it. Although they had hoped to learn more about the fourth dimension at school, it was never discussed. So, the mystery continued and remained unexplained.

Chapter 22

Evening's End

The twenty-minute gong was sounded, indicating the end of the haunted roundup. A heavy pipe whirled round and round in the large metal triangle on the Brewsters' porch. This was the same method of communication used in the old days to call the farmworkers in from the fields for meals. It was amazing how far reaching the instrument's tone carried.

In all, eight cows were rounded up with four more "escapees" getting away. The escapees received duly earned applause for their adeptness.

Travis and Justin from the Ballard farm were the ultimate winners, with three energetic critters to their credit. They had perfected a unique way of double teaming the bovine contenders. While one of them silently hid behind a tree, the other would chase the cow toward him. Once they'd "branded" their captive, they quickly ensnared another into their illusive trap.

The grand prize was Mrs. Mason's award-winning, homemade cherry pie and the right to unveil the new sculpture designed by the local blacksmith, Glenn McGovern. The statue was commissioned to commemorate the two-hundred-year victory for Mt. Hope over the second pirate siege of 1813. The statue would be moved to the ruins of Mt. Hope in time for the annual Inspiration Day celebration.

Amid cheers of encouragement, Justin and Travis tugged the rope that released the covering.

There he was. It was sculpture of young Arnold "Skip" McGovern—just as Ardan and Isabel witnessed. His arms were askew, with a chunk of wood gripped firmly in his right hand. He was in a half-crouched position ready to pounce. Skip was praised for his bravery. By alerting the village in time, he'd not only saved the original settlers but had also enabled the island to continue to grow and develop.

Skip had turned out to be a scrapper his entire life. When he was barely twelve, his father passed away. As the eldest, Skip hired on as a farmhand to help his mother with their large family responsibilities. At fifteen, he worked with the town blacksmith and, later in life, opened his own silversmith shop—picking up his father's and grandfather's vocations.

Skip also helped settle the eastern side of the island, where he started his own family, having two boys and a girl. Skip instilled in his children the same patriotic values he had been raised with. While still in his fifties, Skip was voted governor of St. Delus Island. The town he helped establish grew into one of the largest on the island and eventually became its capital. Shortly after his death, the city was renamed McGovern in his honor. Many of Skip's descendants continue to develop the land, Ol' Humphrey Moore being one of the most prominent in Asterville.

⟨∞∞⟩

The hands on the clock showed that midnight was approaching. When the Murphy family finally made it home, they barely had the energy to crawl into bed. Mitch and Angela tucked their exhausted children in their beds without reading the usual bedtime story.

But before Arden closed his eyes, he looked at the blue moon, realizing that this same occupant of the universe had been observing decades of evolution.

Life is but a blink of an eye to you,
But yet you see so much.
Keep your eyes on me.
I'll be in touch.

Ardan was asleep in minutes.

⟨∞∞⟩

BOOK FIVE
Inspiration Day Celebration

Chapter 23

The Big Event

Mother was busy in the kitchen packing a big picnic lunch for the dedication ceremony. Inspiration Day was an annual event celebrated across the island, heralding their ancestors' heroic efforts against the pirates. This year, the people from around the whole island were invited to Mt. Hope (the original settlement of the St. Delus Island) for the two-hundred-year anniversary of its declared liberation—although the island itself had been occupied a few years earlier. The early settlers chose the name Inspiration Day to honor the great victory over the pirates. Their success inspired them to dig in and build a prosperous nation for the next generations to take pride in. It also set their resolve to never again allow invaders to rob them of their rightful possessions.

Minerva Dawson designed the nation's original flag in 1813, inspired by the new hope derived when the settlers defeated the pirates that year. Thusly, New Hope also became the undisputed name for the settlement. The upper portion of the flag shows a sun rising in a bright blue sky with just a hint of the waning moon on the right. The lower section features a border of a deep blue sea surrounding fields of flourishing golden wheat and barley to complete the story. It served then and still serves as an inspiration to all who live under her protection.

"Mom," Ardan began, "do you think you could pack enough lunch so we can ask Mr. Moore to join us? He doesn't have a wife to fix him any really good meals, and nobody fixes food like you do." The twins loved Ol' Humphrey like a grandfather, but the truth of the matter was, they really felt they needed to talk to him. The two had some unexplained feelings about the pirate raid.

"We can ask, but don't be surprised if he hasn't already planned to picnic with Mrs. Mason," Mother warned. "They're both on the board for the historical society and have worked very hard at putting this huge bicentennial event together. Considering the whole island is invited to attend the celebration, they've spent a lot of time together getting this organized." She gave an impish little smile with a secret wink to their father.

Ardan didn't know what to make of that. He shrugged it off as Mother just being goofy. Mentally, he made a note to somehow get together with Ol' Humphrey—alone. In some way or another, Isabel and Ardan hoped Ol' Humphrey would put to rest the unsettling feelings they still had about the pirates' raid. Somehow, the mystery of Mt. Hope didn't seem to be complete. There had to be more to the story. Ol' Humphrey never failed the twins, and more importantly, he never forgot anything when it came to the history of Mt. Hope.

This year, Inspiration Day would be held on the original site where the battle took place. The sculpture, unveiled on Halloween, was set in place ready to be dedicated on these hallowed grounds. Isabel and Ardan felt a special connection to Skip and the settlers, since they'd had the opportunity to share in the defeat during the pirate raid. Being a witness to history made the children more aware of their own personal responsibilities in this ever-widening world.

"Hurry up, Isabel," Dad called up the stairs. "Time's a wastin', and we want to get a spot near the stage."

"Ready. I'll be down in a sec." Isabel quickly grabbed her sweater and met up with the family in time to help carry a few items to the car. "Hey, Ardan," she whispered. "Do you think it's true. Are the widow Mason and Ol' Humphrey in *love*?"

"What? What nonsense!" he retorted. *The very thought*, he continued in his own mind. *They're old for goodness sake—way too old for that silly stuff. That Isabel, being overly dramatic—again. What will she come up with next?* He shook his head in disgust. *Ugh!*

Chapter 24

So Many People

This celebration proved to be the largest assembly of people the twins had ever witnessed. It was huge. Blankets covered the landscape like a patchwork quilt. A barbershop quartet strolled among the visitors singing quaint songs in perfect harmony. Brodie MacDougall delighted everyone by playing his bagpipes with many traditional tunes brought from the fatherland. Old friends and relatives took advantage of the opportunity to become reacquainted with their long-lost relatives and friends.

Ol' Humphrey Moore, who was a direct descendent of Arnold "Skip" McGovern on his mother's side of the family, was also a member of the historical society for Mt. Hope. Due to the society's efforts, the original town hall, main church, and a few other original buildings had been restored to their former condition.

As the people strolled through the old settlement, they could get a sense of what might have occurred during that fateful night the pirates attacked. The town hall was displayed with pallets depicting the makeshift infirmary ready to treat wounded townsfolk. The church held antique toys and handmade cribs that would have been available at the time to keep the children occupied while still being protected. Every effort was made to help the visitors envision what happened that night two hundred years ago.

A few actors were dressed in historic clothes pretending to be the various leaders—Minerva Dawson, Dr. Jenkins, Mayor Meade, and Skip McGovern to name a few.

This year, Humphrey was given the distinction of presiding over the affair. He and the entire board highly deserved the recognition for all the time and energy they'd devoted to preserving the island's heritage.

Humphrey did share a picnic lunch with the widow Mason, *but* (and that was a very significant but for Ardan) the entire board shared in that lunch. He smugly felt relieved. Ardan could accept that—the board eating together. *Where, oh where, did Isabel get that love crap? Mrs. Mason was a sweet person, but* love? *With Ol' Humphrey?* What was Ardan to do with Isabel and her overactive imagination?

It was difficult to catch a free minute with Ol' Humphrey, but finally Ardan and Isabel seized on a chance opening. They prodded Mr. Moore to tell them some of the stories of the Mt. Hope settlers' fight with the pirates. With the twins' experience on Halloween, they felt a strong pull to the settlement, and Mr. Moore's knowledge of the past surpassed everyone else's. He'd even helped research and write the history book for the island. All of Humphrey's stories were still in his head and at the tip of his tongue. With a little prompting, he was ready to share with all who would listen.

"Will you tell us about the pirate raid?" Ardan begged Ol' Humphrey. Both he and Isabel always felt there was more to the story but didn't know what. Maybe Humphrey could fill in the gap.

Ol' Humphrey liked the Murphy twins. They were different from most children their age—inquisitive, ambitious, and sincere, with a large dose of mischief. These were all good qualities to his tired, old eyes. Mr. Moore smiled mysteriously as he spoke, almost in a whisper, as if he were divulging a well-kept secret. His face assumed a radiant aura, "I'll bet you never heard about the buried treasure the pirates left behind?" The twinkle in his eye left the two more intrigued than ever.

"A real treasure? Like with gold doubloons and jewels and like maybe diamonds and stuff?" Ardan and Isabel asked, almost in unison (the twins often thought alike).

"Well now," he went on, "mind you, it's only a tale that's been passed on for generations. But it's been said—" He paused and looked around to see if anyone else might be listening. Leaning in closer, he lowered his voice even more. "It's been said that, on that first raid, the pirates absconded with so much food, along with the personal treasurers of the townspeople's, that they had to decide what they could take with them. You see, young

Captain Devin didn't have much of a crew in the beginning so, they couldn't carry it all. With the ship so low on food, it was more important to feed his band of thieves.

"Soooo, as the story goes, Devin chose to hide the loot, fully intending to return and claim it. The belief was that the treasure was the main reason for the second attack. And of course, the canned goods our women processed were the best he'd ever had the fortune to steal. The captain wanted more. Having a skimpy crew made Devin realized he needed to recruit more sailors to help manage his oversized ambitions. A potential treasure, easy for the taking, would be an apple to dangle out front while he worked at luring more of his kind to carry out his dastardly deeds. Devin's dream was for vast wealth and dominance over the seas. When he pulled up anchor after his first successful attack, he was already making plans to come back.

"Again, I say," Humphrey nonchalantly continued, "it's only hearsay. No one ever found any kind of a map or anything. Kinfolk have searched every cave and cavern on the island—nada, zip, nothing." He snapped his fingers so loudly the people on the next blanket glanced over.

Again he leaned in, and with a hushed voice, he continued. "Generation after generation have come up empty-handed. But somehow, the rumor manages to live on. Yes indeed, the lure of a treasure exists to this day."

This bit of trivia peaked the twin's imagination. The possibility of a treasure did little to settle that lingering unrest they felt about the pirate raid. A treasure merely festered it. Just think, the very likelihood of a treasure with so many heirlooms from the original settlers—still sitting out there, waiting. Ardan's and Isabel's young minds took great pleasure in the art of pretend anyway, and this tidbit fueled that fire. One scenario after another played in their young minds. Imagine. What if? Maybe.

Chapter 25

Adventure on the Brain

Inspiration Day led into a long weekend. A late Indian summer left the island in a blanket of warmth. Isabel and Ardan went for a walk enjoying the break in the weather. Of course, they talked about the celebration and about the rumor of a treasure.

"Do you think it's possible there might be a real treasure out there somewhere?" Isabel asked Ardan.

"Probably not. Like Ol' Humphrey said, enough people have looked for one," he responded. "It does make for a good yarn to pass on to future generations though. We can even pass it on to our kids."

"I don't know about that. Who'd marry nuts like us?" She laughed. Their belief was that this malady they were cursed with would probably prevent them from being able to find a partner who could accept it.

The two continued down the road chatting and kicking stones along the way. "Hey!" Ardan said with renewed gusto. "Let's gather a few rocks and go down to the bay and skip them in the water like Ol' Skip used to do."

"Good idea. That sounds like fun." Reflecting on the past, she added, "I wish we could have known Skip better. He turned out to be a pretty good guy. Imagine. He became the first governor of this whole island. I wonder if he remembered meeting us. Do you suppose this dimension thing we have leaves any lasting effect on those we meet?"

"I've wondered the same thing. Guess we'll never know." Ardan shrugged.

On the shore, Isabel busied herself perfecting her technique. By putting just the right pitch on the rock, you could get it to skip across the water. The flatter the rock, the more jumps it would take. With the flick of the wrist, you could put a spin on the pebble to make it hop and jump across the surface like a frog after a fly.

When they ran out of their stash of rocks, the two took a minute to absorb the wonderment of the bay. Sitting on the sandy beach, Isabel let her thoughts drift back again to their time with Skip and the pirates.

"This is where it happened—where the pirates landed. Remember how we thought it was part of the Halloween Roundup? We were so naive," she reflected.

"Maybe we should suggest that pirate version to Mr. Brewster—you know, just to put a new twist on the cow roundup game," Ardan said. "That would have been great for this year's celebration. The pirates versus townsmen reenactment."

"I like that idea," Isabel said thoughtfully. "Anyway, we had our own reenactment—so personal we can't even talk about it."

"Yeah. Personal."

The bay was a rounded indentation with both sides jutting out into the ocean. On the southside the land was flatter. The northern peninsula bore an incline that rose quite high by the end of it; that was also where the currents were the strongest. Fishermen took great precautions when venturing out. Farther in on the highland lay the village of Mt. Hope.

"Look at that!" Isabel pointed to a grove of trees on the crest. The moon was making a daytime appearance and looked like it was rising just between two elms standing so tall and proud. "Am I wrong, or does that seem to be a sign? Well, brother of mine," she continued, "you're the one who talks to the moon. What's it saying? Should we check it out?" Isabel was the one teasing Ardan now and enjoying it. "Aw c'mon, silly or not, wanna check it out?"

"Sure, let's go," Ardan called as he raced ahead in a playful mood. "Dizzy Lizzy, I'll beat you there," he teased over his shoulder.

"Don't call me Lizzy. You know I hate that!" she chastised him.

"Itsy, bitsy, frizzy Lizzy." He laughed as he sped on.

If Isabel knew one thing, it was that Ardan was the fastest kid around. Jumping up, she chased after her ornery upstart of a brother, who already had a healthy lead on her.

After the twins' first spurt of energy, the trip became more tedious as the incline grew steeper and rockier (they should have taken the pathway). Reaching the top, Ardan and Isabel took a deep breath of the clean, fresh ocean air. The climb, however challenging, left them feeling refreshed and invigorated. From this vantage point, Ardan and Isabel could look out over the waters. The ocean appeared endless as waves glistened in the waning sunlight. The colors of the seawater blended from a rich turquoise near the shore into a deep indigo blue further out. Seagulls speckled the sky as they searched for their last meal before sunset.

"What's that old saying? 'Red sky at night, sailor's delight. Red sky in the morning, sailor's warning'? Well, I for one am delighted with the colorful display the ol' sun is putting out for us," Isabel stated as she absorbed the breathtaking view. "Perhaps the view is what the moon wanted to share with us. Well, he did a good job. The trip was well worth the effort."

"Oh, so the moon's a he?" Ardan smiled proudly.

"Well, I never heard of a Woman in the Moon. Did you?"

"I'll work on that. Maybe *she's* the one who causes those fierce tides. I think you're on to something here. Thanks, Moonbeam," Ardan teased. "We should probably head back. We don't want to be late for supper. Mom's making a roast tonight." That was one of his favorites. "And I think I got a whiff of apple pie before we left. It doesn't get much better than that."

As the children were leaving, they noticed an odd formation totally out of context for the rest of the region. It was severely overgrown with vegetation. At first thought, Ardan suggested it to be an old root cellar. (Root cellars were used to preserve some foods before refrigeration was invented.) But this would not have been in a useful location. That idea was probably way off base.

"Can you imagine living a few hundred years ago without electricity or running water? Every day, the settlers had to struggle for what's simple for us. Life must have been really tough," Ardan was remembering back to their brief encounter with Skip. "Remember, you had to help carry buckets of water from the well, and I helped carry wood for the fires. To think that was a part of everyday life for the people back then. We sure are lucky today."

Returning to the subject at hand, Isabel queried, "I wonder what makes this hill so different. Want to dig around a bit and see if maybe it is a root cellar? We could surprise Mom with some ancient jars of tomatoes or corn or something."

"Or a *grave*— hey, Vampira," Ardan said. "That's what it is—a real grave with a real *ghost!*"

"Get off it! You just stop talking like that. It's not a grave and there is no such thing as a ghost. And I don't like you calling me all those goofy names either, for that matter. I'm going to make you sorry if you don't apologize *right now!*" However, Isabel didn't press the subject because she was still curious about this mound.

They circled the man-made hill several more times looking for a possible entry. Ardan started pulling at a weed here and there with no results. "If there is a door, it's certainly well camouflaged," he determined. "Maybe it's just a hill after all. Centuries of dirt have done an awesome job disguising anything that might have caused the dirt to start accumulating."

They were about to give up when Ardan decided to pull on one last sapling. With a mighty tug, it released a torrent of rocks from their resting place. Ardan flew backward as it gave way, tumbling him head over heels backward, only to end with him bumping his head. Catching his breath, he struggled a moment or two to stand erect.

Chapter 26

More Than They Bargained For

"Thar ye be! Ain't ye be da lad det kicked me in da shin?" In front of Ardan stood a hideously large pirate. His wild, unkempt hair was drawn back in a bandana. A single gold earring dangled from one of his enlarged earlobes. The sudden appearance of someone in this disheveled demeanor would catch anyone off guard. It certainly threw Ardan off his game. His breath caught in his throat.

Could this be the pirate I encountered during the pirate raid? It was dark then, and everything happened so fast. Ardan tried to put things in perspective.

"I've been awaitin' fer ye, ya scallywag!" The pirate continued his rage against the young enemy who'd accosted him a few centuries back.

Ardan was barely on his feet when the pirate lunged at him. Quick as a wink, Ardan dodged behind one of the elms. Ardan looked around for Isabel. Needing to protect her was by far his greatest concern at the moment. He dashed about but couldn't find her. He could only hope she was safe.

"Come back 'ere, ya whippersnapper," the pirate spat out, his tone a venomous threat.

The buccaneer was neither fast nor steady, but he was *large*. And when he spread out, he controlled a lot of space. It was the leg injury that prevented him from matching the speed of the younger, more agile Ardan. Unfortunately, however, the pirate had Ardan backed to the edge of the cliff. Beneath were the ominous waves crashing against the shore. Making matters worse, the tide was at its peak, causing the fierceness of the waters to be all the more treacherous. Ardan weighed his options both of which left him needing to charge past the aggressor. To the right, the villain could pivot off the good leg and easily catch him. Ardan might have the advantage on the left, where he had clobbered the pirate's leg with his spurs. Ardan was totally out of time. *Decide*, he thought. *I must decide now.*

The assailant was upon him. No more dallying. He dodged to the right but lost his footing and tripped on the rocky terrain. He could almost feel the pirate's hot breath on the back of his neck as he encountered the uneven ground with a hard thump.

"Aarrr!" The pirate jerked backward in a painful reaction to a hostile assault. Bam. Bam. One hit after another struck the callous wretch; each hit connected with its mark. The assailant lurched backward, losing his balance; his arms flailed about in useless motion. He began to stagger aimlessly and, inevitably, plunged off the cliff to be lost back into the space of time.

Ardan was astonished. As he tried to right himself, he felt a small hand reaching down to help him.

"Skip!" Ardan cried out. "Holy cow. Where did you come from? Thanks, buddy. Good lord man, you saved my life!" Ardan could hardly believe his good fortune. To see Skip again was the surprise of a lifetime. Ardan gave him a humongous hug, hating to let go. "Skip, doggone it! Aw, Skip." Ardan was at a total loss for words. Never in the world did he expect to see his friend again. "Isabel and I think of you so often. We wondered if you could remember us."

"I do, indeed. And I was so grateful for what you two did for us that night at Mt. Hope. I wanted to tell you. I wanted to thank you. But I never understood what happened to you or where you went—until now, that is."

Skip himself was just starting to put together the fragments of time exchange. Had he crossed into Isabel's and Ardan's time or had they come to him again? What Skip did know was that he had been in limbo protecting the heritage of the people who had sacrificed so much to develop this land. The treasure was theirs, and he had been guarding it.

"I knew when we met I could count on you. If anyone, it would be you and your sister who would save the treasures of our past." Skip was a boy speaking like the statesman he had become as he explained the importance of the items soon to be unearthed. "It has just taken this long for the time to be right."

"And you, Skip? What of you?" Ardan felt like—no, he knew—he was about to lose a very dear friend one more time. This was a bittersweet moment for him. The inevitable portal of time was once more at hand.

"I've already lived a long full life, and now my last mission is complete. I can finally rest thanks to you and your sister. Take good care of our treasures. You have a gift, Ardan. Do great things with it. Don't waste your life."

The two grasped raised hands through entwined arms and gave the victory cry one last time. "To the defenders!"

With that, Arnold "Skip" McGovern was gone.

Chapter 27

A Reality Check

"Ouch!" Ardan said.

"See, you should have apologized. You got what you deserved." As soon as Isabel said it, she felt ashamed. Ardan was just goofing around, and teasing was just his way. Never had he intended for his teasing to hurt her. She wished she could take back her own harsh words. "Are you OK?" she asked, trying to soften her brassy remarks. In her heart, Isabel did feel badly that Ardan might be hurt. She would never want anything bad for him.

"I'm good, my noble treasure hunter, but hold on to your bonnet. You will *not* believe this," Ardan said, trying to put into words what he'd just experienced.

This wasn't the first time one of them had journeyed without the other. Once, Isabel had disappeared when they'd done a magic trick, but she hadn't been able to recall anything. They had been a whole five years younger at the time. But that experience was the beginning of the twin's ability to exist in an alternate time period.

Because of the lateness of the hour, the two decided to talk along the way home. Ardan explained how Skip had used his skills with rocks to bombard the pirate until he lost his balance, plunging him back into the deep abyss. "I'm sure the pirate won't be back to haunt us again. Now, how are we going to convince our parents we *actually know* where the lost treasure is? Skip has been watching over it all this time, making sure the finders were not just other looters under a new name. He knew we would not claim it for ourselves but would get the items to their rightful owners' relatives."

Chapter 28

Convincing Their Parents

Supper was ready by the time they reached home. Father gently scolded his errant offspring for losing track of time. The children decided to wait until after eating before trying to convince their parents to help them dig for the famous treasure. How, oh how, could they make believers of skeptical parents when even they themselves found it hard to understand?

"You have to be charming, Ardan. This will take everything we have to win the folks over," Isabel implored him as they washed for supper.

"*Charming*?!" Ardan shouted. "Boys aren't charming! You have to be kidding me. I can do almost anything—but *charming*?" He walked away shaking his head in total disbelief of his very own sister's ridiculous idea. He was all boy—all boy. Charming? Not in this lifetime.

⁂

After the meal, when the family was gathered in the living room, Ardan eyeballed Isabel. Who should start?

Isabel took the reins. "Mom, Dad," she began. Slowly, she unraveled the tale of the treasure and how they'd just happened upon it. Even though they hadn't been able to dig up anything, their gut instinct told them that it was the treasure.

Eventually, it took both of them to sell the idea to their parents. After all, they were a well-practiced *team* by now. The telling was especially difficult since they couldn't talk about the pirate or Skip. They yearned to be able to share their unique experiences with their parents—and to be able to tell Ol' Humphrey about the actual facts from that night. Wouldn't he love it? But this was not the time, especially if they expected to sell the idea of a long-lost treasure.

Father got the biggest kick out of his remarkable tale spinners' fabulous story. He commended them on their ability to turn fantasy into reality. "You kids should write stories. The way you can coordinate your ideas is amazing." He laughed.

Even Mother had to chuckle. Seeing their parents in such a happy frame of mind gave the twins a shred of personal pleasure at having been the cause of their high spirits. Even the twins had to laugh at themselves. After all, the story was preposterous. *But,* the folks weren't getting the point either. How could two young children get their older, wiser parents to understand that this time, this tale, this event was not just another story? This was the for sure, real truth.

Finally, Mother gave in. "Tell you what," she said. "How about we pack a picnic lunch and take it down to the beach. It'll be fun, and I haven't had time to relax with a good book for a long time. What do you say, hon?" she challenged her husband.

"Yeah, why not," Mitch accepted. "It's back to work Tuesday. Another outing would be welcome. It'll have to be the last of the season. Now, off you two go. You were supposed to have cleaned your rooms today. Or did you forget?"

Without a quibble, the twins quickly jumped up, excited at the prospects of the next day.

Chapter 29

The Hunt is On

The next morning, Ardan asked his mother if the family could invite Humphrey Moore to join them, him being alone and all. Mother agreed. Besides, father needed to discuss plans with Humphrey for the next building renovation at Mt. Hope. The Murphy hardware store always worked generously with the historical society. Over the years, Mitch and Angela had even helped secure funding for the restorations.

"Just for the heck of it, can we bring some shovels?" Isabel begged. "We can dig in the mound—just in case there might possibly be something hidden below. If we don't find anything there, we can always dig in the sand—you know, to make castles and stuff like that. Please." Again, she was taking advantage of Mother and her softer side.

⚉

At the beach, Ardan could hardly contain himself. "Now, Ardan," father reminded him, "we need to help Mother unload the car. You get the beach chairs, and, Isabel, you get the blanket and Mother's book. Mr. Moore and I will handle the rest."

"Don't forget the shovels," Isabel cried.

"I won't," Ol' Humphrey answered Isabel. To Mitch, Humphrey said almost apologetically, "I told the kids about the treasure at the dedication ceremony. I never thought they would get this carried away with it. I'm sorry, Mitch. But what the heck? I'm willing to humor them. The fact of the matter is, I admire their spirit."

When Angela was settled back with her novel, the twins just couldn't take it any longer.

"Let's go," Dad said, knowing you can't contain water in a sieve—nor could he contain his offspring a minute longer.

Ardan and Isabel needed no further prompting. They were off and running, each with a shovel in hand. This time, the twins chose an easier route. Over the years, a pathway had been contrived as others sought to enjoy the view from the top. Ol' Humphrey would need this safer ascent to retrieve the treasure. Industriously, he used his shovel like a staff for support while negotiating the uneven terrain.

The Murphy twins were waiting at the top of the embankment like conquering heroes. "King of the Mountain," Ardan had shouted victoriously as he beat Isabel by a good fifteen lengths.

Upon reaching the two tall elms, Father asked disappointedly, "Is this it? It doesn't look like much of anything!"

"It's here. Trust us," the children chimed in unison (again with the twin thing).

"Jinx!" Ardan said as he and Isabel interlocked their pinky fingers.

Their enthusiasm invigorated the older treasure hunters, and the digging began.

After a few minutes of pulling up nothing but weeds and gravel, Humphry's shovel hit something other than more rocks. The load he dug up revealed a wad of rotting cloth. With a bit more prodding, they all helped him pull up the first bundle of *treasure.*

Isabel had never seen Ol' Humphrey cry before. He turned away, unable to explain that what he was feeling was joy and pride, not sorrow. The old man dropped to one knee as emotion overwhelmed him.

"It's OK," Isabel said, putting a comforting arm around the shoulder of a man she loved as dearly as her own grandfather. "We all feel the same way."

Each of the treasure hunters victoriously carried as much as they could back to the car. Mother spread out a lunch while everyone brought her up to date on the results of their historical discovery. After the eager participants wolfed down sandwiches and tea, Mother picked up the blanket and joined them in completing the honorable task of retrieving the founders' heirlooms. It took several trips, but the blanket saved them from many more. Thankfully, carrying heavy items downhill was easier than vice versa. Although the climb back up was hard for Ol' Humphrey, he would not shirk what he considered to be an honor that had been bestowed upon him.

Collectively, they all determined the treasure should be unloaded at the museum at Mt. Hope. The historical society board members would catalog the items and do their best to return whatever they could to the proper relatives. Items whose ownership could not be determined would become a part of the museum, displayed for all to share.

This would be an enormous task. As families grew, they'd expanded around the whole island to afford themselves of the many opportunities the land provided.

The first settlers had arrived when the weakened ship they traveled on needed to harbor in the bay for repairs. Having already been at sea for weeks on end, many of the Scottish colonists were too sick and weary to continue on to the mainland of Bodenia. The elder clansmen scouted the uninhabited island and deemed that it had the potential for settling. The Scottish passengers stayed, and in time, more immigrants from many other nations joined them. Over time, St. Delus became a regular shipping stop for the seafaring vessels.

New generations developed orchards, along with fields of wheat and barley brought in from seedlings of various homelands. The rich land embraced the improvements and rewarded their efforts.

One of the bundles from the excavated treasure stood out immediately. A bit of cleaning revealed a silver tea set with the "McG" stamp marking it as being from Skip's grandfather, who had been a master silversmith in Scotland. Skip's mother and father had received the tea set as a wedding gift. The one-of-a-kind possession was the one real treasure Skip's parents had brought with them from Scotland when they'd ventured out on the high seas for a better life. Skip's father, and eventually Skip himself, had carried on with the family vocation.

⟨⟨⟨⟩⟩⟩

It was one of the most exhausting days of the youngsters' short lives. Ardan was tapped out. That night, proud of his relationship with the universe, he approached the window with a new admiration. Mr. Moon (the mister part was now in question) was his personal favorite. And after all, it was the moon that had shown the twins where the treasure was. He felt a unique bond with the illusive fellow. "Ya did good, Mr. Moon! Ya did really good." He spoke as if to a trusted friend:

Leading us to the treasure
Put us in your debt forever.
Especially finding the McGovern silver
That put Skip on his life as a human builder.

The sky was ablaze with twinkling stars. Ardan imagined the Big Dipper had spilled its own treasures—the stars.

BOOK SIX

Camping at Rainbow Falls

Chapter 30

Roughing It

The terrain on St Delus had tremendous versatility. The island encompassed a long mountain range that snaked its way between rich plains. The several inlets often included magnificent waterfalls.

The Murphys' favorite camping spot was Rainbow Falls, where the sun's rays played against the mist of tumbling water flowing over the mountain crest. A rainbow bursts forth with color as sunlight dances through the leaves of tall sequoia trees. Even in the heat of summer, the moving water with its canopy of trees kept the cove cool and refreshing.

Camping was, by far, the most rewarding vacation for the Murphys. The ruggedness and working together during these adventures drew them closer as a family. The Murphys encouraged their youngsters to learn through personal experiences on how to resolve life situations. As problems arose, they utilize family discussions to consider the options to solve them. Early on, the twins were taught how and when to use the various tools sold in the family hardware store. Hopefully, these lessons will be useful throughout their lives.

Everyone assumed part of the responsibilities in setting up the campsite. Isabel's specialty was carrying pails of pure water from the community well. She hooked her bucket to the rope on the crossbeam and manually lowered it to the water below. After a few moments, she'd reverse direction and churned the wheel until the filled pail reappeared at the top.

The duty of gathering wood for the campfire fell to Ardan. He liked to take this time to reminisce about when he and Isabel had joined Skip and the original settlers in fighting the pirates. As an everyday chore, these primitive duties might lose their uniqueness. But, as a novelty Isabel and Ardan found them enjoyable.

"Hey, Adventure Annie. Why don't we ask the folks if we can go exploring for a while after lunch?" Ardan suggested.

"I'd like that," was Isabel's enthusiastic response. "Remember the family of ducks we found last year? I wonder if they came back. The babies should be big by now. Their adult feathers were just coming in the last time we saw them. They were so cute. Maybe the young ducklings are parents this year. Do you think we'll recognize them?" One thought after another quickly flew across her mind.

"Yeah, they sure were cute. Maybe Mom will give us the heels off the bread loaf so we can feed them—if we can get close enough, that is."

Rainbow Falls was also a popular camping spot for many other families. Over the years, the Murphy family had made several friendships with people from other towns around the island. Some people had trailers, but most of them just pitched a tent like the Murphys did.

Lunch would be simple, since the first day was heavily involved with unloading and setting up the base site. The Carter and McShane families joined the Murphys for a quick "power lunch" as it was called. Enough nourishment to carry them through but not enough to make them sluggish. Everyone situated themselves around a campfire and roasted their own hot dogs. A certain warmth came from sharing a meal with old friends, and the outdoors lent a fresh flavor to the simplest of foods.

While helping clear away the lunch, the twins could feel their excitement building. It started slowly with them. They began to feel kind of jittery-like inside. Then the heebie-jeebies started developing. Soon, it turned into full-blown nervous energy. Just thinking about the chance to explore the park again was more than their two inquisitive minds could control.

"Wanna come with Isabel and me?" Ardan asked Christian McShane and Lynn Carter. "Our folks said we could go down to the creek and explore."

"Sure thing," was Lynn's immediate response.

"We'll go ask our parents and be right back. Don't do anything without us," Chris excitedly added.

These four youths had formed a special relationship and already shared in many exploits in the few short years of knowing each other. The chance for another adventure was in the air. They could smell it. When you were with the Murphy twins, things just seemed to happen.

Chapter 31

Seeking an Adventure

The twins were now ten, soon to be eleven. Chris was already eleven, and Lynn was twelve and a half. As they made their way to the creek bed, Chris began to tell the others about the creature supposedly haunting the forest. He suggested they keep their eyes peeled for the possibility of any dangerous beasts inhabiting the woods.

"Some call him Sasquatch," Chris went on. His eyes widened, and his voice assimilated an ominous tone as he recounted the story. "They say he's been stealing food from the campers. I'm not certain—but I think he eats people, too. The creature has only been seen in shadows after nightfall. But witnesses say"—as Chris continued, he drew his hands into claws and raised them above his head—"he's big and hairy and that he smells like rotten fish."

"Aw c'mon, Chris, that's just another one of those stories that's told around the campfire at night. One time, he's Bigfoot; another time he's a ghost unable to pass over and doomed to haunt the earth—*forever!* Heck, the monster might be an alien from outer space with the next telling," Lynn stated with superiority. She was pretty savvy about things. "Those are just spooky, scary campfire tales geared to frighten gullible kids like you." She got a big laugh about Chris falling for all that folklore. "Those stories have been going around since the beginning of time. And never, *never ever* I repeat, has anyone found a Bigfoot." Lynn let her age become the measure of reason.

"OK, Mr. Smarty Pants," she continued to tease Chris, unable to just let it go. "Have you a plan in mind if we do come across one of those so-called Sasquatch creatures? What are we to do to save ourselves if one sneaks up on us?"

"It's simple! All we have to do is outrun Ardan," Chris laughed.

"That's your plan? Outrun Ardan? He's to be the sacrifice kid? Oh, you must have been up all night thinking up that one. Maybe you could be the sacrifice kid." Lynn gave Chris a playful shove and ran off a safe distance.

"Look here," Isabel said, wanting to change the subject before it got further out of hand (not that *she* bought into these ridiculous myths of weird creatures), "a pool of tadpoles."

On a bed of lily pads was a whole community of frogs carelessly basking in the warm sun while lazily watching the flurry of tadpoles trying out their water techniques. The amphibians seemed oblivious to the trespassers who had just invaded their domain.

A little further upstream, the young scouts ran into a flock of ducks. "What do you think, Small Fry?" Ardan asked his sister. "Could any of these be the ones we saw last year?"

"Well, these are mallards and the ones we saw last year were mallards," Isabel mused. "It's a good bet that they could be ours. Wow, look how many there are. Our babies have grown up." She giggled, looking squarely at Ardan with an I-told-you-so look. "And now last year's fluffballs have babies of their very own."

While observing the adorable critters, an overwhelming sadness enveloped Chris. Although he was happy for the twins' excitement in rediscovering old animal friends, it brought back his own loss. Chris spoke in a melancholy voice as he shared his personal heartache.

"Would you, guys help me look for my cat, Sassy? We were here camping earlier this summer. And, well, Sassy must have sneaked into the camper when we packed for the trip—unbeknownst to us. When we unloaded our gear, she ran out. Somehow, she got spooked and took off. We looked everywhere that whole weekend, but she just wouldn't come back. I asked my folks if they thought we might find her this trip. Dad said I shouldn't get my hopes up because she could be miles away by now. I sure do miss her."

"Of course, we'll help you look, Chris. We'd be happy to. After all, we're here on an adventure. Now we have a real mission. We'll find her.

Don't you worry." Lynn rested her hand on Chris's arm to demonstrate her concern. "What does Sassy look like?"

"Well, she's a Siamese cat, and she has six toes on her front feet. I know that sounds crazy, but I've learned it's not unusual for that breed. In fact, some even have had more extra toes than that. And she's so smart. I toss her this small rubber ball, and she retrieves it—just like a dog. It's true. I swear it. She *is* a very unique cat in so many ways. And at night, she sneaks into my room and cuddles up right next to me. Mom complains about cat hairs on my bedding, but she still lets us get away with it." Chris beamed from ear to ear at the thought of his precious friend. "Can't help it. I miss her so much."

"If she's around, *we will find her*!" Ardan stated emphatically.

The mission had now been raised to a level of real urgency. They all started calling for the *kitty, kitty*.

"How come you call her Sassy? Is she mean or something? Does she have some kind of attitude?" Isabel asked.

"No, no, she's gentle as can be. Remember I said she has all those extra toes? Well, our family was joking around about her big feet, and Dad said she was a Sasquatch, you know, a Bigfoot." Chris laughed. "We all thought that was funny, so Sasquatch it was. Sassy's just her nickname."

"*Oh*, I get it now," Lynn declared. "Sassy *is* the real Bigfoot. She's been morphed into this monstrous campfire enigma. Whoo," she howled.

"C'mon, Lynn. This is real to Chris. He just lost his best friend. We shouldn't tease him when he feels so sad about it," Ardan reasoned.

"You're right. I'm sorry, Chris. Sometimes I just say things without thinking first. I didn't mean to imply this wasn't serious." Lynn's apology was clearly evident in her voice.

The small band of compadres continued their quest with renewed gusto. As time elapsed, however, they were drawn off task as children tend to be. Soon the foursome was lured back to the stream. They started to turn up rocks looking for hidden species of grubs, crabs, clams—whatever. Watching the quickness of a water spider intrigued them for a while.

"He doesn't seem to have a care in the world. It's like being hypnotized watching him," Chris observed.

"I have an idea," Lynn proclaimed, sensing boredom creeping into their afternoon. "Let's play hide-and-seek."

"Great idea!" Chris agreed.

"OK with me. But we ought to set a few rules. There's a lot of space out here," Ardan wisely stated.

"How about we only count to twenty—slowly. You must be hidden by then. And no moving around after that. After twenty, you must stay put. Agreed? First one caught is it for the next time," Lynn instructed.

"Well put." Isabel was always impressed with Lynn's ability to organize.

"I'll take first turn at being the hunter." With that, Lynn turned to the big maple and, resting her head against the trunk, began to count. "One ... two ... three."

The other three took off running in different directions. Quick little feet can cover a lot of ground when the stakes are high. There's a certain amount of pride in being the last caught or, better yet, not found at all and getting to come out all on your own when the hunter gives up looking.

Chris, Ardan, and Isabel scattered for the woods, looking for big trees to hide behind or maybe a fallen log. Isabel saw Chris dive into a pile of leaves, and Ardan seemed to be searching the area to her left. So, Isabel aimed for the fat tree straight ahead. She was pretty skinny and was sure it would be a good hiding place.

"Eighteen ... nineteen."

Chapter 32

An Unexpected Event

Rounding the tree, Isabel bounced off a furry obstacle. It grabbed her. She screamed bloody murder and fainted dead away as shock took possession of her in this unprepared-for situation.

Startled and confused, the accidental abductor lifted her limp body and ran off with her.

From Ardan's location some distance away, he heard his sister's scream. He knew immediately that Isabel was in trouble. With his adrenaline spiked, Ardan took off at full gallop trying to find Isabel. Ardan thought he saw what looked like a huge, furry creature running off through the woods. Not able to see Isabel anywhere, Ardan had a sickening feeling that whatever it was had his sister. Instantly, Ardan was in pursuit.

After a quick dash through the woods, the critter ended at the waterfall. He climbed the rock ledge and slipped behind the cascading water into a slim indenture in the mountainside. The hidden entrance wrapped around, eventually opening into a large cavern where two others of his ilk were silhouetted against a low fire.

Slowly, Isabel awakened. Her breath caught in her throat as she tried to figure out this new situation that had been suddenly thrust before her. Her movements startled the leader, causing him to jump backward. With great caution, the hairy creature approached her—slowly, so as not to unjustly alarm her. Surprisingly, Isabel was not frightened of him. Just as strangely, she could feel that he was actually showing compassion toward her.

The other two creatures were obviously upset at the presence of the human. Loud sounds and physical chest pounding emanated from them. Her captor turned his attention to the other two, giving Isabel the opportunity to survey her surroundings. The low fire only produced a faint glow, but she knew she'd never been in this cavern. Worse yet, she didn't remember anything about how she'd gotten here. How would she find her way home when she escaped?

The leader turned his attention back to Isabel, making every outward effort to speak with her. He was almost desperate that they be able to communicate. Finding that she could not understand his language of various grunts and hand gestures, Isabel tried using eye contact. Through this method, she hoped they could read each other's mental processes. As the sasquatch became aware of what Isabel was suggesting and the tension eased, the two learned to perceive each other's thoughts.

This Bigfoot was referred to as Raugh. The other two were Moof and Wour. He explained that, as youths, the trio were wild and careless. And as young rebels, they never adhered to the warnings of their elders.

One night while the youths were foraging for food, they ran across a flotation device, a boat if you will. Always inquisitive about humans and their ways, the boys had mimicked what they'd observed and jumped in. It had proved to be a wild ride, ending with the delinquents here, shipwrecked on this island. Raugh's world was not regulated by years, but he believed they had been marooned on the island for three seasons of winters.

Last year, Raugh had seen Ardan and Isabel and had been inexplicably drawn to them. Maybe Raugh felt he might possibly forge a useful connection with them. Could that justify this magnetic draw he had to them? Regardless, that was the reason he'd risked observing them in daylight, never expecting Isabel would pick the very tree he was hiding behind as her refuge too.

Raugh wondered why the children would run from each other. Normally, he was highly alert to dangerous situations, but this time he had not been aware of any jeopardy. Impulsively, he'd felt he had to save Isabel from whatever peril existed. Risky or not, he'd brought her to the safety of his lair.

Now that they'd met, he hoped for a better understanding of the attraction he had to the twins. For one thing, the two entities *were* able to communicate. That was a good start. He was more than grateful for that.

Humans did so many things the Sasquatch didn't understand. Now was an opportunity to learn about these oddities.

"We want to return to our own kind. It's easier to live secretly when you have your whole community for support," Raugh explained. "Here we live in fear all the time."

Chapter 33

Ardan Searches for Isabel

Ardan followed the hairy creature through the woods but lost the trail at Rainbow Falls. He paced back and forth. The twins had always had a special connection with each other, even more so than other twins have. Very often, they could read each other's thoughts. Just as often, they said the same things at the same time. They even felt each other's pain, which would more likely be attributed to identical twins and not fraternal twins. Ardan tried to draw on that intuitive link now. *Tell me, Isabel. Where are you?* he thought. *Talk to me.* Ardan always felt protective of his beloved sister, not that she was fragile. She was more than capable of handling herself. He just needed to be there for her.

On one of his pacing rotations around the falls, Ardan spotted a clump of fur. He reached for it. The texture was different from that of most animals. Running the fur through his fingers, Ardan felt Isabel's aura. She was here. Ardan knew he was close to finding her.

The sunlight flickered across the falls, revealing a dark pattern behind it. Ardan had not noticed that before this very moment. What was it showing him? Ardan climbed the formation beside the falls and could see a slight space behind the cascading waters. He flattened himself against the wall and slowly shuffled forward along the narrow shelf. He was surprised to locate a slender opening. Entering the dark gap, Ardan blindly followed the interior walls with his hands. There was a flickering glow ahead. Ardan tensed. He could feel the hairs on his neck begin their eerie transformation of standing straight out as he reached the open cavern. He sensed Isabel was near. He knew he had to follow his instinct. With the greatest of caution, he proceeded.

Almost immediately, furry creatures pounced upon the young human. They'd smelled Ardan coming and were ready for him. Arms and legs were flailing about everywhere. Ardan put up a good fight but was easily brought down. He knew his adversaries were not animal, but he did not feel they were human either. They were exceptionally big—and strong. He heard Isabel screaming his name in the background. Was she safe? He was fighting off the vermin as best he could. Isabel needed him.

Raugh quickly arrived on the scene and brought the action to an abrupt halt. Isabel was right behind him. Again, Raugh reasoned with his fellow Bigfoot while Isabel checked that Ardan was not injured.

Once the situation was under control, Isabel conveyed to Ardan what had happened so far and showed him the way she was able to communicate with Raugh. In the past, the twins had been able to converse with others by using thoughts as opposed to verbalizing, but to understand a creature without a common language as a base was a monumental challenge. When their *discussion* with Raugh reached its conclusion, the twins realized their mission was to help the Sasquatch get back to the mainland.

The boat the adolescent Bigfoots had traversed the ocean in was hidden in the cove. But as Raugh related, it was leaking, and the loud contraption (engine) didn't work. The twins surmised it had probably just run out of gas. Fortunately, the boat was equipped with a sail. The owner had apparently installed the engine as backup and liked the versatility. Continuing, the twins learned the sail was torn. It sounded as if the mast was still intact and that there was no major damage to the hull.

Calling upon the basic training and skills their parents had instilled in them, Ardan explained that the Bigfoots could fill the cracks in the hull with tar, stressing that a second application might be necessary. He described how to make tar by heating the sap from pine trees until it thickened. He also advised the Sasquatch to add beeswax to the finished product to prevent cracking when the tar dried. Isabel promised to leave a pan and spoon at the edge of their campsite. She explained how to cook the tar. The Sasquatch nation had long ago mastered the art of making fire.

Utilizing the dirt covering the floor in the cave like a chalkboard, Ardan demonstrated how to rig a sail. The explanation made more sense to Raugh with the help of the drawing. Lastly, Ardan drew a map of St. Delus Island and the mainland of Bodenia to show the direction the trio of Sasquatch would have to travel. Ardan was carrying a compass, since he and Isabel planned to do some exploring this weekend. The wiggly directional arrow mesmerized Raugh and added more to the mystique of these humans. Although the gadget was new to him, Raugh was quick to pick up on how to use it and of the value the compass would be on the open waters. Bodenia was due west and, in the best conditions with a motorized boat, about twenty hours away. With just a makeshift sail as fuel for their vessel, they recommended the Bigfoots prepare for a several days at sea.

The Murphy family had a tarp they used as an outdoor canopy to protect them from inclement weather. At the end of the weekend, the twins would simply forget to pack the tarp and ropes used to tether it. Raugh would find it at the campsite when the Murphys left. The canvas would make a strong sail.

Moof and Wour had finally lost their inhibitions and had been sitting near the twins and Raugh. When translation was related to them, Moof and Wour showed their gratefulness in their own way (if beating your chest and roaring is being grateful, that is).

There seemed to be one drawback. Whatever that was appeared to be emotional. The twins could not understand the exchange of "words" used by the trio of beings. In the ruckus, Ardan and Isabel were not able to make eye contact with Raugh, leaving them completely out of the conversation. If there was a way, Ardan and Isabel wanted to help.

When Raugh gave his attention back to the twins, he explained that the boys had found a very small creature and had basically made it, as humans would say, a pet. They were afraid to take her on a tumultuous ocean voyage, but they were also reluctant to leave her to her own resources. Moof and Wour left and brought back a Siamese cat. Not only that, but she had given birth to three babies.

"Sassy!" Isabel and Ardan cried out in unison. "Chris will be so happy." They explained as best they could on how Sassy had been lost and that Sassy was the very thing the children were searching for. The twins assured the Bigfoots that Chris was a loving owner and would give the mother and kittens a perfect home. At this point, the twins' own emotional needs were hard to ignore. They had dear friends they desperately wanted to rejoin—especially now that they could share the return of Sassy. They could not imagine what Chris would think of the kittens.

Sassy had filled the loneliness the Sasquatch felt in this foreign land. When she gave birth, they believed they were given a purpose in caring for her. The thought of giving up this tiny pet and her kittens was heartbreaking, but the prospect of going home again was pulling at their heartstrings. Being marooned had given the boys new respect for their parents, and they ached for that love and support once again. The adolescent trio trusted the young humans' advice on repairing the boat. They were sure, too, that Sassy would be safe with the humans. All they cared about now was going home.

The time had come for the Murphy twins to say goodbye. Having found Sassy was understandably making them all the more anxious to get back to Chris and Lynn.

"One last but *very important* detail we need to warn you about," Ardan shamefully acknowledged. "*Stay as far away from humans as you can!* It is unfortunate. But if caught, you will be treated as a wild, newly discovered species. You will probably be held in a caged area and be scientifically observed the rest of your lives."

Isabel was just as apologetic but had to agree with Ardan. Humans would not be able to resist themselves, no matter what the long-term detriment to the sasquatch would be.

Chapter 34

A Joyous Reunion

"Come out. Come out, wherever you are," Lynn was hollering. "I give up. Chris is already captured. He's the next hunter. Come on out."

From around the large tree, Isabel and Ardan emerged, holding three squiggly kittens and one happy mama cat.

Chris *freaked*. Lynn squealed, almost frightening the lot of them. "How did you find Sassy? Where did you find her?" Chris cried out. Not waiting for an answer he reached for Sassy. "Are those hers?" he asked, spying the babies.

The children could hardly keep their hands off the rescued family. Although still babies, the kittens' eyes were open and full of apprehension. Keeping their mother always in sight was a comfort for the offspring. They sensed that she appeared to be very, very happy with this new breed of caretakers. Chris counted the toes of the babies to see if any had inherited their mom's oddity. "Nope," he said, "only Sassy has the special trait."

"You know," Lynn stated with a great deal of pride, "we did it. Mission accomplished. We wanted to find Sassy, and we did—or, anyway, you two did. Even better than that," she added with a laugh, "we got more than we bargained for."

"When you're with the Murphy twins, things happen! Bring it in," Chris stammered, indicating it was time for a group hug. "You guys, you're the best friends ever."

With one cat for each child to carry, they hurried back to camp to show off their booty. Once there, the children were heralded by everyone in the campsite. Never in this world had Chris's family believed they would see Sassy again. She looked remarkably well for having had to fare for herself and a new litter in the wild. Isabel and Ardan never let on that Sassy had been given the very best of care from very loving hands.

Chapter 35

Now They Are Eleven

The end of summer meant the twins would be celebrating another birthday. Eleven. Where did the time go? This birthday would be a simple one, with just the immediate family attending. After making a wish, everyone was treated to a slice of cake and a heaping scoop of ice cream. With Grandpa's sweet tooth beckoning to be satisfied, he asked for a scoop of chocolate *and* a scoop of strawberry ice cream.

In the process of distributing the goodies, Uncle Randy quietly slipped out to the garage and brought back two small boxes. "Hope you like your birthday presents," he said. "Aunt Cheryl and I just couldn't think of anything else to get you."

"Thanks! We'll love whatever you got us," Ardan and Isabel joyfully said in unison. "Jinx!" again speaking as if of one voice.

Excitedly, they pulled the lids off. "*Oh. My. Gosh!*" Isabel shouted as she lifted up a tiny Siamese kitten. Looking over at Ardan, she saw him displaying an identical gift. "Are these Sassy's kittens?" she asked.

"They are. Since you played a major part in saving them, your folks thought you were big enough to take the responsibility of raising them," Aunt Cheryl added. "This was by far the hardest secret I've ever had to keep. I really debated giving them to you sooner—before I got too attached to them. Now then, you have to come up with their names."

The rest of the afternoon was consumed with watching the frisky kittens exploring their new surroundings. The pair finally curled up together in the warmth of a sunny patch on the living room carpet.

Isabel settled on Ishkabibble as the name for her girl kitten because she dribbled milk down her chin while drinking. Ardan thought Mergatroid would be just as unique for his boy kitten, who was already showing mystical promise. The furry creatures would always be a fond reminder for the twins of their brief encounter with Raugh, Wour, and Moof.

"As soon as the kittens are old enough, we'll take them to the veterinarian and have the 'wander' taken out of them. They'll be better cats and live longer," Uncle Randy promised the twins.

Aunt Cheryl shook her head at the corny expression. Why didn't he just say, he'd have them spayed and neutered? The kids knew what that was. Their lives weren't that sheltered. Having pets fixed was universally promoted as a way to keep the population under control and reduce the stray animal epidemic. An extended lifespan was the bonus. Have the *wander* taken out? She could only shake her head in disbelief.

Chapter 36

Getting Word Back

Ardan carried Mergatroid into his bedroom and settled the kitten next to him for a good night's sleep. "Merg" snuggled right in and was soon purring. Ardan was just starting to drift off to sleep when he suddenly bolted upright in bed. Merg jumped, too. Ardan grabbed the excited kitten and sneaked across the floor to Isabel's room.

"Isabel, are you asleep?" he whispered.

"No, I'm awake," she answered.

Upon seeing each other, Mergatroid and Ishkabibble chased around Isabel's bed. The litter mates were happy to find they still had each other for company. They were not alone. Mischief is always better with a teammate.

"Did you get the message from Raugh?" he asked.

"I did. Isn't it great?" she responded.

Raugh had communicated that he, Moof, and Wour had finally made it back to Bodenia safely. The three delinquent youths were well and had a big, up*roar*ious reunion with the clan. Raugh thanked the twins for their help. The compass had been a lifesaver, especially when they'd encountered a squall and the boat had kept twisting around in the high waves. The trio had landed miles away from their homestead and had to carefully work their way across many populated areas. But they were home again—happy and well.

Raugh did inform his fellow tribesmen that, although the twins were helpful, not all humans could or should be trusted. They would be sure to avoid humans at all costs.

The twins used the same power of telepathy to tell Raugh they were happy for him and that Sassy and her brood were being well cared for. They hoped Moof and Wour would like knowing that the twins were owners of two of the kittens and that the other one would get to stay with his mother at Chris's home.

"I'm overwhelmed. To think we had a part in all this. I almost feel guilty, though, in thinking we could maybe take credit in helping to save Raugh and his friends," Ardan revealed. "Is that bragging? Is it wrong to feel good about helping them?"

"I don't think it's bragging, Ardan," she consoled him. "I think it's just a feeling of pride that we were in the right place at the right time. We can simply accept the thanks from our new friends and be grateful we were able to help. After all, it isn't like we can tell anyone about this. Now, that might be bragging."

Back again in his room, Ardan showed Mergatroid the wonders of the universe. The sky was clearly showing off her beauty. "See, Merg, isn't it magnificent?" Ardan said. "There is so much out there to explore. Maybe one day I'll have that chance."

Opportunities come from the blue
Never knowing when or where,
But I will be mindful of every clue
And do my best to be there.

The utter vastness of space held in the universe only magnified the warmth he was feeling in his heart.

BOOK SEVEN
Growing Up Sasquatch

Chapter 37

The Early Years

Side note: As your author, I will attempt to translate the language of the Sasquatch into English. Many of their expressions do not have an equivalent word or phrase in English, but I will try my very hardest to help you understand their lifestyle as conveyed to me.

Situated in the most northern part of Bodenia lies a rugged territory of several thousand acres. This land is extremely remote and considered uninhabitable. Thus, it has not been explored to any extent by the human race. This is precisely why the Sasquatch found it to be the very haven necessary for their unique survival. Over the last several centuries, the Sasquatch have homesteaded the forests and caverns, adapting themselves to the harshness of the elements.

Just as with every other living species, the Sasquatch have evolved with each succeeding generation and have learned many useful skills, often by observing the very humans that bring them so much fear.

Fire is by far the most beneficial tool for their continued existence. This simple discovery of many prior centuries has afforded them cooking and heating opportunities, along with *light*. As simple as that seems, it was light that allowed them to explore the depths of the numerous caverns. Here in the belly of Mother Earth, they were able to establish permanent living quarters that not only protected them from nature's elements but also provided them seclusion from prying eyes.

For as long as Raugh can remember, Moof and Wour have been a part of his family unit. They all live together with their individual parents and siblings in the same cavern. There are other of these "family units" living similar lifestyles in nearby caves. The various units often join together—especially for the big hunts. Each group is diligent in updating the others on whatever new knowledge they might have gleaned. Not only is there social comfort in these meetings, but the gatherings also reaffirm their mutual security. Every Sasquatch has the back of every other Sasquatch.

Although curious about humans, the sasquatch are also suspicious of these strange-looking, simulated Bigfoots. They've wondered what went wrong in their society that made these humans lose their hair and grow to look so odd. Though saddened for them, the sasquatch are determined not to make that same mistake in their own culture. And so, they simply continue to observe, careful to only implement ideas they feel are safe and useful.

It's not to say that the sasquatch themselves haven't been proficient in developing tools and methods of implementation on their own, for they have. Centuries of evolvement have afforded them with a relatively comfortable lifestyle. They often wish they could share their ideas with the humans and perhaps develop them together, but fear keeps them from exposing themselves.

❧

"Aargh, let's go down to the river," four-year-old Raugh called to his wolf puppy.

Sasquatch offspring have that same unexplained inner drive human children have—a drive that keeps these youngsters in constant motion. Raugh is no exception. In fact, shortly after taking his first steps, the rambunctious child started running. His father never remembered Raugh as walking, only running. As Raugh grew, he enhanced his active lifestyle. When he wasn't running, he was jumping and leaping. Elders could only shake their heads at these offspring. If they could but capture and maintain that level of energy, the long hunts would not be so personally draining.

Moof and Wour (around six and seven respectively) were eager to get in on Raugh's action. "We can play chase-the-stick with Aargh," Moof said, giving the mutual pet a roughing over. Aargh had been raised by the clan after he'd been found isolated as a mere cub. The boys enjoyed watching him twist his agile body in midair while focusing on the coveted stick. Then chomp! Aargh never missed.

"What say, squirt? Try our luck at catching some fish for supper? We'll teach you the trick at where to grab them so they can't wiggle away," Wour offered to his mite of a friend Raugh. "It's about time you learn to carry your own weight around here," he added with a wink.

Already close-knit friends, Moof and Wour easily opened their tight circle to include Raugh. The older boys found Raugh's childlike ways amusing. Sasquatch learned at a young age to watch over each other. They would always protect the four-year-old, with the help of the vigilant Aargh, of course.

Although gentle with the clansmen, Aargh could revert to his wild roots should he encounter danger. His acute sense of smell had alerted the boys more than once to unseen dangers when confronting wild forest creatures. Those wolf instincts were always lying just under the surface, ready to protect his adopted family.

"I'm not a squirt. I'm big, *and* I'm just as strong as you are." Raugh charged at Wour, tackling him around the knees. As Wour fell, Raugh mocked him. "You're too easy, Wour," Raugh championed. "You're the little sissy!"

"You just think so, you pint-sized gnat, you." Wour grabbed Raugh, hoisted him over his shoulder, and took off at a dead run. "Sissy my foot. I'll show you who's the sissy."

Excited by the chase, Aargh pounced at the opportunity and sped after the boys as they made their way to the river. Aargh reveled in the attention of the three boys as they goofed around. Minutes turned into hours before the spirited trio realized.

As promised, Moof and Wour showed Raugh how to stand quietly in shallow waters with his legs spread wide apart—waiting for an unsuspecting fish.

"Be patient. Don't move a muscle," Moof advised Raugh. "When one meanders between your feet, grab him right over the gills and hold on tight; they bite, and the fin across the top is spiky. Be fast. Quickness is everything. There," he said, triumphantly displaying a fat fish. "You have to hold him real tight, or he'll wiggle away."

Many of the wily swimmers managed to escape the untested Raugh, but he was finally successful in capturing a fish of his very own. Although smaller than the ones Moof and Wour had caught, Raugh's fish nonetheless brought him pride in his own accomplishment. He beamed with well-earned pride. Soon their sack of woven vines was full. It was time to head for home.

"Next time we'll practice spear fishing," Wour said. "But first you have to learn how to find the strongest, straightest tree branch, and then you have to learn how to sharpen the end. And then"—he laughed—"you have to learn how to use it. Can't have you spearing your own toe, you know. Think you can handle all that, squirt? You spear your own foot, and we'll have to call you 'littlefoot.'" Oh how the boys enjoyed teasing Raugh, mainly because he was by far the most beloved of all their friends. "Littlefoot! How does that sound, little buddy?"

"I can learn anything you two nincompoops can throw at me," Raugh declared with spirited resolve, "and then some!"

Still riding high with the excitement of this, his first catch, Raugh burst into the community lair with his hands high above his head displaying his contribution to the evening meal. He was sure his father and mother would be so proud of him. "Look what I did," he shouted, holding the still lively fish. "I caught it all by myself."

The pride he felt was quickly drained as he realized that something was seriously wrong in the family dwelling. An emotional blanket of uneasiness hung in the atmosphere. The boys looked around in fear. What was it? Their keen senses felt the tension displayed on everyone's face.

"Raugh." Father quietly drew his son into his arms. "We just lost your little sister. Mother is so terribly heartbroken. She's going to need all the love we can give her right now. This won't be an easy time for any of us."

What? These were harsh words for the young Raugh to comprehend. Little Woobie had been all right when he'd left for the river just a few hours ago. She was just now getting old enough to respond to his funny gestures, and he enjoyed acting up for her.

"But, Father," Raugh stammered in disbelief, "she was playing with me just this morning. Why – while I was holding her, she grabbed my finger and giggled as I pretended to pull away. Then she reached up and pulled at the hairs on my face. She likes to do that, Dad. I don't mind—really, I don't … And then she laughs when I yell because she yanks too hard. She has such a funny laugh. Dad … she's … so … funny …" His voice trailed off. Was she gone? Could their cute, little Woobie Coobie be gone?

"Raugh, dear Raugh." Father held his boy ever more closely. He desperately wished he could ease his young son's pain. "Maybe that was your sister's way of saying goodbye. Perhaps she wanted you to always remember her as being happy and that *you* were a big part of her happiness. She loved you, Raugh, so very much. You were a good big brother to her. She loved you with all her heart, and when someone dies, their heart goes with them. Raugh, you will always be with her, just as she will always be with you. We all will remember our beautiful little girl. She may be gone, but we will never, ever forget her."

No, she couldn't be gone. She was too young. This had to be a cruel joke. Raugh pulled himself free of his father's arms and urgently ran to his mother. She would say it wasn't so. Mother would make it all right again.

One look at his dear mother's face—so full of sorrow, so tearful—and Raugh knew. Heartache was etched deep within her swollen eyes. No longer able to contain his own tears, the young child cried, unrestrained in his mother's arms. At only four, Raugh felt his world had come to an end. He knew what death meant. He was never to see his little sister again. A painful ache enveloped his entire body as grief consumed him. His throat was so constricted he felt he would choke. Mother's warm embrace was therapeutic to both of them as she cradled her little boy in her arms gently rocking back and forth.

Aargh, too, understood. Slowly, he crawled on his belly to the grief-stricken boy and postured himself at the saddened child's feet.

The one enormous difference between humans and Sasquatch is in life expectancy. Sasquatch do not have as many living generations. Without the benefit of doctors and medicine, their life span is much shorter. Oh, they have some of nature's remedies, with moss, root plasters, and the like for minor ailments, but broken bones or major medical issues shorten their lifespan dramatically. Bigfoots don't have birthdays, so keeping track of actual years is difficult. If you could put a number on their potential life expectancy, a good guess would most likely be forty-five, fifty at best.

Chapter 38

Wild Adolescents

In Raugh's particular unit, he, Moof, and Wour became known as the intrepid trio—always together, always pushing the limits. Although Moof and Wour were older and should be an example for Raugh, they were the real mischief makers. Containment fell on the younger Raugh when and *if* possible. The three were often just one step away from being banished by the community.

A devil-may-care attitude was beneficial to the very survival of a Bigfoot and was even encouraged in youngsters. But this wild trio managed to disregard the rules and push back at authority—like the time they almost exposed the whole Sasquatchewan nation when they thought it would be a lark to creep up on a group of campers and scare the living bejeebers out of them.

Wour suggested they sneak up on the humans to see what kind of reaction they could get. Completely ignoring Rule One (never ever let a human see you—and certainly never interact with one), the troublemakers silently tiptoed up on a group of humans as they were enjoying an evening of companionship with friends around a flickering campfire.

"*Raaraugh!*" Wour let out his infamous war cry.

"*Wooorugh, aaugh,*" the others joined in, making it appear as if there were an entire pack of wild creatures encircling the perimeter of the campsite with an eagerness to charge.

The humans jumped up, believing they were actually being attacked. Total chaos ensued. Women grabbed their children and dove into their fragile canvas tents. The men ran around in circles looking for weapons of any sort to fend off the vicious predators.

The trio laughed so hard they barely had time to make their own escape before the humans organized a protective offensive of their own and tried to chase the culprits down. By all accounts, no matter how close the call, the boys deemed the encounter another hilarious adventure! One for the books. Truly *epic*.

However, that episode led to an all-out hunt jeopardizing the exposure of the entire Sasquatch community. The local ranger called in extra support and searched the expansive area for the perpetrators. They combed the wooded terrains within virtual feet of the Sasquatch habitat.

Eventually, a grizzly bear was singled out as the culprit in the campers' frightening experience. Because it had happened at night with only a flickering campfire to illuminate the dark, the park ranger justified his decision that what had scared the campers had to have been the large bear and her half-grown cubs.

"We've scoured the entire campgrounds and beyond," the ranger declared to the alarmed campers. "The only thing around that comes close to what you described is that feisty, ill-tempered mother grizzly and her equally contemptuous two-year-old cubs."

The campers *insisted* that what they had seen was almost humanlike and not even close to being a bear, even if the bear stood on its hind legs. No sir, what scared them was not a bear—of that they were *very* certain!

"It was dark. I'm sure that, in the excitement, everyone became confused," the ranger reassured them. "I've watched over these campgrounds for some twenty odd years now. I can assure you I know my critters. But we'll keep an eye out for any signs of your 'creatures.' Meanwhile, we moved ol' mama and her cantankerous offspring to a remote area far outside the camping reserve. They'll have a whole new territory to explore. And Lord help the wildlife there."

What luck. The grunts and guttural sounds of the Sasquatch were animal-like in comparison. So, the grizzlies took the fall. This action turned out to be a benefit to the Sasquatch as well, considering the mama grizzly and those misfit cubs of hers were incorrigible neighbors.

"Guys," Raugh reminded Wour and Moof, "we have to think first before we pull another stunt like that. We got lucky *again*, but if it weren't for the fact of getting rid of Ol' Chomper, we would still be in some serious trouble."

"Awe, Raugh." Wour slapped his overly, cautious friend aside the head, "You're always the worrier. Lighten up. Ol' Chomper was tough to live with. She wasn't the least bit good about sharing. We did the clan a favor. All's good, buddy boy. No denying we're better off. You can say, 'Thank you, Wour!'"

"Not likely," Raugh stated.

Openly siding with Wour, Moof gave Raugh a noogie and leaped away in search of another opportunity. Keeping up with these sidekicks was a challenge, but he didn't want to be the one left out of the action either. The pack was on the run!

"Let's not forget, my furry-faced friends, we have to fill that hollowed-out log with berries before we head back home." Raugh again displayed responsibility. "If we want to eat, we have to help out. It's the Bigfoot way." Early on, a Bigfoot learns that you work for what you get. Survival of the strongest was the harsh reality in their world.

"Just one more swing across the creek," Wour said, grabbing an available hanging vine.

Moof chose to hop from stone to stone across the cold, clear water.

"Wait for me!" Raugh shouted as he relinquished any attempt at rationality. "Meet you at the berry patch!" An unspoken challenge hung underneath the simple statement.

Aargh was like a shadow—a physical extension of their bodies. He was, however, a mischievous shadow that enjoyed nipping at their heels when he had the chance.

Almost considered adults at this stage in their society (ten, twelve, and thirteen-years-old), the intrepid trio were still young enough to be mired in a world of juvenile-enhanced mischief that seemed to follow their every move.

"Hey, bros," Wour shouted. "Tonight let's forage for some human food down by that town along the big waters. We can stir up their animals and get 'em all bellowing." With a laugh, Wour cut loose with an authentic howl that was fast becoming an integral part of his identity. Just the thought of setting off the sissy town "wolves" filled his imagination with visions of chaotic madness.

That was another thing; *whatever* happened to the human's wolves? What had they done that had changed a perfect wolf specimen into one of those awful-looking, spineless four-legged creatures that followed them around yapping and begging for food? Had the animals forgotten how to hunt? Humans were strange in many ways.

"OK, but we have to keep on the edges of town and stay away from the brightness!" Raugh stated, trying to lay down some ground rules for his fun-loving buddies before they were to start on their evening hunt.

There was one more complication, and that included Aargh. The boys hated sneaking away without their buddy. But whenever they planned to embark on a hunt that carried potential interaction with humans, Aargh's aggressive manner would make them more vulnerable. Under no circumstances could they take that chance. Aargh had to be left behind.

"I wonder why humans throw away so much food?" Moof quired. "We can probably find enough to bring back to feed the whole unit. It isn't very tasty, but it's easy pickings." The youth wondered how many times bears or racoons were blamed for their rummaging through the human's trash cans. That was just one more bit of inside humor the boys enjoyed.

So as not to get in bigger trouble, the boys filled the log with berries and dragged it back to their lair. Come nightfall, they would take their hunt for food into the human's environment.

Chapter 39

An Unexpected Event

Creeping along the perimeter of the seaside town was like a game to the trio. The risk at being so close and not getting caught was exhilarating. Moof and Wour especially were addicted to the unpredictable events their devious minds contrived.

"Lookie here," Moof said as he spied a boat. "I wonder if we can make this *thing* move like those hairless creatures do." Moof was trying to visualize what he had seen the humans do with this *thing* to make it rip through the deep waters of this vast ocean. He could almost feel the wind blowing through his hair. He could imagine the wetness from the high waves billowing off its sides. Yeah, what a rush that would be! Gotta do it!

The boys gleefully jumped into the contraption and started to play with the odd instruments. They giggled like little girls seeing their reflections in a creek for the first time. Moof pulled at some ropes, causing the boat to drift away from the dock. Wour twisted and turned one object after another. Then he turned the right (or wrong, depending how you look at it) metal shape, and the engine revved. Holy cow. The lads were thrown off their feet. The craft, with the youth pinned to the floor, began to race full speed ahead, and the trio had no idea how to stop it.

Wour was the first to pull himself to his feet, and he moved toward the round form he had seen the male use. He quickly found how easily the craft steered. Once the boys recovered from their initial shock, they found gliding over the surface of the water fascinating. No wonder the humans indulged themselves in this aimless activity. The three had always wondered how much water was in the ocean. Was there an end somewhere in this large expanse that was not visible from shore? Maybe now they would have that answer.

Returning to land became irrelevant as the trio found themselves fully engrossed in their immediate activity. You could compare the Bigfoots' experience to the same euphoric high a human might get on a roller coaster. Like maybe coming down from the crest of a high wave would be the same as plunging down the coaster track from its peak.

Before they realized it, the wayward adolescents were far out to sea when something happened. The noise from the object that moved the boat sputtered and stopped. The vessel was now solely reliant on the ocean's current. Wour found the round wheel wasn't as useful as it had been initially. In the pitch-black night without any visual sight of land, the young Sasquatch were now at the mercy of the sea.

One day turned into two and then four, maybe five before Moof glimpsed a landmass on the horizon. "Land," Moof shouted to his sleeping buddies. "We're home at last."

Raugh, Wour, and Moof came floating to shore on the crest of waves created by the rising tide. The weary youth were much the worse for wear when they reached the beach.

Exhausted and hungry, the three were sure they were finally home. Without worldly knowledge, they were not aware that there might be land other than Bodenia, and so Moof, Wour, and Raugh were happy to be back to where they believed they'd started.

"This place doesn't look familiar, but we can find our way home," Raugh said confidently.

"If I never get in this *thing* again, it'll be too soon," Moof said, giving the loathsome hunk of wood a mighty kick. Exiting, he breathed a sigh of relief as his feet hit terra firma—dry land at last.

"We still better hide this *thing* to cover our tracks of having been here," Raugh warned. "You never know how many humans we'll have to sneak past before we find home." They hid the watercraft deep in a ravine, believing it would be a prudent measure in protecting their abrupt appearance.

Too quickly, the Sasquatch would live the consequences for breaking the rules. Over the next several months of exploring the island, the boys realized they were on a landmass that did not include their families' habitat. The intrepid trio were now homeless. Out of necessity for their own survival, Moof, Wour, and Raugh set up a home base in a secluded cavern behind a waterfall.

The only bit of luck in this whole fiasco was that they were not alone; they had each other. As Sasquatch, the youth had learned how to forage for food and how to protect themselves from unforeseen enemies. They would make do. They had to.

Raugh ran across a camping area located away from but near the falls. It afforded them the same easy human food they'd found on the homeland. How did humans get to this island? he wondered. And so many of them—there were towns all over the place. Sadly, however, they never ran across any Bigfoot. If there were humans, why weren't there Sasquatch?

A year earlier, Raugh noticed a young boy and girl. For reasons he could not explain, he was drawn to them. He also did not understand where this boy and girl went after only a short stay. It looked like they were making a home, but then they'd tear apart their nest and were gone only to do it all over again at another time. Raugh only saw the human children twice that first year. He was elated to find that they were back this summer. And again, he felt the same magnetism. Why? he wondered.

One day as Raugh watched from afar, he observed the two human children interacting with other young humans. Out of curiosity, he followed their activities from the river bottoms to the woods to the meadows. Why was it he was only drawn to this one boy and this one girl and none of the others?

Never did Raugh intend to meet with the human children, at least not until he didn't have the option that is. As he was hiding behind a large tree and watching their activities, the young girl literally crashed into him while she was running from danger. The shock at seeing Raugh made her faint. As a caring being, he simply could not leave her lying there as vulnerable prey, at the mercy of the unforeseen predator. So, Raugh broke the Bigfoot rule; he brought a human to his lair. Now they were all exposed.

Chapter 40

A Helping Hand

Raugh found that Ardan and Isabel were able to communicate with him, confirming the reason for the great magnetic draw he felt toward the humans. While the twins advised the Sasquatch on boat repairs and navigation, the bond grew deeper.

Raugh was especially interested in the concept of many other landmasses separated by oceans on this thing called a "planet." Although there were no other Sasquatch on this particular island, Raugh wondered if these other lands Ardan spoke about might harbor some of his kinfolk—somewhat like the way the many human races had populated the world. Were Yeti related to the Sasquatch? And would he have the chance to find out?

"Raugh, I wish you could go to school. You have such a natural curiosity," Ardan said. "If you could just have the opportunity." The sad reality was that it would never be possible. Such a loss. Raugh might have contributed greatly to the world by giving it a new perspective.

"The more I see around me, the more questions I have," Raugh hungrily replied. "Why are you so different outwardly, and yet deep inside we are exactly alike? We did not know humans were capable of deep emotions." Thinking back to his own family, Raugh said, "I wish I could show you my family unit. We could learn so much from each other. If any humans could break the barrier of misunderstanding between our cultures, you two would be the ones." Raugh said this last bit wistfully, realizing this, too, could not be.

Moof, Wour, and Raugh spent the balance of the summer readying the boat for a trip back to Bodenia. Just as promised, Isabel left a large pan at the perimeter of the campsite for cooking the tar. The trio filled the cracks in the hull and tested the boat over and over again to be sure the leaks were well sealed. The last challenge was to retrofit the tarp Ardan had left into a sail. Although not easy, the Bigfoots accomplished the deed and realized they would soon be able to head for home. Instinctively, the trio knew winter was approaching. The time was now or live another cold season away from their loved ones.

On the night of departure, the ocean was calm. "Well, it's time." Raugh sighed, not really looking forward to another excursion across the wide, deep waters. When they'd disembarked the first time three years ago, he'd vowed it would also be his last boating experience. After fighting the elements on a moving mass of liquid that was trying its best to swallow them up, the trailblazers had lost their lust for exploration. But this was the only way home, and home was a powerful incentive.

"I gathered enough food to last us at least five days—in case we run into trouble like the last time." Moof, too, was reflecting on the trip that had landed them on the island of St. Delus in the first place. They felt lucky to have survived it. But the only alternative would be to remain alone on this island. Their desire to rejoin the pack was more compelling. They would risk the perils of the sea one more time.

"Well, I for one am anxious to get back to my family," Wour said in a soulful voice. "I didn't realize how homesick I was until we started making plans to go back. I wonder what changes have happened since we left."

"I think I've learned my lesson. Our elders had a lot of common sense behind the rules they made. Having experienced firsthand the consequences, I'm a believer," Moof added.

Had they not met up with squalls the first night on the trip home, the boys should have been on the land by noon the third day. Thanks to the compass Ardan gave them, the Sasquatch continued to head west—west to Bodenia. Although the winds played havoc on their navigation of the open waters, the intrepid trio's sheer determination saw them through.

The boys realized they had been traveling more southwest than straight west but chose to disembark as soon as they saw land, figuring they would have better luck on solid ground.

The trek across Bodenia was long and tedious. The trio had to skirt around many huge cities—cities that were a far cry from the simple towns and villages up north in the region the sasquatch called home. The trio would have a great deal of information to share with the clan—that is, if they found home again.

Chapter 41

Home Again

When they finally entered Sasquatchewan territory, the boys were exhausted, but the need to reunite with their families kept pressing them forward. As they finally entered the family cavern, the smells of home brought warm recognition to their homesick souls. After the families' initial shock of strangers breaching their abode, the boys were welcomed with total disbelief.

Raugh's mother and father cried for joy as they hugged their son. "Raugh, I thought we would never see you again," his mother sobbed. "It was unbearable!"

Father kept slapping Raugh on the back, as though if by touching him, he was confirming that his long-lost son was really alive and in their midst. "I can't believe it. I can't believe it. Raugh, it's so good to have you home. Where have you been?" His father peppered him with one question after another. "Why didn't you come home sooner? Why would you leave?"

Moof's and Wour's families were just as flabbergasted to see their sons were alive and standing before them. In the three years of separation, the boys had grown into tall, handsome young men. Emotions for all concerned ran from pride at the boys caring for themselves under circumstances they were yet to learn to regret that those years had been lost to each other.

Not to be forgotten, Aargh tore across the den and leaped on the youths. Soon the old friends were wrestling on the ground as if the time apart had never existed. All that mattered now was this time together. Forgotten were the years of separation.

❧

"We have Ardan and Isabel to thank for our safe return," Raugh reminisced with Wour and Moof when things settled down for the night. "We owe them our very lives."

"I never thought humans would be so friendly," Moof reflected. "I wonder if the time will ever come when we can all live in harmony?"

The boys stepped outside and walked into the illumination of a full moon. Looking up, Raugh said, "I know Ardan looks at the moon a lot. He uses it like a sounding board—a nonjudgmental friend of sorts."

Raugh paused, reflecting on their adventure. Overcome with gratitude, Raugh said, "I'm going to try to contact the twins. I think they'd like to know we're safe and at home once more. I've no idea if this will work since we aren't face-to-face, but I'm going to try."

Raugh closed his eyes and put all his focus on reaching deep inside himself for that illusive portal of thought transference. Clearing his head, he concentrated solely on communicating with the twins. In this self-induced hypnotic state, he felt as if to be in a sort of time warp.

After a prolonged interval, Raugh was able to relate the good news to Moof and Wour. He had indeed made contact.

"The twins are well and relieved to hear we are safe. You'll never guess." Raugh laughed. "The twins adopted two of the kittens."

"Wow, that makes me so happy!" Wour grabbed Moof and danced around in circles. The boys loved those little critters. And to think that the twins would be the forever owners was an unexpected relief. The young humans were even more endeared to the Sasquatch boys by this one additional act of kindness.

Moon and stars alike,
Keep your vigil through the night.

Raugh felt at peace with the universe.

Chapter 42

Sasquatch Epilogue

Over for the next several months, Raugh, Moof, and Wour spoke to the various family units. They used their unique experience as an opportunity to educate the clansmen on the things they had learned during the three years they'd lived on the island of St. Delus.

"The biggest surprise we learned was that humans think, love, and learn much the same way we do," Raugh said as he spoke to one of the family units. "We always thought they were more like mechanical 'objects.' But in actuality, they have compassion for all living things. We were amazed to find they are what is called 'educated.' The big units" (machines) "they operate were actually created by them. We always wondered where and how those things appeared and how the humans knew what to do with all of it.

"Moof, Wour and I intend to work on a school system for our society," Raugh continued, fully absorbed by the desire to offer an opportunity for the Sasquatch Nation to achieve an education. First, we'll establish a written language, which will serve as the basis for teaching. And"—he pointed at two impish boys—"we want you to learn from our mistakes. No need to repeat the errors we made. We don't intend to break your spirit - just to provide you with a more intellectual approach. I think, when you find that by directing your ideas and energy to the betterment and not detriment of others, you'll also gain satisfaction in your accomplishments. That satisfaction will become as addicting as mischief making."

Raugh reflected back to his own misguided ventures. Those were unsure personal times when he wondered what was ahead for him. Specifically, he'd wanted to know what was in his future—now, this minute. In his self-absorbed, impatient world, Raugh felt insecure. Perhaps that was why he'd acted up. He was looking for a purpose to his existence. By just allowing time to grow up, Raugh had found that purpose. Looking at these youngsters, Raugh knew they would also find their own direction—in time. Patience was the difficult factor for impatient youth.

While on their speaking tour, the trio found an uninhabited cave and made it their own "digs," as humans might say. Wour was the first to find a soul mate. Soon after, Moof, too, was overcome by a charming young female of his own.

Although not committed as yet, Raugh had his eye on a girl two caverns over. The two often split from the pack after Raugh's many lectures and found they had mutual interests. Her name was Soovy, and she expressed a desire to work in his teaching program.

⟨≋⟩

Author's note: The future is a work in progress. The intrepid trio did create a written language and named it Woobie for Raugh's beloved little sister. I, for one, hold great hope for the Sasquatch Nation. I believe they are employing ideas that will ensure their continued existence. As time progresses, should I learn more from Raugh, I will relate that information to you. In turn, if you are the one to make contact, I would appreciate your sharing what you have learned with me. Many thanks.

⟨≋⟩

BOOK EIGHT

In the Game

Chapter 43

Approaching Summer

The twins were about to finish the seventh grade and were looking forward to summer. It wasn't that they didn't love school and all that, *but* they really wanted to delve into their own special interests. As avid readers, they explored the various topics that would feed into their current interests.

"Have you figured out what you want to be when you grow up?" Isabel asked of her sibling. "I think I'd like to do something in medicine. Doctor, nurse, physical therapist. Crazy, huh?"

Whether Isabel realized it yet or not, the karma in her life was repeatedly guiding her toward life in the medical field. For instance, she'd worked in the infirmary when the pirates invaded, there'd been the hospital visit with Matthew Tyler, and she'd learned about plants used in healing from the Sasquatch. Yes, if there was a hand out there guiding Isabel, then it was leading her toward a medical profession.

"Na, I can't think farther ahead than what's for supper tonight," her brother replied. Whatever happened with your being a dancer, little Miss Twinkle Toes? Guess I missed when you grew up."

"That was so first grade. Since then, I thought about being a veterinarian when we got the kittens. Then there was that bakery with a reading center I considered, given how well Mom's goodies go over at potlucks. And oh, a detective after we caught the dognappers. The world's a big place, Ardan. Who knows?" Isabel's mind never slowed down. Her ideas came at her as if from a conveyer belt. Zip. Zip. She never missed a beat; instead, she gave each inspiration its due consideration. Limitation might have to come first, if and when she was to focus on her true vocation. Till then, it appeared she'd have to struggle through on overload.

Ardan was playing it cool as always, but Isabel knew he was already leaning toward his own special interest. Since a kid, Ardan had been fascinated by the enormity of the universe. In probability, that would be the logical field of study for him. As the twins grew older, he tended to be the more focused of the two. In translation, the twins' personalities were polar opposites.

Two years ago, Ardan had bought a telescope with the money he'd saved from helping Dad and Grandpa at the family hardware store. This Astro-Spacecam 500 wasn't the top grade, but a better one could come later. For a starter, it would serve his purpose. With this telescope, he had the ability to connect an adapter to a phone and take pictures, which, as it turned out, was totally awesome for making comparisons.

Maybe it was the unknown. Or was it the very vastness of space that interested him the most? Either way, this summer, he intended to explore the skies for as far as his Astro-Spacecam would take him.

Ardan was in awe of the astronauts. He wondered what g-force would feel like. What about the possibility of finding more galaxies other than their own? But most importantly, could any of this be connected to that fourth dimension he and Isabel experienced?

That was the underlying question the twins faced way too often in their young lives. No one else even seemed to know about alternate time travel, let alone discuss it. It was becoming apparent each succeeding year that the twins would have to discover the answers all on their own.

"Hey, I know. You'd make a good shrink. We could be the study for your thesis. Whooo, weirdos who think they're time travelers," he goaded her.

"I can see it now. I'd be getting my diploma in a straitjacket instead of a cap and gown." She chuckled. The very thought threw her into one of her giggle fits. Anything said from that point on was simply more fodder for this embarrassing malady. Ridiculous as it was, Ardan loved this aspect of his zany sister's personality and often capitalized on her weakness. He wouldn't stop until they were both in tears.

"OK, my little dingbat, let's pull ourselves together and head our creepy cruisers over to the library. It's almost time to make our deliveries. Our customers need their weekly dose of reading material."

Volunteering was important to the entire Murphy family, and the twins had come up with the idea a few years ago of delivering books to those who couldn't get to the library for whatever reason. Each Wednesday during the summer months, they rode their bikes to the Asterville Library and picked up the new orders. When they delivered the new books, they also retrieved the returns, along with a list of their clients' next request.

As it turned out, these deliveries were multipurposed. It gave this inquisitive pair the chance to meet with some very interesting patrons. Older people enjoyed reminiscing about stories of the past. With the recovery of the historical treasures from the pirate raids, memories long forgotten had become fresh again. These silver-headed classics took pleasure in sharing tell-all tales about their own relatives. Skeletons poured from open closet doors. Life seemed so much more exciting in the olden days, even if the stories were probably only half true. With Isabel still in her silly mood, she couldn't hold back. The simplest word tickled her funny bone—which, of course, only encouraged the senior patrons to embellish the disputed facts even more. They enhanced their stories to make their ancestors more interesting and, after all, it was just innocent fun – right?

"Sorry, folks, but I have to get this chucklehead back to the trolly wagon, or we'll never get done today. This has been a lot of fun. If I don't have to put her away, we'll see you next week," Ardan half apologized.

Outside, Ardan said, "You can dress up, but I can't take you out." He shook his head.

"I know, but honestly, they *were* funnier than usual. Hey, I was holding back. I actually tried coughing to get control. What did you think about the old spinster who lurked around the village with her pet Raven flying reconnaissance intel?"

"Now *that* had to be completely made-up," he laughed.

The next stop on the list was Jonathan, who suffered from muscular dystrophy. Reading was his greatest pleasure. His caretaker always had a cold glass of lemonade and cookies ready when the twins arrived.

As they chatted, Jonathan and Isabel shared information on their mutual interest in medicine. Jonathan didn't let a little thing like a wheelchair get in his way. He was a sophomore, and during the school year, he was on the sidelines at every athletic event—bringing towels, water, or a simple bit of encouragement. He was the inspiration in a tight game or the moral support if the team lost. Jonathan made the most of his life without regrets and was already planning his future as a therapist for people who've had traumatic experiences—physical or mental.

"You know, I've been wondering, should I add the use of therapy pets in my training to help in patient recovery?" Jonathan said. "What do you think?"

"Great idea!" Isabel said. "That technique has proved to be very beneficial. Maybe not in every situation, but I would think it would be a useful tool to have in your evaluation. When we get back to the library, I'll look for some books on the subject and bring them next week."

"I think you're on to something. There are some great organizations out there training rescue dogs. In fact, I heard of one starting in the capital—McGovern Rescue of Pets (McGRiP). Sounds to me like you're already on track for your future. Isabel and I are struggling," Ardan added.

"Aw, it'll come to you when the time is right." Jonathan laughed sounding wiser than his physical years.

They left feeling better, seeing how Jonathan was making the best of life's unfortunate twist of fate.

The current books holding the most interest for the Murphy twins dealt with science fiction—time travel in particular. They often wondered if the author was actually writing about his (or her) own experiences. Could these authors be trying to share their own personal events, but couldn't openly suggest these things really happened—especially to themselves? Then, there were the authors who simply piggybacked off the original ideas. In time, it became more apparent which was which.

Ardan and Isabel sometimes brought up the subject of time travel to their housebound customers, but none seemed to hold an interest in the supernatural. The children were still left without a smidgen of hope of finding anyone else who might be a fourth-dimensional traveler, let alone provide an answer to an alternate physical state of being.

Although books could be read on an iPad, you couldn't always get everything you were looking for online. And to some people, the feel of the volume in their hands gave a more intimate relationship with the story.

Chapter 44

A Friend's Gift

Margie McClain was a close neighborhood friend. Mother always enjoys having her for tea. Working as a school crossing guard gave Margie a real handle on the pulse of Asterville. The children loved her jolly greetings at the beginning and close of each day. Unable to have children of her own, Margie worried over each and every child as if she were their true grandmother. Were they having difficulties in school? Sick? Lonely? Could she help? On weekends, Margie often tutored students having trouble with their studies—always adding a touch of humor to keep learning enjoyable. She believed laughter was healthy for the soul, and Mrs. McClain's laugh was undeniably unique. It had a musical quality, with tones that seemed to glide up and down a melodic scale.

"Enjoy each and every day—good and bad alike," she would say. "Tomorrow brings its own surprises, and you want to be in the right frame of mind to take advantage of it."

Her husband, Brian, was the physical education teacher and coached the various sports teams. As a couple, the McClains were a true asset to the educational system of Asterville.

This day, Margie brought over a video game and handed it off to Angela. "This is supposedly educational, along with being a game of skill. But we could never get the crazy thing to work," Margie said in total exasperation. "We were hopeful to somehow apply it to the Science Club, but it seems to be stuck at the very beginning. Your family is so much more up on these 'techy' things." For emphasis, she put her fingers in the air, indicating quotation marks around the operative word—"techy."

"Maybe those enterprising youngsters of yours can figure it out. If not, just toss it. We got it secondhand, so we won't be out any. My guess is that it's a manufacturers flaw or goof-ups by previous owners. So tell the twins not to waste a lot of time with it."

The women shared a good neighborly chat. Mrs. McClain expressed her worries over the newly planted crops after the difficulties of last year's drought and ensuing fire, when so many acres on the eastern side of the island had burned. The twins' parents, along with many residents around the entire island, had traveled to assist where they could. Some helped in putting out the fires and clean-up, while others prepared meals to keep the firefighters and displaced homeowners nourished and hydrated.

Ardan helped Grandpa, who had stayed behind to run the family hardware store, while Isabel and Grandma maintained the home responsibilities. During that time, the twins were able to enjoy the luxury of their grandparents loving care on a daily basis.

Focusing on happier times, Mother and Margie talked of all the changes at the Mt. Hope Museum. The discovery of the treasures that had been originally stolen by the pirates had given new breath to the island's history.

There was a suggestion that Humphrey Moore was becoming even more fond of the widow Hazel Mason. Several years of working together at the museum had served to strengthen their relationship. The two older folks were fondly admired by all, so this was warmly considered a positive move.

"They deserve a meaningful relationship at this time of their lives," Mother lovingly said.

"So right," Margie added her own feelings. "Life can get lonely in an empty house, and they have so much in common. It's nice to see them happy."

The afternoon seemed to fly by. Too soon, Margie McClain said goodbye to her dear friend, leaving the mysterious video game behind.

Chapter 45

At the Controls

The game was a welcomed distraction to the twins' summer routine. Supposedly, the game would introduce concepts of environmental issues, all while showing the impact of potential problems and possibilities of cures. Deep stuff. It would probably be a good fit for the Science Club. The players were to battle various levels of interactive activities as they met these challenges. The three levels represented different elements—water, soil, and air. If not the Science Club, then maybe the 4-H group would find it useful. Yep, the twins were intrigued. There might be some benefit to this game after all—if it worked, that is.

"I don't know if you would have particular interest in this, but since Mrs. McClain was so sweet to leave it for you, I just couldn't refuse it. Maybe you could just try it when you have time," Mother had said with little to no expectations.

"Interesting," Ardan had declared. "Thanks, Mom. C'mon, Miss Lame Game, let's try it right now." Ardan had taken hold of the box and headed directly upstairs to the open rec area between their bedrooms.

"Hey, watch it!" he scolded Mergatroid. "One of these days, you're going to trip someone by jumping in front of moving feet like that." Merg, who'd been only a kitten when received as a birthday present, was fully grown now. He liked to anticipate Ardan's moves and beat him to the punch, so to speak. Merg only glanced behind to be sure Ardan was following and acted totally oblivious to the scolding.

Ishkabibble, Merg's litter mate, leaped on Isabel's shoulder for a free ride up the flight of stairs. The two "kittens" believed they were an interactive part of the twins' lives and were positive the human children could not function without them. The attachment had been immediate. Merg and the Bibb were showered with love and affection from the start. Hence, they felt entitled to be in the middle of everything—smack-dab in the very center of activity.

The twins' interest in the unusual was undeniable, especially considering the strange adventures they'd already experienced in their short lives. Video games themselves were not the norm in the Murphy household, although they did have a few simple miscellaneous games that gave the twins the general concept of how to interact with one. This game, however, was one they'd never heard of before. Hopefully, it would have possibilities worthy of their time.

"Wow," Ardan said. "This is going to take some serious studying. Here. You start reading the instructions while I bring this over to the TV and plug in the controls," he said to Isabel.

After a few tries, the twins were able to open the app. Well, it did at least give the appearance of working—for now. The undaunted duo couldn't be sure how well it would respond on the different levels.

Mergatroid jumped at Ardan's hand and knocked the control stick to the floor. "Heaven's to Mergatroid!" Ardan shouted, imploring the old saying that he was named after. "You scared me! What's gotten into you?"

Merg continued his nervous prancing. The Bibb was equally irritated and joined her brother's frantic antics. The cats obviously did not like this new thingamajig. And it wasn't only because it would take precious attention away from them; they just didn't like it—at all!

"C'mon, you rambunctious cats. You're not kittens anymore. Act your age, and pretend you're a tiny bit disciplined, will you?" Isabel smiled at Ardan. "I think we've spoiled them."

"OK, you little hairballs, give us some space. Go find a catnip toy or something," Ardan fondly suggested. "We'll play with you later. Promise."

Turning back to the subject at hand, Ardan asked, "Who do you want to be, Twitter Bug?" (He loved assigning unusual names to his sister, knowing he could get a robust response.) "The girl, Almighty Blastro, with explosive powers or the boy, Super Hunk, with superior strength in his arms and legs? Ah, how about the tumbler, Dizzy Dean, or maybe the invisible man, Air Head?"

"Well, you can bet your bottom dollar I'd never lower myself to be a boy! And by being the girl, I'll also be able to rely on her *superior intellect'* I'll be Almighty Blastro with extraordinary blasting powers," she stated, completely satisfied in her choice.

"I think I'll be the Super Hunk with the strong, athletic body," he said while flexing his own muscles. Isabel couldn't help but smile and shake her head—what a nut.

"How do I even know you?" she replied.

Getting past the stage of choosing the characters was like adding oil to free a locked gear. A tweak here and a nudge there. Finally, the screen opened to a clear waterscape, brightly shimmering with light from a sunny sky.

"Remember, Double Trouble, we're a *team* in this. It's not a competition. You need me," he warned as they sat on the brink of challenging their combined skills against the machine.

Chapter 46

Level One: Water

Level one seemed to be a water challenge. Just hop from lily pad to lily pad. An easy first step. The twins each took hold of a controller. Ardan gave a slight grimace toward Isabel, and off they went. The task proved not to be as simple as it had first appeared.

Isabel activated her character and soon learned that she could not linger on a pad or it would give way, and she would be dunked. The lily pads were extremely weak. One life gone. Then another. Always, she'd be sent back to square one. Ardan wasn't having any better luck with his character.

They also found that the further they advanced their counterparts, the faster the water ran, and there wasn't a button anywhere on the controller to harness the speed. To keep up, Ardan and Isabel had to totally engross themselves in the game. All too soon—*they were the game*!

Struggling, Ardan reached shore first. Caught completely by surprise, a very frightened Isabel went down again in the swift current. Even though she was one of the strongest swimmers on the swim team, Isabel was engulfed in a serious struggle to keep her head above the swirling liquid. Looking around, Ardan reached for a lifeline and found one in the form of a hanging vine. Utilizing the superstrength in his arms, he thrust the vine to Isabel and yelled for her to grab hold. Ardan hit his mark just in time. An exhausted sister grabbed the offered salvation with both hands and allowed Ardan to reel her in.

"I feel like a drowned rat," she declared, trying to shake the water off, much the way any wet animal might do.

"Sorry, Sis, didn't bring the towels," Ardan responded while jumping up and down, attempting his own version of drying off. "I don't know what in the world just happened here. How did we get into this mess?"

"I'm more worried about how we're going to get out of this mess. What did we get ourselves into?" she wondered aloud.

As they gathered their second wind, while bouncing around on the embankment, Ardan and Isabel tried to understand what lessons they were to have learned and where the game would take them next. What weakened the lily pads? What caused the foam on the water?

They were still contemplating these ideas when the embankment they were standing on began to erode. With the ground rapidly giving way beneath their feet, the twins quickly leaped onto a large rock formation protruding from the water. At least this was solid and did not give way like the lily pads and bank had.

Relief was but a split second, as they realized that the rock was not a safe location either—not with the currents whipping around them. The thrashing water was breaking over the surface, making it super slippery.

Ahead were a series of rocks, but many were spaced far apart. Isabel didn't believe she could navigate them. Not knowing how many lives they had left, the team decided Ardan would try leaping from one rock to the other to reach the opposite side of the river. Ardan was the stronger and taller of the two. His human passion for running already made his legs strong and muscular, and with the enhanced superpowers that came with his Super Hunk character, he was the obvious choice. Ardan accepted the challenge.

Once he reached the other side of the river (which had now traversed into a choppy mass of liquid), Ardan looked around for another lifeline. The only option presenting itself was to tie some of the largest limbs together with some ivy that was entwined around the shrubs. Working at superspeed, he tossed the makeshift raft into the water. Isabel slipped off the wet rock as she dived for the lifesaving craft. She missed, and under she went again. Gasping for air, she bobbed up from the frothy waters. Unable to right herself, she was being dragged downstream by the current toward a whirlpool. She was already feeling the pull of the circling water as it ferociously tried to draw her ankles into its turbulent trap. As another large boulder broke the surface in the rushing waters and as she came close enough, Isabel used every ounce of energy she possessed and made a life-or-death lunge for it. When she made contact, she clung to the solid mass as if superglued.

Ardan had already pulled the raft back and was running down the shoreline to keep pace with Isabel. Again utilizing his superstrength, he tossed the raft out once more. Isabel's new position was less precarious than the last one, giving her a better shot for recovery. With relief, she was able to latch onto the log contraption. Once back on shore, another thought came to them. Had outside influences played a factor in the bank's erosion? Or was it a natural evolution of the earthen shoreline? What had caused the water to foam, current or pollution?

"See that rainbow downriver?" Isabel excitedly asked Ardan as she peered into the distance. "I think I see a flag or something similar right behind it. I believe that could be the end of this level."

"I see it. You could be right. Let's go for it. I think the raft will be our best option to navigate these waters," he calculated.

"Let's go for it and fast," Isabel concurred.

Having already survived several water trials, the duo spotted a growing wall of jammed logs, brush, and discarded trash looming ahead. The speed at which the twins were approaching the wall left precious little time to react. Quickly, Isabel threw her arms forward and blasted a hole large enough for the raft to burst through its shattered opening.

"OK, Superwoman, what next?" Ardan asked, relieved they'd been spared a lethal crash.

"Well, I think the rainbow is still our best bet," she responded. "Let's just keep riding the waves."

Amid surging water, the raft again picked up speed with a renewed gusto, as if it, too, wanted this level to be completed.

Before them, the river seemed to disappear. In this game, was the world flat as people centuries ago had believed? Were they about to fall off the edge into a dark abyss?

A deafening roar made them instinctively cover their ears. What new trial awaited them? Not now, not another demon. Not when they felt they were so close to the coveted finish line.

"Oh no," said Ardan shouting at the top of his lungs to be heard. "I think it's a waterfall!"

Again, Ardan called upon his superpower. He took the drag rope off the raft and swung it over a massive tree branch. "Hang on to me, Isabel. We're going to swing our way over to the rainbow. Hold on tight!" he instructed. "Now let's start acting like a pendulum. Swing, my little oscillator, *swing*!"

Like Tarzan, the energized youth achieved enough momentum to propel themselves over the falls and to the solid landmass on the other side of the rainbow. There, back on a firm foundation of soil, the tired but gleeful duo captured the first flag.

"Whew," Isabel exhaled. "That was one wild ride."

Having completed the water level, the twins tried to recount the obstacles. Assuredly, many problems were natural occurrences, a gift from Mother Nature herself. But—and that was a big *but*—man was careless as well, either purposefully by inappropriately discarding waste or accidentally by neglecting to scientifically study the adverse effects of pesticides and fertilizers before employing their use. So much to absorb.

Chapter 47

Level Two: Soil

"I don't know, Freckle Face, if it's just me or not, but we're not very tall," Ardan said as he observed the discrepancy in their size to that of other objects around them. "Corn is what? Six feet high, maybe? That would make us only eight, maybe ten inches or so?" Ardan could not believe their diminutive stature.

"This is putting us at a very unfair disadvantage," Isabel warned. "I can't fathom what lies ahead. Do we still have our powers?" A quick test showed their powers were still intact.

As they trekked through a field of corn, an influx of locusts beset them. The pests were consuming the crop at a gluttonous pace. Regarding the twins as human morsels, the locusts contemplated enlarging their appetites to include flesh. Without question, it became apparent that it would be wise for Isabel and Ardan to remove themselves from the equation as quickly as possible. They ducked and darted as best they could. Every clump of dirt represented itself as a hurdle. Every pebble became a boulder.

Above, a particularly large locust was rubbing its hind legs together anticipating a hardy meal. Taking aim at Ardan, it swooped in and wrapped its prickly legs around the defenseless lad. Ardan was swept away in a flurry of commotion. Out of sheer instinct, Isabel raised her arms and blasted the vermin, displaying a vengeance she hadn't realized she was capable of prior to this perilous attack on her sibling.

Ardan tumbled through the air, landing in a pile of dried tassels and leaves that, fortunately, broke his fall. Isabel was quickly at his side, hustling him to an opening in the ground. Like the rabbit hole in Alice in Wonderland, the twins slid down the earthen gap, hoping it would be their sanctuary.

Beneath the earth's surface, a new reality awaited them. The crops were no safer here than they were above ground. Busily gnawing on roots was an army of white grub worms. They were devouring the roots down to the nubbins. Eventually, even the slightest breeze could fall the stalks, like stacked dominos.

"Ew, it's even grosser down here than it was above," Isabel said as she winced in disgust. Her body shuddered.

Realizing they had been invaded, the grubs turned to give the intruders their undivided attention. Red eyes glared in the direction of two terror-stricken children. Putting one stubby leg before another, the bloated matriarch started squirming toward them.

"Run!" Ardan screamed. "We can outrun them. Go, go."

When they were faced with a fork in the tunnel, the twins had to make a choice on what route to take. "People are inclined to go right. I'm guessing animals think the same way. Rodents always prepare an alternate escape exit in their dens. Let's hope we get lucky." Isabel tried to apply reason, if not female intuition, to their unfortunate dilemma.

After a short distance, the twins stopped dead in their tracks. Ahead was the mother-of-all-rats blocking the way out. Her wiry hair bristled. Her sharp teeth glistened as she sneered at the pint-sized invaders. Isabel bit her knuckle to hold back the scream welling inside her. Ardan stretched a protective arm in front of his sister, not knowing which way to turn.

From a cloud of dust, two paws pounced upon the predator followed by an open jaw with even larger teeth than the rat's own spiked appendages. Above, a hungry fox had been listening to the sounds of a fat, satisfying meal moving underfoot. Isabel was thankful she had not screamed aloud, as that might have frightened the fox away.

With the predator removed from their escape route, the twins were free to exit the underground passage.

"Remember when Grandpa and Dad attended the farm seminar last fall?" Ardan asked Isabel. "They talked of natural ways to discourage pests from homesteading farm fields. Rotating crops not only deprived the bugs of expecting their favorite meal, but it also changed the nutrients in the soil so as not to deplete one or another. And they learned so much more, like no till and contour farming to help prevent erosion."

Breathing fresh air beat the humid, smothering atmosphere encountered below. Judging by the amount and variety of trees around them, the duo determined they were in a forest, as opposed to an orchard. As they looked about, the twins saw a vast array of wildlife. To say the least, the area was on the verge of overcrowding. With the human population explosion being witnessed all around the Earth, the many wooded areas were being depleted to accommodate the humans' needs. Proper selection in replacement of trees being harvested did not appear to have been a consideration. More land, too, was being cleared to house and feed the masses. Loss of habitat was not only evident but of extreme concern. How could a reasonable balance be reached? The future held some serious problems.

The tiny duo decided to simply forge ahead, rather than remain where they were. It was unclear what to expect, but standing still was not going to get them to the end of this oppressive game.

"I see a flag on the peak of that mountain way over there," Ardan said while looking about for a clue to their next step. "Could that be our way out?"

"You're guess is as good as mine. I sure don't see anything else," Isabel replied. Maybe Merg and Bibbs had sensed something and weren't just being pests. The twins should have paid better attention to them.

"Ardan," Isabel said in a whisper, "don't look yet, but I think we're being followed."

Indeed. Tracking the petite pair was a large grizzly bear. He had been following their scent since they'd left the rabbit hole. Curiosity attracted him to this unique option to his daily diet. Encroachment of his territory left food at a premium, so he could not afford to pass up an opportunity, even if it was only a "tidbit." This tidbit promised to be high in protein.

Sniffing the air, he pulled himself up to a massive height of eight and a half feet to show off his superiority. Since he knew he was at the top of the food chain, he saw no need to hurry. There was no other animal around to match his strength or his cunning intellect.

Ardan cautiously turned and caught his first look at the predator, who was sizing them up for what would appear to be an easy mark for the furry beast.

"Teamwork, Shorty. We'll need to rely on each other's powers if we are to get out of this one. I don't think we'll get a second life to try again," he warned. "This is for real."

In unison, the twins stood as tall as their ten inches allowed and spread out their arms to appear larger—much like other species do in times of peril. With feet and arms akimbo, they screamed, "Hi-yaa!" as they took a defensive position.

Although caught by surprise, the beast was not to be intimidated by a couple of tasty ants. The smell was intriguing, and his desire was only intensified with the impassioned display for survival. Back on all fours now, the giant lumbered toward the children.

"I'll wait until he gets close enough for maximum impact," Isabel stated.

With eyes bigger than melons peering down on the underlings, the bear opened his savage mouth. Faster than the blink of an eye, Isabel jolted the beast's throat with a full blast of her lightning power.

"Jump on my back, Isabel. I can run faster with my superpowers!"

While the grizzly recoiled in pain, the twins raced toward the mountain. Ardan started grabbing at tree roots and ledges to pull them up the rough surface. Using his super arms, Ardan threw nature's version of a rope over the rocky ledge at the crest of the mountain. With practiced skill (like the time they'd scaled a similar mountain to warn the villagers of the pirates), the twins employed the hand-over-hand technique to scale the rugged terrain to its apex.

"We made it!" Isabel sighed. "I'll bet that ol' bear won't be able to swallow anything for a week."

The youngsters realized how grateful they were to have each other to get through these rough times.

The team had worked. They'd captured the second flag.

Chapter 48

Level Three: Air

Weary from the two previous levels, the twins were even more anxious for the game to be over.

"What next, Ardan? I hope this level is easier."

"I believe this one is air. How hard can that be? Maybe we'll soar to Mars or even Neptune." Ardan wasn't really hoping for that. The prospect just popped into his head, and as usual he spoke before he thought. He always said he didn't know what he was going to say until he heard it himself.

"Oh, no!" Isabel worried. "Say it isn't so. Not space travel."

"Of course not. But I have no idea what's next. We've come this far. We can handle anything … right? Hey! Are we normal size again?" He glanced about, trying to find something to relate to.

"Thank the Lord. We are normal. So now what? How do we go about traversing this level?"

Foreseeing the future was not in their forte—although they alluded that it was in their magic show. No, something had to physically appear to give them direction.

"There we go, Almighty Blastro. Let's check that out," Ardan said, pointing to a patch of color in the distance. As the two approached the brilliant gift, Ardan added, "I believe our transportation has just arrived."

"You're kidding," Isabel said in despair. "What is this? Big kites?"

"No, little Miss Aerospace. I do believe these are hang gliders."

"Again, I say, are you kidding me!?"

"You'll love it. Remember how excited we were on those big school swings? Before we fell off, of course. Remember the feeling of flying? The wind in our hair? Well, this will be even better. Finally, some fun in all this." Ardan's enthusiasm made Isabel a little less apprehensive. She wasn't totally at ease, just a tad better.

"OK, bro. Show me what to do. And excuse me for stating the obvious, but where are we going? There must be a point to all this, after all." Isabel began looking across to the next mountaintop for something relevant to the game. Nothing jumped out saying, "Here it is."

They were still on the cliff where they'd captured the flag from the soil level, and with nothing else in sight, it seemed the hang gliders were to be their mode of transportation. The question still was—*to where?*

"Ready?" Ardan asked as he strapped on his gear. "Let's just go for it and get this over with. Something'll pop up. Run as fast as you can to the edge of the cliff and then simply jump off the edge and let the wind and air do the rest."

"Simply jump off the edge. You say that so easily. Are you crazy? That is not *simply*!"

"OK, maybe it's more of a 'leap of faith.' But it appears this is the only way. You can do it. I have all the faith in the world in you. We're a team, remember. I'll take the lead, and you can be my wingman. Follow me."

"I'd like to assure you that I have your six, but ..." She hesitated.

At that, Ardan took off running, with Isabel fast on his heels. The air currents gracefully raised the wings of the colorful gliders. Almost weightless, the twins were in the air and flying. From their lofty position, they had a true bird's-eye view of Mother Earth in all her splendor. As Ardan promised, the rush was more than they could have imagined. It was majestic.

As if part of a Disney painting, an artistic mist ringed the distant mountain, giving it an appearance of an enchanted neverland. The children were euphoric. They could feel the stress of previous levels melt away. This was indeed relaxing. After all, why would they think every level had to be horrible?

Unfortunately, this feeling of relief was not to be enjoyed for long. The reality of the game was to rear its ugly head once again, and "horrible" was, indeed, back in play. The gentle, sweet-smelling mist had become heavier and incurred the odor of sulfur. Smog? Were they in smog? Thick, unbreathable smog?

"Ardan, I can't see anything. Are we in fog or smog?"

"My guess is we're getting a lesson in air pollution," Ardan replied between coughing spells. "There's a distinct odor connected to this."

The duo soon lost visual contact with each other in the thick, dark sky. "Ardan, where are you? I can't see you," Isabel called out.

No answer.

"Marco," she yelled at the top of her lungs.

Pause.

"*Marco!*" she screamed, incorporating the game they'd played so many times with friends. But this time it wasn't necessary to use a blindfold.

"Polo," she heard in the distance.

"Say again," she shouted. "Marco."

"Polo. Follow my voice. I think I found an opening."

Together again, they aimed their crafts toward the lighter atmosphere. The skies opened back up to the wonderous beauty they'd previously enjoyed. What had caused that hideous episode? Volcano ash, burning forests, factory burn off, car emissions? Another lesson to be taken into consideration?

As they navigated down to a slightly lower level, the twins noticed an ominous, large, blackish cloud approaching. It was quickly blocking out the sun.

"Oh no, Ardan. Remember the news last week covering that hurricane? Well, this looks very much like that looked."

"That was so destructive! Whatever it is, it's coming fast. Suggestions Isabel? What can we do?" Ardan's voice displayed his mounting fear.

"Let's land on that ledge down there. I'll blast a hole in the side of the mountain where we can ride out the storm. We should be high enough to be out of the way of any flooding."

Isabel let forth with her superpower. It took two hits to get a deep enough cavern where they would be protected from the savage winds and gully washer that was about to overtake them.

It seemed like hours before the danger, which included several tornadoes, past. The two could relate to the importance the Sasquatch attached to living in caves. Their friends had so much natural ability to cope with worldly conditions.

When they looked out to survey the damage, the twins realized that, in their haste, they'd neglected to bring in the hang gliders. Now what were they to do? With their gliders lost to the ravages of the hurricane, they could only hope for another option to miraculously direct them.

"We're fully entrenched in the air level. I think logically we should go up." Ardan looked to Isabel for confirmation.

"Drat it all, more climbing. I'll never even think of climbing a hill when we get out of this," Isabel said with consideration of her tired muscles.

The climb wasn't as rough as they'd feared. In fact, with their normal size, it was hardly a challenge. The weary travelers could almost forget the horrors that had proceeded them thus far and again could take in the beauty of the land.

"This really takes the cake." Isabel was totally taken off balance when they reached the top. "Say it isn't so, Ardan. Tell me my eyes are playing tricks on me."

"Wish I could, but it looks real to me," Ardan said.

They cautiously walked around the monstrosity. The metal vessel had but one gleaming ladder leading straight up to a hatch located in the upper section.

"Ardan, this has to be your doings!" Isabel stated in disbelief. "You and your dreams of being an astronaut have been implanted into this game. Well, I am *not* traveling in a spaceship! This is the last straw."

"I can't blame you, Isabel. This doesn't look too promising to me either, but what else can we do? We're stuck in the middle of this game. And honestly, I'm at as much of a loss as you are."

There was literally no other option. This was the way out.

Reluctantly, they began to climb the long flight of steps to the open portal, step by agonizing step.

Almost by instinct, Ardan closed the hatch and secured the latches. They donned the space suits waiting inside and strapped themselves in for the ride of a lifetime. Lights on the control panel started to bounce.

"I believe we're getting our orders through a series of blinking lights. How good were you playing Simon?" he laughed. "I'll take the helm again if it's all right with you."

With Isabel's nod of confirmation, Ardan assumed command as if he'd been born to it.

"Go for it," Isabel said. "I'm happy with second chair. Does that make me the copilot? Or is it co-commander?"

The duo responded to the synchronized sequence of blinking lights. As they hit the final button, the boosters hit full power.

"We have liftoff," Ardan announced.

Pinned to their seats, the airmen hit g-force within seconds and passed through the ozone layer a second after that.

"How're you doing, Space Monkey?"

"Hanging in there. And you?"

"Unbelievable!"

When they broke free of earth's gravity, the novices got their first experience of weightlessness. It left them in a playful, giddy mood. They tried floating, pushing off, catch.

"Quick. Look out the window. We may never get an opportunity like this again." Ardan was astounded at the view of earth shrinking from the size of a gigantic ball to a marble in the blink of an eye while the reverse was happening with the moon, which was looming larger just as quickly.

"Look at all the activity in the sky. Does this show up on your telescope?" Isabel asked.

"No," Ardan replied. "Mine's not sophisticated enough to catch all of this space debris, let alone most asteroids or meteors. If they're big enough and close enough, I can track them. But that's nothing compared to what's actually out here. After this, I really want that bigger model."

"What's that thing over there doing? It looks like it's coming straight for us!" Isabel grabbed Ardan arm and pointed out the front window.

"How do you steer this thing?" Ardan frantically searched the control panel. "I think it's going to crash into us!"

In a nanosecond, the spacecraft arrived and instantly stopped dead in its tracks—right in front of the young cadets, who by now had braced for impact. It began to hover, as if checking them over. First, it circled to the right, allowing its occupants to look directly into the capsule, before doing a complete comprehensive search around the entire spaceship.

"What do you think they're doing?"

"Looks like they're as inquisitive about our being here as we are about them," Ardan guessed.

With a *whish* the alien ship was gone, leaving behind of fiery trail.

In the past, Ardan might have mistakenly thought this to be a comet. Without question, he really wanted to upgrade his telescope. There was so much more to look for after this experience.

"I couldn't see inside the vessel, could you?" Isabel asked.

"No, I didn't see any life forms. I've also never known of any of our aircraft that can do those maneuvers—unless it's one of those top-secret military programs."

A sudden movement in their own spaceship left the youngsters grabbing for their seat belts. The autopilot seemed to be taking over? Or were they in the control of the aliens? *Where were they going?* they wondered. All the young cadets could do now was hang on and hope for the best.

With a sudden jolt, the craft stopped. No movement. No lighted panel. The spacecraft was dead. The twins appeared to be on their own without an obvious lifeline.

"I think we've landed somewhere," Ardan said, looking out his portal.

"*Look*, Ardan! Here on my side. It's a flag. I don't think there is even a breeze. It's just all spread out without a ripple."

"Isabel, we're on *the moon*! That looks like an American flag. I'll bet it's the one that that American astronaut—oh, what was his name? Neil ... Neil Armstrong. Yeah, I'll bet it's the flag Neil Armstrong planted on the moon." Ardan felt like he was living out the fairy tale of his dreams.

"That's it. Our final flag. Let's get out of here and get out of this game—once and for all! Well, Captain, do you want to put your footsteps in the moondust first?" Isabel offered.

"Mission accomplished!" the twins said in unison.

169

Chapter 49

Wrapping It Up

The attack came fast, knocking the twins off their feet. There had been no advance warning. Quicker than they could say spit, they were hit from behind.

"Merg! Gimmie a break, fella."

"You too?" Isabel said laughingly as she looked over to her brother, who was sprawled out across the floor. Ishkabibble had pounced on Isabel with the same gusto as her furry brother. The cats were happy to see their counterparts back home again.

"I'll give you credit, Merg. You tried to warn us. Little did we know. You OK, kiddo? Are you any the worse for the wear?"

"Well, I never want to do that again," Isabel said as earnestly as she could. "Just saying."

"I think we should tell Mom that this game just didn't work and trash it. I'd hate to think some other kid might go through that experience." Ardan was firm in his assessment.

"I do believe I learned a lot. I think my next project at the science fair will be on the elements—water, soil and air. Na, I think I'll just pick one. There is so much to research, if I want to do a good job of it, that is."

"Great idea, Whiz Kid. I think I'd like to take air if that's OK with you." Ardan became excited at the prospect. "We can work on it this summer to get a head start. Spacewoman, you come up with a doozy every once in a while!"

That night, Ardan had new respect for his "Man in the Moon" (who, by the way, he never saw).

As you patrol the skies,
Are you watching everything?
Do you see the wonders in disguise?
Or are they strange only in my eyes?
I do want to give space a fling.

BOOK NINE
Running for Student Council

Chapter 50

Taking Responsibility

"So far, high school isn't so bad," Isabel said, regarding their freshman year. "We're, like, the underdogs and all, but I feel like we have so much more freedom."

"Yeah, freedom with a lotta stipulations," Ardan added with a knowing warning.

"Do you think we'll ever get sent to the principal's office?"

"You're joking, right? We've never been that bad," he scolded her.

"Or have we?" she coyly responded. "How quickly you forget."

"If Archie makes it through, we're safe. Seriously now, I've been thinking of trying out for the basketball team. Coach McClain thinks I'd be a natural," Ardan said changing the subject. Ardan's record at the Asterville grade school was pretty solid. "And it's an activity to fill the winter months. Isabel, you should try out for the high school swim team. You'd be good at it."

"Wow, imagine us—athletes. Olympics, here we come. And thank you very much, I *have* been thinking about it. Competition's going to be tough though. I understand the kids from the other two schools have some pretty big fins with turbo kicking power."

"Oh, you'll make the team easy. I have all the confidence in the world you can cut it." Ardan nodded his assurance.

"You know." Isabel hesitated. You could tell she'd already given the subject prior thought but wasn't too sure how Ardan would take to it. "You should run for student council. You're so organized, and, Ardan, you could make a difference. I'd be your campaign manager. You can't lose with me on the team."

"Cute. Say I do run. What would be my slogan—whoopie cushions for all?"

"That'll get you the fun lovers votes. You'd be halfway there." Isabel laughed.

⬨

The next afternoon, Ardan had his head buried in homework when Isabel entered their study room. This area between their bedrooms had become the twins' sanctuary. Over the years their playroom/craft room/ classroom had adjusted to keep up with their growing needs. Gone was the brightly colored alphabet border. A laptop and printer replaced the worn-out flash cards and stubbed-off crayons. Little by little, the room matured with them.

Isabel's bedroom morphed from princess pink to a soft buttercup yellow. When she woke in the morning, she already felt energized by the sun-filled atmosphere. Even cloudy days couldn't hamper her spirits, as the warmth of the color superseded the gloom. Yes, Isabel was what you call a "morning person." She was ready to go as soon as her feet hit the floor.

Ardan gave up his sapphire-blue colored ceiling with its glow-in-the-dark stars for a more sedate oyster-white ceiling with celery-green walls. Nice and soothing to meditate at the end of the day. Indeed, Ardan was the night version of his older sister (older by a whole eight minutes). When he looked out across the star-filled sky, the youngster simply left behind the trials of the day. Ardan was a "night hawk."

⬨

"Did you think homework would be this heavy? It's like tripled, even quadrupled, since grade school!" Ardan exaggerated. He was kidding, of course, but it gave him the chance to release his emotions related to what was really troubling him. Since Isabel had brought the subject up, he'd been wrestling with the idea of running for student council.

"Isabel, you have me thinking. Do you really think I should run for the freshman seat on the student council? Could I make a difference?" Ardan was clearly perplexed.

"Ardan, I'd have never suggested your running if I didn't believe—no, I *know*—you can handle it. Honestly, you're smart and you're caring," Isabel said, taking pride in the possibility of her brother's stepping up.

"OK, say I go for it, what comes next, Miss Campaign Manager?"

"Well, first you'll have to go to the principal's office and get a petition. Then—and I *will* help you—you have to get the required number of signatures."

Ardan could tell Isabel was wired and ready to hit the political trail with gusto.

"I've been thinking of a slogan. How's 'A vote for Ardan is a vote for action!'?

"*Or*, you could go for something catchy—like, say, 'Ardan will reinstate Murphy's Law'. You know, if something can go wrong, it will. Or maybe 'Ardan, Ardan. He's our man. If he can't do it, nobody can!'" With that, Isabel did one of her feeble imitations of a cheer that was in obvious need of a major makeover.

"Your cheerleading skills aren't any better than your ballet routine," Ardan said remembering her prancing around trying to distract the audience during their magic show. However, he appreciated her using humor to take away any hint of apprehension he might be harboring. But in perspective, he wanted to look at this as a very serious responsibility.

"I just want you to enjoy this opportunity—win or lose. Give it your all, do your utmost best if you win, and always keep smiling. Mrs. McClain would tell you to love every day—good or bad. 'A cheerful attitude will get you through the stressful times,'" Isabel said, remembering the encouragement of their grade school crossing guard.

"You're right—as always." Ardan added the last bit almost under his breath. "I won't let it get me down. But some stress is good stress. I tend to work better when I'm under the gun, so to speak. First, let's run this by the folks—just to see what they think."

The two decided to spring the idea on their parents at the supper table. In the past, their outlandish ideas were usually revealed over a hearty meal. Their often-astonished parents generally viewed their ideas favorably. This time, however, the youth hoped for some mature advice to go along with their support.

177

Chapter 51

The Candidate

Right before school the next day, Ardan went to the principal's office. The secretary gave Ardan his petition and explained the details of filing, stressing the deadline.

Tri-township High School (THS) was a combination of grade schools from three neighboring communities and was centrally located in the larger city of Barshire; Asterville and Rohnsted rounded out the trio.

It was a shock of sorts to the twins, not only at being the school underdogs, but also at not knowing the other two-thirds of the freshmen student body. In the Asterville grade school, they knew all their peers. Over the years, with rotating classes, they had intermingled with all of their Asterville classmates. Things were different now. The halls were crowded highways of activity without traffic constraints. With only five minutes to navigate between classes, you had better think ahead for everything you would need for the next several periods. Freshman lockers were located at the far north end of the building. Somehow, most of their classes seemed, to them at least, to be in the south end, intertwined with staircases.

"Well," Isabel said as they reentered the hall, "we should start getting signatures between periods. We'll have to be sure they're freshmen though. I found out I have a sophomore in my biology class. He was sick a lot last year and is doing some makeup classes."

"I asked Jay Reynolds if he could help us this weekend making posters and handbills," Ardan added.

"Great. He'll be a good one for the team. I thought about asking Margaret Willis to help but I heard Archie McNabb is running, too. I believe she's working on his committee. You know, I think she's had a secret crush on him since kindergarten."

Thinking about Archie always brought a smile to Isabel's face, especially when she thought about his centipede creation in kindergarten and how it had played into Matthew Tyler getting well.

"Isn't that weird that two of the three candidates should be from Asterville? I think a lot of Archie. He's a good friend. Wish I'd have known ahead of time that he was going to run. He always ranks in the top of—gosh, just about everything."

"Do you mean you wouldn't be running if you knew Archie was?" Isabel was surprised.

"I don't know. I wouldn't want any hard feelings to come of this."

"Well, there shouldn't be. You both have a lot going for yourselves. I can't see either one of you holding grudges."

"Guess I shouldn't be borrowing trouble. Archie and I have competed in other things without it getting in our way. This is just so new. I don't know; high school's different. I only want to do what's for the best."

"Well I can guarantee you Archie's a bigger person than to let this upset him enough to lose to a friendship over it. Besides, he might win, and *you* might have to be the responsible loser." Isabel would never conceive of this race as being a dividing factor in a long-term friendship. Nope. The boys would weather it. Besides, the third entry could be the actual winner, and all this would be a moot point.

"Hey, bud!" Ardan was startled by an enthusiastic grip across his shoulder. "This is so great. You and me running for the same spot on the council. It's almost a comfort to have a fellow Asterville*ian* to run against. If that's not already a word, then I'll coin it as one of my own. I got a million of 'em. You should see me at Scrabble," Archie declared in his usual jovial manner. Archie had proved himself over the years as an outward leader—a bit of a wacky outward leader but one who never shirked his responsibilities.

If Ardan had ever thought this competition could decisively divide old pals, his worries were put aside. Archie's personality was infectious. Everyone who knew him instinctively liked the uncontested class clown. Although he loved pranking people, he was never harmful or mean-spirited in his actions.

"I expect we'll make this a good, stiff competition. So what's say we make our fellow students sit up and actually want to get involved in some real issues. I'm excited, Ardan. You're the best opponent I could have wished for. You're gonna make me work for this," Archie said with a broad grin. "You'll be tough to beat! But you can be sure, *I will beat you!*"

"You just try, old man. Give it your best shot. But remember, that's me breathing down your neck every step of every day, and as I'm passing you by, I'll wave," was Ardan's playful rebuttal to his old friend.

"OK, guys. Enough with the trash talk. We'll be late to class." Isabel thought it prudent to step in before they were all tardy.

That weekend, the Ardan committee gathered at the Murphy house to start rolling out posters and flyers. Jay, as it turned out, was a talented artist. Isabel incorporated his designs with her computer skills and ran off a supply of handbills. New friend Marcus Wilson from Rohnsted was handy with words and came up with a catchy campaign slogan— The Smartest Cookie is Ardan the Rookie! Also included in the body of the flyer were some of Ardan's accomplishments—civic, scholastic, and athletic. Rounding out the team was Vicki Thomas, another Asterville friend who was chosen for her organizational skills. She laid out a timetable to keep the group moving without distractions.

The petitions had been judiciously turned in, giving Ardan the OK to start posting his signs. It didn't take the team long to cover all the bulletin boards at school and hand out flyers to their fellow classmates. After school, the twins were going to hang a few posters around each of the towns in the grocery stores and laundromats, where parents might see the information and maybe/hopefully talk about it at home to their voting students.

"Since we're already in Barshire, let's cover a few places on our way home. We can catch a later bus. Mom knows we'll be late," Ardan said.

"Awesome. Then on the bus, we can talk about that speech you have to give at the assembly Friday. I'll bet Marcus can help you with the wording. And thanks to Vicki, you have time to prepare for it. We're learning as we go about how this campaigning stuff works. By the time we're seniors, you'll have your feet well planted under you and you can run for council president." She laughed.

"Let's not get ahead of ourselves, Miss Eager Beaver," he said. "One day at a time." You could always figure the gung-ho Isabel for a rapid projection of where life could take them.

"Do you even know my real name? You know, the one on my birth certificate? The one Mom and Dad actually gave me?" she asked rhetorically.

"But of course, *Mon cheri*. It's but one of those mythical concepts that appears to fit your ever-changing ideas on what you want to be if—oops, sorry, 'when'—you grow up. It's even written in disappearing ink so that the appropriate moniker will magically reveal itself as you make one critical career choice after another. I can never be incorrect. It's just there. Each name fits every flip of your imagination," he replied.

"I can't get ahead of you." She resigned herself with a shrug of her shoulders. "What was I thinking?"

"You got that right, Miss Shilly-Shally."

Neither of them had known anything about this speech thing in advance. Now *that* might have been a deal breaker. Ardan had talked in front of a class when presenting a project assignment or at small team meetings. But this speaking in front of the entire student body, on stage in a large auditorium, was not something he looked forward to.

As they moved around Barshire posting their literature, the siblings chatted about school and the new friends they were making. Absentmindedly, they wove themselves to the edge of town. They'd have to think about getting back to a bus stop before it got much later.

Chapter 52

Another Transition

"That's peculiar," Isabel said. "There's already a sign on this post."

"By the looks of it, it's been here awhile. Would it be rude to replace it with ours?"

"What's this? The president's dead?" Isabel was having trouble reading the weathered text.

"There's a reward of $50,000 for a Wilkes guy and another $25,000 for each of his two accomplices. Hey. This stuff is from world history," an astonished Ardan uttered. "It's about Lincoln. Wasn't he a president in America and somebody shot him because he didn't like his politics?"

What the children were looking at was an actual handbill dating back to 1865. This was the first time real photographs were used instead of artist sketches to portray the culprits. The quality was still an antique, brownish color, but otherwise it looked like any other typical wanted poster of today.

"Rethinking about running, are you?" Isabel teased "Looks like it can get pretty rough out there. You might need a bodyguard instead of a campaign manager."

Already used to quick, unannounced transformations, the astute duo simultaneously realized that they had just crossed over into another alternate universe. It was hard for the twins to explain *how* and *when* they know the conversion had taken place, and it was something they couldn't prepare for because it was new and different every time. It was the *why* that usually took time to reveal itself in an aha moment.

Galloping horses could be heard in the distance. By all indications, they were approaching rapidly—perhaps in great numbers. Not knowing who was coming, the children chose to move into a thicket of pine trees behind them. From their hiding place, they could still hear the activity on the hardened dirt road they had just vacated.

Lieutenant Edward Doherty was in charge. He slowed the calvary to give precise instructions. He spoke to his squad leaders. "Our best leads put them in this general area. I want to make a thorough search of this stretch of highway. You sergeants, take ten men each. We'll drop units off in sections about a mile apart and meet up together at the far end, where we'll camp for the night. You're looking for any signs of horses leaving the main road. It might not be much more that some bent stalks or muddy hoofprints. The culprits are probably taking refuge in the woods away from the traveled highway. Whoever finds them, send a scout back to the rest of us. Is everyone clear? OK then, assemble your squads. Now let's catch the cowards!"

With the army scattering in organized chaos, the twins moved further into the pine forest. They were still uncertain what time frame they were in. The conversation they'd overheard hadn't used names or places.

"Whatever can we be doing here, Ardan?" Isabel wondered. "I'd bet this isn't even our country anymore."

"Neither was Bodenia our country when we helped catch the dognappers. But this—this seems just way too crazy. Do you think this is tied into the murder of Lincoln? Was that wanted poster a clue? Let's move on until we have an epiphany of sorts. Something'll just jump out at us, you'll see," Ardan said with a reassuring voice.

Almost as soon as the words were out of Ardan's mouth, a man jumped out of the undergrowth, confronting them with pistol in hand.

"Who are you and what are you doing here?" the man yelled. "Who *are you*?" he demanded when he didn't get an immediate response.

Startled, Isabel stuttered, "Ah, we're lost. We were coming home from school and lost our way. We're new in town and ...a—"

"What's going on?" whimpered a man who was resting against his saddle. His bandaged leg was stretched out over a makeshift pillow of dried brush.

"I found these youngsters sneaking around," the man with the gun replied, dragging the twins to face his fellow conspirator.

"Well, bring the young urchins closer, David, where I can get a look at them." The man's voice was deep and authoritative, like some sort of Shakespearian transplant.

From the pictures on the poster, the twins surmised that David must be David Herold, a confederate sympathizer and fellow conspirator. It also showed that the other man was probably John Wilkes Booth, an actor and the actual assassin. The twins now believed that the soldiers they'd overheard earlier must have been Yankees, since, as they remembered from history, the Confederates had surrendered five days before the president was shot. Then *why*, if the war was over, would Booth want to kill the president? Booth had to have heard the news of General Lee signing the surrender document at Appomattox. For goodness sake, people were rejoicing in the streets, relieved at there being an end to the horrendous war that had divided the nation—a war that had split families in two. So many lives had been lost. The country had suffered so much grief. Everyone was hoping and praying that now the healing could begin. Why? Why on earth would he kill Lincoln?

Herold said, "We can't let them go. They'll run to the authorities sure as we do, and those dastardly Yankees are close at hand."

"You are correct as always, David. They will go with us," Booth said. Despite his agony, his diction was spot on. "We can decide later what we will do with these intruders. For now, good man, there is an urgency we reach Garrett's farm. He will put us up, and I need some whiskey for this pain. The bottle Dr. Mudd gave me is long gone, and the pain is excruciating."

Booth broke his leg after he fired the fatal shot to President Lincoln during a stage performance at Ford's Theater. As he jumped from the president's balcony box to the stage, his foot became entangled in the patriotic bunting that adorned it. Limping, he raced to the alley, where his horse was saddled and ready for a quick escape.

Shortly afterward, he linked up with David Herold, and the two rode to the home of Southern sympathizer Dr. Samuel Mudd, where he received treatment. However, the balding doctor kicked them out when he learned what Booth had done.

Last month, the Booth band of rebels had only been talking of kidnapping the president. As it turned out, with Lee's surrendering, Booth's intent had become more radical. Now he wanted to kill the president and those who were in line to succeed him. The vice president, the speaker of the house and even the secretary of state were in their crosshairs. The new plan was thwarted when either the dignitaries were not where they were thought to be or Booth's accomplices plainly chickened out. In the end, only Booth followed through with this deadly assault.

Herold hauled Ardan by the arm to where their gear was piled and forced him to assist in readying the horses. Ardan tried to resist but was slapped across his face with the back of Herold's hand as he reminded Ardan that Booth had a pistol pointed at Isabel. Ardan would give his own life before he would let anyone harm his sister. He elected to bide his time and wait for a proper opening when they could safely make their escape.

Then Herold made Ardan help manhandle the heavy saddles and throw them on the horses' backs. Roughly, Herold assisted Isabel behind Booth, while he kept Ardan in his own personal charge. It was almost a blessing for Herold to have someone to take his anger out on, and Ardan became the unfortunate target. None of this whole catastrophe had gone the way the scoundrels had planned, and now the Yanks were hunting them down. Several times over the past few days, they had heard the thunder of horses in dedicated pursuit. The culprits' stress intensified as the Yanks cast a wide net over their escape route. It was keenly apparent to them that the soldiers were drawing in those strings, ever so much tighter.

With the offenders mounted on their weary horses and Ardan and Isabel perched behind them, the four headed for what was hoped to be a safe harbor.

It had been ten days since the Good Friday shooting of Lincoln. Booth couldn't believe he was being hunted. When he shot President Lincoln, he had been certain he would become a national hero and that he would be rewarded by both sides of the Civil War. As a famous actor, he was accustomed to adoration from his fans. In a fantasy of his own making, he believed his brave effort to destroy the hated opposer of the people's rights to own slaves would elevate him to a godly status.

They reached the Richard Garrett farm only to learn that Garrett would not give the notorious criminals sanctuary. Garrett would only allow them a brief overnight respite in his barn before moving on. Even though it was evening and traveling would be safer, Booth was worn out. They would take a short break.

With the Union Army scouring the area, Garrett (although a Southern sympathizer) wanted as much distance from the murders as possible. He did not want any personal ties linking him to this vicious plot. Garrett also expressed his anger at the presence of the two children. He wanted them off his land as well. The original scheme was woefully out of control.

Appling a bit of foresight, the farmer brought out some bread and milk so he might be remembered kindly, should the children live to tell the tale.

Ardan and Isabel were then tied and shoved in a dark corner of the barn. With their prisoners out of the way, the perpetrators began drafting a new escape route. Herold was becoming more and more agitated and expressed his desire to surrender—much as General Robert E. Lee and his men had. Herold believed he would receive reasonably fair treatment and maybe even be let go, just like a uniformed Confederate soldier was sent back home, instead of becoming a prisoner of war. Better that, than to be cut down as a hunted fugitive. Booth was adamant that he would not be afforded such a waiver. The entire audience had seen him as he'd leaped from the president's box yelling, "Sic Semper Tyrannis" (Thus Always with Tyrants). He'd now accepted the fact that he would not to be as kindly received as he'd once believed.

When Herold tied him up, Ardan used a trick he learned while practicing his magic act. By holding his wrists in a certain way, the ropes would not be as tight as Herold intended.

"Remember I said 'it's all in the wrist' when we practiced our magic act? Well I was right. My ropes came undone already," Ardan told Isabel. "Here, let me get yours."

While the twins freed themselves, they discussed their own plans. They had contemplated escape earlier but were hesitant because the men had weapons and were obviously killers. Each hour made the necessity to flee more apparent. The hour was still early, but the twins could already hear Booth and Herold talking—sometimes heatedly. Isabel and Ardan had to formulate a plan of their own.

"Ardan, you may not approve of this, but because you are so fast, I think you should make your escape and run to the authorities. Wait." She held her hand up to squelch her brother's protest. "Hear me out. This is such an important part of history; you have to get help. I'll distract Booth and Herold like I did in the magic act so you can slip by them. There's no way we both can get past them and not be seen. They have guns. We have to be tricky." She reached out and took her brother's hand. "I'll get out as soon as they realize your gone and start looking for you. Ardan, this is the most important thing that has ever happened to us. If Herold and Booth get away, they'll get deep into the South, where they'll find sympathizer protection. History could be changed if you don't act now. I remember reading that the Union soldiers were given a tip as to where Booth and Herold were hiding. That anonymous tipster very well might be you. I think we are here because we are a legitimate part of that history."

"Are you done now?" he responded. "I can't leave you. No way. History or not. These men are desperate. Who knows what they're capable of?"

"You have to! Be reasonable. They're killers! Someone has to put an end to such a horrible deed. Ardan, you have the speed. Besides, I'm cute. They won't hurt me," she said with a twinkle in her eye. "We have to hurry before they decide to leave and take us with. They may intend to do away with us when they get off Garrett's land. If they can kill a president, we're nothing. Honestly, you can show the Union soldiers exactly where to look."

Isabel was to circle around to the far side of the barn, where she would divert their captors' peering eyes to her. This would allow Ardan the precious minutes he would need to escape. Isabel had Ardan retie her wrists (loosely this time). Stealthily, she crept away from her brother. When she felt she was far enough away from Ardan, she started to scuff her feet in the dried hay, making distracting noises. With the full attention of their captors, Isabel requested permission to use the outhouse.

"Excuse me," Isabel started, "I hate to intrude, but … I need to … ah … use the facilities." She had that sweet, innocent routine down pat, having used it to get out of tight spots before.

"You're more trouble than you're worth," Herold snapped before she could finish. Turning to Booth he continued his rampage, "I knew it was wrong to drag them along! They're nothing but trouble—*trouble!*"

"What else could we do?" Booth shouted back with equal distain. "But what are we to do with them now is the bigger question. They'll slow us down, and we need to get south as quickly as we can." Booth was torn between his options. Clearly, Garrett didn't want the youth left with him. "You go with her. No, wait. May as well drag the lad, too. Then settle them back down while we get organized. When we get deeper into rebel territory, we'll have time to discuss their demise. But for now, we must hasten our departure."

Isabel needed to stall them just a bit longer. Ardan had already cleared the barn but would need a few more minutes to get past the long drive. These men were becoming more desperate, and she could not discard the fact of their weapons. "First, could you undo my ropes. Sorry to be a bother, but"—she fidgeted about and stammered—"it might ... be ... you know ... difficult ... to ... a ..."

"Drat it all! John, this is impossible!" David Herold threw his head back and cursed his fate. "John, I'm not cut out for this. I'm just not. I'm an aristocrat, not some backwoods roughen."

"Just get the other child. We'll work all this out when you get back."

Within seconds, Herold shouted, "*He's gone*! The kid got away. Come back here, missy," he said, grabbing Isabel by her freed wrist. "Where did your brother go!"

"I can't imagine. Are you sure you looked in the right place?" *Stall, stall,* Isabel thought. *Just stall!* "You know, he might be trying to find the outhouse. He knows I was wanting to use it before we left."

"Don't play dumb with me, girly. Now what?" he yelled at Booth. "What do we do now?"

"Gather your gear and fetch the horses. Drat it all."

Nothing was going right for the men—absolutely nothing.

<hr>

Fortunately for Ardan, he ran into the advanced guard of the Union soldiers almost as soon as he cleared the farmer's lane. After a brief update, the lieutenant pulled Ardan up on his horse, and the troops advanced to the Garrett farm. There were nearly fifty men in his platoon. In all, some ten thousand federal troops, detectives, and police officers were out looking for the assassins—one of the largest manhunts ever complied.

With his soldiers encircling the barn, Lieutenant Edward Doherty ordered their surrender. "There is no chance for escape, John. You and David come out with your hands above your heads."

"I'm the only one here," Booth yelled back, lying in hopes of protecting David.

"We know better. Come out. Surrender while you can!"

It didn't take long for Booth to realize it was over. Looking at his friend, he yelled to the lieutenant, "I have a man in here who wants to come out on his own. He's unarmed!" Booth nodded to Herold and sadly bade his comrade farewell. "Good luck, my friend."

Booth looked around for Isabel but, unbeknownst to him, she had already made her escape through an opening at the rear of the barn.

David Herold raised his hands and turned himself over to the Yankees without a glance over his shoulder to his fellow cohort. His fate was now in the hands of others.

"You come on out, too, Booth. You're surrounded." After a short pause with no response, the lieutenant warned, "We'll set fire to the barn if we have to, so come out now."

One of the soldiers was already starting to stuff straw through some loose boards. "This is your last chance, Booth. Come out while you can."

On command, the young corporal ignited the dried materials. A marksmen, Sergeant Boston Corbett, had Booth in his sights. When it appeared Booth would not come out, the rifleman fired. He intended to only wound Booth, but at the last minute, Booth turned, and the shot entered Booth in the back of the head about an inch lower than the entry wound Lincoln had received. It wasn't known why Booth turned at the last moment. Was it to try and put out the fire or, just maybe, it was to see if Isabel was safe? No one would ever know.

Booth was carried to the porch of the Garrett home. They had wanted Booth alive—to stand trial as an example. An urgent attempt was made to bring the local doctor to the scene. But by the time the doctor arrived, he could only confirm that Booth was beyond help. John Wilkes Booth succumbed to his wound some seven hours later.

As poetic justice, it should be noted that he died the same death he dealt to President Abraham Lincoln—a fatal shot to the back of the head—and lingered almost the same amount of time. (Lincoln died approximately nine hours after he was shot.) Various accounts were written of this event. Times might differ. Intent? Speculative at best. But the utter uselessness of this horrendous act would mark history forever. Slavery was on the way to being abolished at long last.

Chapter 53

The Vote

As far as Ardan was concerned, Friday came too soon. The morning assembly was set up for each class to have a specific amount of time to hear the candidates give their speeches. Voting would occur shortly thereafter. Freshmen were scheduled first, with the upper classmen following in succession. At the end of the day, the entire student body would reassemble for the results and finish with a pep rally for the upcoming football game. Go, Panthers! Go!

Since Marcus Wilson was gifted with words, he helped Ardan compose a speech. Ardan began by showing his enthusiasm to represent their class. In closing, he promised, "I have worked hard in the past to support various project in my home community and will take that same energy representing you on the student council. I will not take this duty lightly. With your vote, I intend to give it my all."

Archie drew the last position on the docket. With a smile and a thank you for the opportunity, he started with a script but soon set it aside. Taking the mike in hand, Archie slowly made his way to the edge of the stage. He looked his classmates in the eye and began speaking directly to them, as if they were each in a private conversation with him. Archie just talked, not preached, unscripted and strictly from the heart.

"We all have an opportunity. Yes, even as lowly freshmen, *we* have a tremendous opportunity. We can make a difference here and now." He continued moving from one side of the stage to the other, crossing the wide expanse with impassioned purpose. "I have some solid goals to suggest that are in easy reach. Together we can accomplish projects for our school and community."

He had his classmates' attention. With some shifting in their seats, you could see students straighten up and actually start to pay attention.

"Let's start with a simple project for each of our own villages. Remember the devastating fires a few years ago? Remember, too, how the firemen struggled with resuscitating the smaller family pets? They had human oxygen masks, but they were too big for most of the family pets. Well, we can fix that! We can hold fundraisers and supply our fire trucks with the proper equipment—*pet oxygen masks*. They come in three sizes to ensure proper face coverage of small and large alike."

You could tell Archie had already taken a detailed look into the project. By the applause filling the auditorium, the idea sparked real interest. After all, who didn't have a cherished pet within the family?

"Hunger is another little addressed issue. Since the fire, many jobs were affected. Homes were destroyed and had to be rebuilt. In this aggravating, long process, the daily lives of our fellow citizens have suffered. We can host food drives. I'm sure local churches would be willing to help with the distribution with *us* doing the heavy lifting. These few ideas will take a lot of promotion, legwork, and support from the entire student body."

Kids actually started cheering. Archie was an effective motivator. Ardan and Isabel themselves felt a swelling of pride in their friend. He actually hit the floor with constructive challenges. Something told the twins that this was just a starting point for their friend. Archie's mind continued to spin with ideas. And he wanted to apply that energy for the good of the entire community. It was Archie who would lead the way for the youth to show they were willing to carry their own weight in civic duties.

At the end of the day during the big assembly, Archie was the overwhelming winner as the freshman representative to the student council! In fact, all day his speech was the most talked about topic in the hallways, even creeping into the classrooms.

When Ardan was finally able to reach his old friend, he not only congratulated him but pledged his full support. Their eyes locked in true friendship. Archie was the kind of kid who shared achievements with all.

"There is no *I* in success," he often said. "We all need to pull together" was his motto.

Archie was a man of action. Again, it would be worth going to school every day just to see what Archie came up with next.

⚭

The full moon filled Ardan's bedroom with a brilliant glow.

Old friend, I can tell
You hold great hope for the future
This generation will do well
Count your stars as we mature.

⚭

BOOK TEN

Isabel Choses A Medical Summer Camp

Chapter 54

Growing Pains

The twins were growing up fast, with still so many unanswered questions floating around in their heads. The future. What was their place in life? Where were they headed? Christmas was approaching, and the ambitious duo was in the process of deciding which summer camp they wanted to register for at the close of their junior year. Their parents had encouraged them to attend specialized summer camps this time. Gone were the juvenile summer camps of mostly fun and games. It was time to grow up. The need to reach out into the future was becoming all the more apparent.

Many of the twins' classmates had already decided on their futures and the necessary schooling needed to achieve those goals. The twins (well, more Isabel) wondered why it was so difficult for them. Even the class clown, Archie McNabb, had decided his calling was in civil engineering. He saw the problem and decided to help with the solution. The aging bridges and roadways over the entire island of St. Delus were in need of replacement or, at the very least, major repair. Archie loved a challenge. This, he decided, was it. His love for public service could be traced back to the days of getting the student body involved in food drives and other community projects.

Although both Isabel and Ardan had special leanings, they had yet to zero in on the specifics of their chosen fields.

Isabel was still agonizing over this age-long issue. "Have you decided yet on the direction you want your life to take?" she asked Ardan again. "I'm still leaning for something in medicine—lab tech, doctor, pharmacist. I just can't seem to pinpoint it." Isabel had been a volunteer at the Asterville

Hospital since ninth grade. Understanding her unique interest in medicine, their family doctor saw to it that she was given the opportunity to help in a variety of positions around the hospital. He wanted her to get a feel for all the medical field offered.

"Well, I definitely want to be an aviator. How far that will take me or in what specific field, I'm not sure. I'd take astronaut as the ultimate goal though. You know, sometimes opportunity just falls on you when you least expect it and I want to be prepared. You never know what door will have the open sign—that or our old nemesis Murphy's Law will slip in again. You know, if it can go wrong in any way, well, it just will," he said. "So, little Miss Snake Oil Doctor, looks like we're really taking off in different directions."

He realized he'd miss his little sister (although Isabel was eight minutes older, she was only five foot eight to his six foot one). Most of all, he'd miss the pleasure he took in teasing her. For as long as he could remember, he'd enjoyed picking on her. Even if he had to explain it, he couldn't. After all, she was his wingman. They were each other's best support system. Maybe it was a universal guy thing, but teasing Isabel remained his awkward way of complimenting her.

"Can you see me following in Florence Nightingale's footsteps?" she replied. "Over and over again, medical issues keep cropping up in our 'extracurricular activities.' Maybe medicine's where I'll find the answer to the fourth dimension."

"Extracurricular activities. What a creative way to disguise our time travels. Regardless of whatever we call it, we'll probably never be able to talk openly about it to anyone else," Ardan said woefully.

That's Isabel, Ardan continued with his thoughts. He reminisced about her many adaptations to whatever curve life threw her way. She had a mind in perpetual motion. As quickly as something new would present itself, she would absorb as much information as she could on the subject. Then like a "brain flush," the old simply washed away as her attention was diverted to a brand-new topic. "I can only store so many megabytes in my computer," she'd once told Ardan, indicating her brain with her forefinger. It had sounded funny at the time, but it was probably more truth than fiction. "I can always pull it back from the trash bin if I need it," she'd said, again with that silly grin of hers that was barely able to contain an out-and-out giggle. He'd probably miss that the most—her uncontrolled laughing fits. So much trouble they got themselves into. They were good times.

First of all, Isabel would have to focus if she were to make a life commitment. Ardan was certain that she would do well in any chosen field, since she was, as it was called, a "quick study."

"Well, no surprise here. I've already made my choice on a summer camp. I'm going to register for the Advanced Space Academy. Last year, I really got hooked after I went to the First Space Academy," Ardan reflected. "The adventure that's offered in space is all the more interesting since I attended that first one.

"Isabel," he went on. "Remember that video game Mrs. McClain gave us? Once in a while, it creeps back into my thoughts. I can't help wondering if space aliens are real or if that was just part of the game. Many theories exist. Top-notch pilots swear they've seen spaceships. But again, I guess that might remain another of those mysteries we'll never find an answer to. Maybe in studying about the universe, I'll learn about that aspect—and, just maybe, about the fourth dimension. One day, one or the other of us should be able to figure this out."

"Let's hope you're right. The world holds so many questions," Isabel lamented.

Of the two, Ardan remain true to his original interest. Since his first telescope, his appetite for space had been unquenchable. Even though the pair was on the brink of following individual lifestyles, Ardan was sure they would always remain close, despite the obvious physical separation that was bound to happen. It was hard to believe, with the twins having been through so many shared experiences together, that their personalities remained so uniquely different.

Chapter 55

First Trip away from Home

Isabel nervously started to pack her suitcase. This was her first time on her very own. Last year before she had the chance to think about a summer camp, Grandma was diagnosed with cancer. Isabel wanted to, no, she insisted on being Grandma's caregiver while she went through chemo treatments. The idea of a stranger or even a friend coming in and watching over Grandma did not appeal to Isabel. Tender, *loving* care would be exactly what her grandmother needed more than anything else. Besides, Grandma stepped up and cared for Ardan and Isabel while their parents helped out during the big fire on the eastern coast. Now, it was Isabel's privilege to return the favor.

So now with the opportunity in front of her, Isabel elected to attend a summer camp at the University of Benson Medical located just outside the city of Freemont. Freemont just happened to be where she and Ardan had become involved with the dognappers.

Thank goodness the university had sent a checklist to help her organize. In all this confusion, she surely would have forgotten one essential or another. It didn't help matters that Ishkabibble had her nose in every item she pulled from a drawer.

"Bibbs!" Isabel shouted a warning to her mischievous cat. "I've already refolded my clothes twice thanks to you. I don't need, or even want, your help right now. I have a million things to do. Now scat. I'm not going to be gone that long." She gave her friend a playful lift to the floor. "I'll be back before you know it."

Ishkabibble and Mergatroid were five years old now but had never lost their inclination for mischief that was usually attributed to kittens. The Bibbs's favorite choice of amusement was not mere cat toys. No, no. She went for the useful items—items Isabel actually needed. Bibbs's specialty was in smuggling things, like say, pencils, paperclips, Isabel's hospital badge, and especially Isabel's treasured scrunchies. The tiebacks were the only thing Isabel could count on as a fast solution to her wild, untamable head of hair. If the Bibbs could laugh, watching Isabel's frantic searching would bring it out. Instead, she would nonchalantly sit back, washing her pretty little face with her dainty little paw as she observed Isabel from the corner of her eye.

Merg had his own favorite game he played with Ardan. Every day when Ardan left for school, he meticulously hid each and every one of his cat toys, careful to search for new and difficult locations to amuse his favorite play buddy. Once he managed to hide a catnip mouse in Ardan's jeans. When mother went to wash them, she screamed, ever so unladylike. Funny how her scream sounded a bit different than when Ardan made similar discoveries.

Just like people, animals all had different, individualized personalities. Merg and Bibbs had to rank as two of the craziest.

<hr/>

The whole family woke early to take Isabel to the Barshire Airport. The plane would be quicker than taking a ferryboat. The flight was referred to as a "puddle jumper" and was probably the most used method of transportation to get off the St. Delus Island.

Mother wanted to be sure her daughter had a hardy breakfast before she boarded her flight, so that meant no sleeping in. This was the first time Isabel had left their island by herself, and mother wondered if this was a sign of things to come. Would Isabel eventually establish herself somewhere other than St. Delus? The Murphys were already prepared for the fact that Ardan wanted to enter the space program in some capacity. That alone mandated his relocating.

Father had previously arranged for Uncle Hank Henderson, who lived near the air terminal in Bodenia, to meet Isabel's plane. The drive to the university was only another half hour from the airport. Uncle Hank, who was not related by blood but through a strong friendship, assured the Murphys he would be available to watch over her. Undeniably, Isabel took great comfort to know she had a support system nearby.

Chapter 56

Campus Life

The enormity of the campus was overwhelming for the young lady on her own. Uncle Hank stayed with Isabel as she went through registration. Once they learned of the dormitory's location, he drove Isabel and her bags to her living quarters.

A very cheerful RA (resident adviser) was there to greet them and take her to her room. "Your roomy has already arrived. You'll like her," the RA offered. "Her name is Audrey Spencer. She's here from London and has the cutest accent."

"Knock, knock! Are you decent?" the RA quired. "Audrey, your roommate is here."

"Bonkers. Please, bring yourselves in," Audrey answered.

"Audrey, this is Isabel Murphy from St. Delus Island. Isabel, meet Audrey Spencer all the way from London, England. You two will get along famously. Oh, and this is her uncle—ah, Hank, is it?"

"How do you do, Audrey. I'm just here long enough to get my niece settled, and then I'm on my way." Hank nodded. Isabel was sure Hank would call her parents with the complete lowdown.

"I took the bed on the left if that's cricket with you, Isabel. But, I'd bloody well change if you want," Audrey offered.

Uncle Hank was pleased to see that Audrey was not going to be demanding. In fact, just the opposite. Her and Isabel's personalities would blend together nicely. He left feeling completely at easy.

"You girls settle in. Don't forget the orientation right after supper in the cafeteria. Six o'clock sharp. Meantime, mingle. A lunch is provided at the bistro in Myers Hall. If you can't find the map they sent you, I have more at the desk." The RA hurried off to get back out front to greet the other arrivals.

Audrey, it turned out, was a surprise last child of older parents who tended to shield their gift. Being out on her own was a novelty. Audrey was at Benson Medical to look more deeply at being either a critical care nurse or a physical therapist. She, too, was looking to define her future.

"You're fine, Audrey. I'm happy over there by the window," Isabel responded when they were left to their own devices. "Is this your first excursion on your own?"

"Yes, indeed it is. You might say I've had a tad of parental overprotection. That's not meant to criticize my parents by any means at all. They've given me everything I needed. But willies, I'm just anxious to 'take flight,' so to speak," Audrey remarked in her beautiful accent.

"I agree totally. My parents have allowed me a lot of leeway. But I want to 'test my wings,' too. I have a twin brother who's always been my safety net. I know he won't be there forever, so this is my debut at being self-reliant." Isabel was putting on a brave front—inside, she wasn't as sure.

⧼∭⧽

Each morning, Audrey and Isabel chose seats close to the front in the lecture hall. For the next few days, the morning itinerary called for a host of leaders from the many fields of medicine to speak to the assembly of summer campers. Afternoons would be spent in a variety of activities exposing them to the inner workings of the medical field. They were also encouraged to take advantage of the huge campus library to fill in with the information they were all there to gather.

"Wasn't the bloke on forensic science fascinating?" Audrey asked.

"I wouldn't have suspected you could get so much information from a rug fiber," Isabel responded. "I just don't think I could handle delving into all that decomposing material every day. Interesting—just not my leanings. I did, however, find an interest in laboratory research of new drugs and vaccines."

"I bloody well hope I can come away with a specific vocation from this humongous field," Audrey drawled.

⟨IIII⟩

Lectures were set up in forty-five-minute intervals. In the first twenty minutes, the leaders described their particular fields, followed by fifteen minutes of questions and answers.

The last specialty speaker strolled across the stage to the lectern. He was tall and young in appearance. According to his bio, he lived right here in Freemont.

"Welcome to the world of veterinary medicine," he began in a deep voice. "My name is Jeff Swanson. Three years ago, I was in your seat—a summer student looking for assurance that I'd chosen the right vocation. I had already decided on veterinary medicine but needed to find a specific. Should I go into general practice? Zoo? Lab? Every general field has a whole stream of satellite occupations to support it. I needed to know where I fit in. I hope your time at Benson Medical will answer your own personal questions."

As he spoke, Isabel realized that this might be the Jeff she and Ardan had met when they'd encountered the dognappers. The memory began to take shape as he spoke. So, he was becoming a veterinarian. She couldn't wait to text Ardan. He would be so surprised—if, of course, this Jeff and that were one and the same.

When the lecture was over, Isabel anxiously approached Jeff. Maybe he wasn't who she thought, but if he was? She wondered if their fourth-dimension experiences imprinted on those they interacted with. Skip McGovern from two centuries earlier had remembered them, but Jeff was a present-day crossover. Would he remember? Well, she was about to find out.

"I don't know if you remember me, but we met some ten, eleven years ago. Do you still have Bandit?" she asked hesitantly.

"I do. And you are?" his brows furrowed as he struggled to place her.

Oh, no, she thought. *He doesn't remember. How am I to get out of this? Well, my foot's in my mouth now. Might as well keep going.*

"My twin brother, Ardan, and I met you after the dognappers took Bandit. I'm Isabel Murphy," she replied, extending her hand.

"Oh! Good grief, Isabel!" Jeff could hardly believe it. "You've grown up so much. I've always wished you'd come by sometime—you know, when you visited those friends of yours again. I've wondered what'd become of you. And to meet again, here, of all places. Amazing. Simply amazing."

"I'd say we've both grown up," she said, realizing how tall he was. "I doubt very much that I could have recognized you on the street either."

"Well, we still live in the same old house. When I finish my studies, I'll be moving to Park Forest. I've been offered a partnership with our old family vet."

It seemed the two could not stop smiling and talking. Although the dognapping was long past, apparently the bond developed from that adventure still existed. "Can you meet me for lunch in the cafeteria? I'd love to catch up," Jeff pleaded.

"I'd like that. It would be so fun. Of course, I can. Do you mind if my friend Audrey joins us?"

"Not at all. Bring her along. I'll hold a table," he replied.

⊙〰〰〰⊙

Isabel could not contain her excitement. Although this slot of summer camp goers was only hosting two groups of thirty each, the cafeteria was crowded with regular college students taking advantage of odd summer classes. Jeff stood up to wave Audrey and her over. He couldn't be missed. When Jeff unfolded himself, he stood an impressive six foot eight. Even though everyone seemed big to a five-year-old, Isabel recalled his parents as being quite tall.

"So, how's Bandit?" she asked as an icebreaker to get the conversation going.

"He's great. He's been my rock. Keeps me focused," Jeff replied. "And Ardan? He's not with you, I take it. What's he doing these days?"

"Well. Next week, he'll fly to America to attend a special camp for space training. I think he was born in a space suit. The universe is all he thinks about."

"Do you have a picture? I think of you, rightly so I guess, as kindergarteners."

"Oh, I have some on my phone, but it's back in my room," she stammered. She couldn't explain why she felt so disoriented. The shock of the past coming back to life, she guessed.

"Can you come for Sunday dinner? I called my mom after we met. She really wants to see you again. You could bring what pictures you have then. She'd get a kick out of it—if you can come, that is. The folks would really like to see you," he pleaded. "The invite includes you too, Audrey. My mom is excited at the chance to have some girls over. All my sisters are married and, unfortunately, moved to where the jobs took them. It's just me and my younger brother at home, but he's away at a different college. The house feels empty."

"That would be delicious. I'd love to. I'm already learning about campus food," Isabel replied with a skewed face. "My mother is such a good cook. I'm spoiled. What do you think, Audrey? Are you game?"

"That'd be absolutely crickey! Never dreamed I'd get to experience the home of a local Bodenia family. That'd just be the bee's knees. Of course, I'd like to come. Can't wait to tell the blokes back home. Goodness, just look at me waffle on and on," Audrey said with embarrassment. "It's just that—well chips, I couldn't have thought something like that would be possible."

"Now, don't go expecting too much," Jeff cautioned. "We're just ordinary people. I hope you won't be disappointed."

"Never. So sorry, Jeff. I didn't mean to mislead you. This is my first time away from home. My family is pretty straight, too. People always ask, 'So how's the queen?' like I could possibly know." She laughed at her own plain life. "I'm just wondering if our ordinary is the same as your ordinary."

"This is great then. I'll pick you both up. Sunday, say twelve thirty?" Jeff asked.

☾༄☽

Mrs. Swanson excitedly greeted the young ladies at the door, too impatient to wait for Jeff to escort them in. "Isabel, right?" she said as she reached out for her.

"Yes. What gave me away—my curly, red hair?" Isabel laughed.

"I do remember how the sun shone on your *rare* but *beautiful* hair," she responded tactfully. "No one appreciates what they have. Personally, I'd kill for curl over my own straight mop. It just clings to my face, flat as a pancake." She was as charming as Isabel remembered her.

The twins had remarked on how easily the Swansons had made them feel welcomed when they'd met those many years ago.

"Ardan sends his best. He's sorry he can't be here," Isabel said.

"And, you must be our ambassador from England," Mrs. Swanson teased. She held Audrey at length a moment to get a good look at her before embracing her with the same warmth she'd awarded Isabel. "Come. Come in, please. Sorry to keep you hanging in the doorway."

With perfect timing, Mr. Swanson came in from the backyard. "Good. You're here. Welcome. We thought we'd treat you ladies to a good old-fashioned barbecue. Hope you won't be disappointed, but when Jeffery told us how excited Audrey was to visit an *authentic* Bodenian home, I thought we'd go all out and fix some *authentic* Bodenian favorites. And, we do love our barbecues!" His face was one big smile. "We're so happy to have you girls here." He bent over to give them each a quick hug before ushering them out to the patio.

The weather was perfect for enjoying an afternoon outside, especially after being closed-in all week. The Swansons' joy in the outdoors was reflected in a beautifully landscaped yard. Many of the concepts were credited to their son Dean and his interest in agriculture. Dean was their last child, barely a year younger than Jeff, and was away at college.

"Lemonade anyone?" To everyone's delight, Mrs. Swanson came out with a tray full of iced drinks. Shortly after, Mr. Swanson placed several dishes of *authentic* foods on the table, hot off the grill.

Isabel had to sidestep a few of the questions the Swansons asked, so as not to reveal that she and Ardan had been in Freemont during one of their time travels. Although she was used to "white lies" to cover these episodes, she felt guilty about deceiving Jeff and his family. Better to lie, however, than to have them label her as a fruitcake, she justified to herself.

All afternoon, Isabel felt Jeff watching her. It left her flushed and uncertain. What was he thinking? Had he seen through her cover-up? He said very little. The conversation was mostly consumed by Jeff's parents, who were very excited to have two beautiful young women in their home—impressive young women with admirable ambitions.

Before the girls returned to their dorm, they thanked the Swansons for their hospitality.

On the ride back to the dorm, Isabel was consumed by an indescribable loss at having to say goodbye. Although the visit was short, she felt like the Swansons were old family friends. Jeff, with Bandit at his side, pulled at feelings she had stored deep within. She yearned to have been a part of their lives. She felt she had missed out on a very warm friendship. Isabel shook off the ridiculous notion. Goodness, her life had been fulfilling. She couldn't have asked for more. Still, she'd felt saddened to say farewell to Jeff when he dropped them off. Of course, they'd stay in touch. Wouldn't they?

Audrey felt double blessed. The day before, Uncle Hank had invited the girls for a lunch at his home and treated them to a quick tour of the most popular tourist sites. Audrey would be going back to London with some fond memories. If not for her roomy, this trip to Benson Medical might not have been as memorable for the transplant from England.

Chapter 57

Buckling Down

They were only there for two weeks, and the time was flying by. Isabel was pleased to see that Audrey was as dedicated as she was to getting the most out of this lifetime opportunity. Audrey was definitely going to work in physical therapy. She had already spoken with counselors to set her plan into action. Her parents had given her the OK to start with application papers at Benson. With her strong academic background, it looked promising, and she learned the institution had plenty of room in its foreign exchange program for another applicant.

Isabel was getting closer to zeroing in on her vocation as a general practitioner/surgeon. Her next classes would cover many of the aspects of a working operating room.

During one such class, Isabel was sent out for a tray of instruments. They were to learn the proper names of the utensil, as well as handling and exploring their individual uses. As she approached the classroom door, it automatically opened for her as if anticipating her arrival.

"Great timing. Rush those instruments right over to surgery and then come straight back. We have a new batch of arrivals that need immediate attention."

The woman who spoke looked vaguely familiar, but the lighting was dim and Isabel couldn't take the time to figure out how she knew her. The urgency in the woman's voice left no time for dallying. Isabel raced off in the direction the woman had indicated.

The stench was overwhelming. Moans of men in deep pain echoed everywhere in a loud stereo effect. Lighting was poor. She wanted to stop and open a window. Little Asterville Hospital had it all over this, whatever it was.

In the middle of the chaos, teams of doctors were doing their best to treat the wounded. Apparently, supplies were sparse, for every team was yelling for her.

"Over here!"

"Hurry it up!"

"Did you bring bandages?"

Isabel didn't know where to turn next. Fortunately, a young nurse ran up and grabbed the tray. She gave Isabel a weak thank you as she rushed to distribute the precious commodity.

Isabel could hear the pain and suffering long after she left the surgical unit. It was everywhere. Without question, Isabel knew she was in another transition. It had been a few years since her last excursion into the fourth dimension. She deeply wished for these episodes to end. She'd mistakenly thought they had. The years of covering up, lying, and being evasive were wearing on her. She was never comfortable knowing this only happened to Ardan and her.

Like a light switch, she now recognized the woman who had given her the first order. She was Florence Nightingale—her idol in the flesh.

From books she read, she knew she was in a time of preanesthesia surgery. There would have been little to no painkillers—before, during, or after surgery. No wonder there was so much unchecked pain and suffering. Occasionally, a shot of whiskey or a smuggled bit of opium might find its way into the operating room to numb the surgery, but as she was to learn, that was indeed rare. Between the body going into shock and the medical profession not yet knowing about blood transfusions, surviving surgery was a monumental challenge. Recovery was an even bigger hurdle. More patients died from diseases and infections they contracted afterward due to unclean conditions than from the original wound itself.

From her previous hospital experiences, Florence knew the necessity of maintaining hygiene. Florence Nightingale had arrived at the military hospital with a corps of thirty-four nurses shortly after the war started. Previously, the front was not considered a proper place for women, even for trained nurses. In the midst of the Crimean War, necessity called for these angels of mercy to be the first allowed at a frontline hospital. The need had superseded the antiquated ideals.

Some of these nurses assisted the surgeons, while others worked at keeping the wounds cleaned and bandages changed. Those soldiers who could were put to scrubbing the facility. The many duties had everyone working long, crucial hours.

The "Lady with the Lamp," as nurse Nightingale was called, also believed in keeping morale up as a healing benefit. A gentle touch, a warm word of encouragement went a long way in recovery. She worked many long hours, well into the night.

Drawing upon her years as a hospital aide, Isabel quickly picked up on the routine. Pleading eyes ravished in pain reached out for help. On top of her other duties, Isabel tried to fill their needs, be it a sip of water, a wet cloth on the forehead, a kind word, or a simple touch from a concerned human being. She did the best she could to ease their anxieties. Record keeping was sorely lacking from what she was accustomed to, but all the patients had the same obvious basic needs. The nurses did their best. When time permitted, letter writing was a high priority.

⁂

Commander Lord FitzRoy Henry Somerset (referred to as the Lord Raglan) had just been brought to the hospital and placed in a private room of sorts. He appeared to be suffering from extreme depression. The Crimean War was not going well.

As the chief commander, he was feeling the full impact of being the sole person responsible for decision-making. He had recently sent his men into battle to overtake the main stronghold of Sevastopol. This was a primary objective for the allies. Win this; win the war. Plans were meticulously put in place. Every detail was gone over and over again. The only thing was that the supplies did not arrive—neither supplies *nor* reinforcements were forthcoming. Logistics, for a battle commander, are crucial. One part of the plan was reliant on each of the other segments to make it work.

"Lord Raglan." The soldier had saluted his commander. "We await your word."

The commander was bent over a table pouring over the strategic plans. It looked good on paper. Everything was in place—wasn't it? They'd attack at dawn with the sun shining in the enemy's eyes. But the shortage of food, ammunition, and manpower was still nagging at the back of his head.

Put in a very difficult position due to intense, heavy outside pressures, Lord Raglan ordered the full assault to move forward. He hoped the strategy would allow for a swift overtaking of the enemy. If they could accomplish the deed in great haste, perhaps the deficiencies would not be as relevant.

The city was huge and heavily populated. Intel underestimated the number of Russian soldiers holding the city hostage and in how well they were equipped. It took history to show that the differences in manpower and munitions were estimated to be at least three to one in the Russians' favor.

"Charge!"

"Forward, ever forward!"

"Fire at will!"

Orders rang loud and fast. Yelling in battle lingo was evident everywhere. Oh how they fought—side by side. To no avail. The allies had used advanced pounding of the city with their newer long-range cannons, only to be hammered back with a bigger retaliation. At one-point days later, they might have had the advantage, but the allies needed to pull back due to lack of ammunition. Their casualties were enormous. Men were tired and hungry. It was October and cold. Pulling back, however, left the door open for the Russians to draw in their reinforcements from outlying areas, fortifying the city's perimeters and making the eventual win for the allies longer and more costly.

Shortly after the siege began, Lord Raglan was relieved of his duty and brought to the hospital, emotionally drained from guilty stress and suffering with the Crimean fever.

Since he was not considered critical or needing surgery, Isabel, as an aide, was assigned to settle him in.

"How are you feeling, Commander?" she asked.

He tried to wave her away. He did not want to speak. He couldn't.

"Sir, let me get you settled in. The doctor is trying to locate something to relieve you of your pain," she said.

"Take care of my men. God, take care of my men. Leave me," he pleaded. His voice was barely audible. "Please, just leave me."

Isabel arranged the pillows under the commander's head and tucked a sheet across his shivering body. When the door opened, Isabel expected to see one of the doctors. What she saw instead was a battle-weary soldier, eyes glazed over from pain and agony. He stumbled through the door and leaned against the wall for support.

"Is this him?" the soldier called out.

"Who are you looking for? Oh, here let me help you." She moved to assist him as he started to lose his balance.

"*Stop!*" he yelled. "Stay where you are."

Isabel hadn't noticed the pistol that was hanging at his side, until he drew it up with his bandaged hand. The other arm was in a sling. Taking a better look, she noticed his clothes were bloodied and torn. His boots were barely held together with tied-up rags.

"Is this our fierce, almighty leader? Is it?" he demanded.

"I'm Commander Somerset. What can I do for you, son?"

"Do for me? I think you've done enough already! Thanks to you, I lost my entire squad. For *what*?" His anger filled the air.

"I … I'm sorry … I'm so sorry," the commander uttered.

"Not enough. Too little, too late! *Sir!* I'm here to make things right for those who can't." The soldier began waving his pistol as an illustration.

Isabel took a step forward to draw the attention of the young soldier toward her and away from the commander. "You don't want to do that." She spoke calmly. "Not really. That's your grief talking, not you."

"Let him go. He's right, you know. I should have waited for supplies— more men. Another chance would have opened up later. I should have waited." Somerset had been carrying the same burden the young man was accusing him of and was himself in a deep depression because of it. He could not forgive himself. The burden was too much—too heavy.

Isabel was determined to take control. "Frankly, that's not a concern of mine. What I am concerned about is this young man doing something he will surely regret later."

Bang. Bang again, the pistol retorted. The bullets came dangerously close. The smell of sulfur mingled with the smoky spray.

"Get away from my 'esteemed' commander! What I *regret* is losing my men!"

"All right. Is this better?" Although Isabel moved away from Somerset, she was now closer to the soldier in this very small room.

The young soldier appeared to be at the end of his strength. He bent, ever so slightly, as a new pain gripped his body. In an instant, Isabel jumped forward and knocked the gun from his hand. The soldier gave way to the pain and crumpled to the floor in a disheartened heap.

Kneeling beside him, Isabel tried to raise his head. He looked her in the eyes. Saddened. Resigned. "Don't tell my wife," he pleaded. "Please. Don't tell her. We have two children. Let them know I love them." Those were his last words—words he barely had breath enough to eke out. Mentally, he'd already put himself home with his wife and children— home, where he felt warm and safe, home, where he was loved. They were his last thoughts, thoughts of his beloved family.

Ringing through Isabel's own tortured thoughts came a portion of Lord Alfred Tennyson's poem, "The Charge of the Light Brigade." The phrase "Theirs not to reason why / Theirs but to do or die" carried new, personal meaning for her. She would never forget this soldier in his last moments. Sill cradling the young man in her arms, Isabel bowed her head and wept.

The commander succumbed to his condition ten days after the failed raid began, two days after the encounter with the soldier. It was said he died of guilt, never recovering from the infamous decision to attack while being undersupplied. The death certificate mercifully attributed his death to the Crimean fever.

There was no time for mourning or regret. Saving lives was the priority, and there was no shortage of patients. Isabel continued to treat the other patients.

The Crimean War of 1853 to 1856 was eventually concluded with the signing of the Treaty of Paris. The Russian attempt at enlarging her territory was defeated by the alliance with France, the United Kingdom, Turkey, and Sardinia.

Nurse Nightingale returned to Britain, herself in a weakened condition. The Crimean fever eventually took its toll on her body. She became bedridden at the tender age of thirty-eight. Out of tragedy grows opportunity. She proved much can be achieved through dogged determination. From her bed, she continued her work at making the nursing field better. She laid out the curriculum for nurses' training, the basics of which are included in the manuals used today. Heads of state consulted her at her bedside, including the health adviser of the Civil War in America. The Lady with the Lamp lived to be ninety-eight—useful to the end.

Isabel considered herself blessed to have met and observed her idol. She'd been in the fourth grade when she'd dressed as Florence Nightingale for the Halloween Roundup. Never could she have imagined such a chance opportunity. This particular time travel experience served to cement Isabel's choice in life. Medicine would be her calling. She would study hard to become a top-notch surgeon/practitioner. She wanted to provide the best, most updated care to any who would seek her help.

Lying in her bed that night, Isabel wondered if she would be left to handle these "extracurricular activities" alone, now that she and Ardan were on different life paths.

Chapter 58

Cementing the Experience

Audrey was her usual cheerful self. "I've had so many great experiences here in Bodenia. My parents can't wait for me to get home and show them the pictures. I have some on my phone that I could send, but they're not into our generation of technology. They've warned me my day will come. Guess I shouldn't feel too superior. But secretly," she added, changing the subject, "I can't wait to come back to Benson Medical to start my training—in just a few months actually."

Audrey had received notice she was accepted at the university and would be coming back as an exchange student in the fall. "Can you believe it?" she grabbed Isabel and started jumping around in circles. "I've been accepted! I'm coming back!" She waffled on in her delightful way.

"Well, I'm going to apply to Benson myself. I picked up the paperwork." Isabel couldn't wait to share her news, too. "Maybe we'll both be coming back. I'll be a year later, but…"

◦✺◦

Too quickly, the last day dawned. The roomies were trying to get everything stuffed into their bags. "I'm off my trolley. I know I'll be back, but I just had to latch onto a few souvenirs for the blokes back home," Audrey said.

Isabel knew she would miss Audrey—and her quaint ways.

Packing, for Isabel, was much easier this time without Bibbs's help. Oh but, how she missed her buddy and would be glad to see the little mischief maker again. "It's a good thing for expandable sides on suitcases.

I'd never get all this to fit otherwise." Isabel laughed. "And I don't have any keepsakes."

"Do you think we'll get to hang out like this when you're a freshy?" Audrey asked.

"Our dorms will be separate, but we can get around that easily enough. And you'll have a whole year up on me to scope out the good hangout spots. Meanwhile, you have my phone and email." She looked at Audrey to nod assurance. "I know Uncle Hank has already adopted you. Your folks will appreciate knowing you have someone dependable who's close at hand."

The RA knocked on the open door. "Excuse me. Isabel, you have a gentleman caller. He's in the lounge." She smiled.

"Who?" she asked. It was too early for Uncle Hank.

""I don't know, but he's awfully cute." The RA winked.

"*Jeff.*" Audrey smiled. "It has to be Jeff. Quick. Get a shake on it, ol' girl. Then I want a good chin-wag when you get back here."

Isabel had to admit she did feel a twinge of excitement. She'd like it to be Jeff, but they'd actually said their goodbyes last Sunday at the barbecue. This was unexpected, if it actually was Jeff—unexpected but certainly not unwelcomed. Isabel couldn't explain the flip-flops in her stomach.

"Isabel. I just had to say goodbye one more time. We'll keep in touch, right. I don't want to lose contact with you again. You and Ardan, of course," Jeff added nervously. "I just have one more year here at Benson. So, I'll be doing my residency by the time you come back—if it works out, that is. But the animal hospital is practically next door … so." he was embarrassed at his own stammering. Why should this be so difficult?

"I'm sure we'll find a way to keep in touch. It's been so great," Isabel said shyly.

"I can help you with your studies—you know, show you the way to ferret out the basics. The fundamentals are the cornerstone; everything builds from there. And Latin—I was shown a way of learning that's simpler. The Latin terms aren't nearly so intimidating then. If you want, of course."

"Well, thank you. No one in my family went into the medical field but I did help my Grandmother last year as she went through treatments for cancer and I've been volunteering at our local hospital. I'm hoping that'll be helpful. But I'm sure I'll need all the extra assistance I can get."

"I suppose I'd better get going and let you finish whatever you still have to do to pack. Your uncle is probably on his way. I just wanted to see you and say—not goodbye but till we meet again?" He reached in and Isabel felt a flush in her cheeks. He paused awkwardly.

Is he going to kiss me? Isabel thought. She wasn't prepared. His eyes were so soft, so blue. She could get lost in the spell they cast. His hands felt hot on her arms.

Jeff had always been wrapped up in his studies. Interactions with girls left him awkward—embarrassed to say the least. The same story could be repeated about Isabel. She was always more comfortable being one of the boys. She felt more at ease being one of them than being a suitor. With Jeff, she was off guard. This was a first. She had experienced a quick puppy love a time or two, but nothing to match the emotions she felt now.

The outstretched arms were innocently reverted to a hug—albeit a warm and lengthy hug.

Walking back to her room, Isabel tried to shrug off her emotions as being part of saying goodbye. Goodbyes were always so difficult.

When she said goodbye to Audrey, however, her new best friend, the twinge was there but it was definitely different.

BOOK ELEVEN

Ardan Goes to Space Camp

Chapter 59

Following His Heart

Ardan was breaching that point where simply being excited collides with full-blown exhilaration as he was preparing for his second trip to America. He would be attending another summer camp program designed especially for youth interested in space discoveries. Even as a youngster, he'd been absorbed in the universe, and these camps only added to his aspirations. His desire was like an itch that continually nagged to be satisfied or like that song that repeats in your head and won't go away. Space was the black hole sucking Ardan in. Space was his own personal nemesis that wouldn't go away.

Last summer, he'd attended the Space Academy, where he'd been given an overall view of the many divisions that went into the development of space intelligence and penetration. For every person in space, there are hundreds of people doing miraculous jobs to make that opportunity possible. Personnel from the various departments spoke to the students, explaining the real genius involved in designing the complete space program.

By far, getting to use the actual equipment used to train astronauts topped the list. The students were able to experience the gravity chair, explore and work in weightlessness, perform complicated experiments, and use the multi-axis trainer (or spinning chair), a seat mounted in a revolving circle within another revolving circle—a unique gadget that appeared to be designed with the sole purpose of emptying your stomach. Advanced technology helped, to a degree, by keeping the inner ear stabilized.

Here students were introduced to virtual activities through the use of computers. At the end of the school, individual teams were assigned to solve a dilemma while conducting a simulated space mission. This was where teamwork paid off. A big part of the program dealt with that very aspect—team work, depending on each other. At the camp, they ate, slept, and studied together on site. Friendships made here would remain solid throughout their lifetime. Although the robotics portion held a strong second fascination for Ardan, actual flight remained his ultimate dream ending.

⁂

Last summer

As a youngster, Ardan had spent Saturdays and summers helping at the family hardware store. Grandpa and father knew that Ardan would not follow in their footsteps. So, they encouraged him to chase his own dreams.

The summer between his sophomore and junior years, Ardan applied for a job at the Barshire Airport with the owner of a small, private air service—Sawyer Air Transport. After a trial period, the owner knew he'd picked the right young man. Ardan was reliable and willing to take on the nastiest of jobs. The opportunities around planes were endless, and they all proved to be immensely interesting to the inquisitive apprentice. Ardan soon moved from janitor to learning the mechanics of the planes.

"Son," Mr. Sawyer said, "I've been watching you. I'm impressed at how you pour yourself into your work. I admire your work ethics. What do you intend to do after high school?"

"As far-fetched as it sounds, I'd like to become an astronaut," he said. "My goal is to go to America and get my engineering degree—at West Point, I hope. Math and computers are like my second language. At West Point, I'd also get the physical discipline along with my studies. But they only take so many exchange students. So, we'll see? I've worked hard keeping my grades up. Anyway, that's about it. I'm hoping."

"Sounds like you've given it some real thought," Mr. Sawyer said.

"Unfortunately, it's mostly all I think about. Why I didn't apply for this job with you right after school ended was so I could attend the summer

222

Space Academy NASA holds. I absolutely loved it. Next year I'm going to go to the Advanced Space Academy. I'll see where it goes from there."

"I heard some scuttlebutt that you might have been the kid who went to that NASA summer camp. It's not common around here. Glad to know you were the one. So now, I have a deal for you, if you're interested," the boss offered. "How would you like to learn to fly these things?"

"Interested! I'd give my right arm for the chance," Ardan joked. "No kidding? Really?"

"No kidding. Now, this won't be a handout, mind you. I always believe you get more out of things you've actually worked for. So, here's my proposal. You work here at the air transit free; in return, I'll give you flying instructions. It's a win-win for both of us. What d'ya think?" Mr. Sawyer asked.

"*Deal!*" Ardan answered before Mr. Sawyer could change his mind.

"No so fast, young man. You have to get your parents' approval first. I'll draw up the proper permission papers, since you're still underage."

So that was how Ardan had learned to fly—along with the valuable knowledge concerning the mechanical guts of an aircraft.

Licensing wasn't as easy as it sounded. Ardan had to first study basic aerodynamics, weather, and FFA regulations and go to the central airport where there was a flight simulator for preflight practice. Of course, there were the fifty or more hours of flying time with the flight instructor before he could solo. And then he had to pass the tests, written and physical. All in all, Ardan would be forever indebted to his boss, who, as the kindhearted person he was, gave him the better of the deal.

⟨♒⟩

Present

Isabel emailed Ardan about running into Jeff Swanson and mentioned that she and Audrey, who she'd described in an earlier message, were invited to his home for Sunday dinner. She confessed she was a little nervous about keeping the secret in how she and Ardan had found themselves in Freemont so many years ago. The Swansons would never understand that the dognapping visit was during one of their "extracurricular activities."

The twins were also careful not to put anything in writing that indicated time travel. Their texts were in their unique twin double-talk.

Over the years, they'd developed this form of gibberish to get around these adventures. Ardan was sure Isabel would handle it. She'd had a lot of practice. He only wished he could join them. He'd love to meet with Jeff again.

As Ardan began to pack, the Bibbs got really upset with him. When Isabel had packed, she'd left, and Bibbs missed her terribly. The Bibbs and Merg were suspicious that Ardan was up to the same trick. By double-teaming his packing, the cats believed they would prevent him from going down that same dreadful path. Isabel had had a lengthy talk with Bibbs before she'd left, but Bibbs only remembered feeling sad and lonely. The feline companions were no more receptive to Ardan's explanation. Separation was just too hard for the furry little pests to comprehend.

But Ardan couldn't help it. He was joyful as he packed his bags—no hiding it. Another great adventure was waiting for him. And when he returned, he had his job at the airport to look forward to. Last year, he had been fortunate to get licensed on propeller planes. This summer, Mr. Sawyer was going to train him on the jets. They were small personal-sized jets, but to Ardan, it was like going from an old jalopy to a Lamborghini.

Chapter 60

New Set of Challenges

He just stood there for a moment, taking in the view, remembering last summer. Nothing appeared to have changed. It was as if time had stood still, waiting for his return. This was where Ardan felt at peace—where he belonged. He also knew becoming an astronaut would require hard work if he wanted to succeed in this business.

When he arrived at the dorm, he ran into several of his friends from last year. Excitedly, they greeted each other and rushed to catch up on the year spent apart.

"How are ya? Ya ol fart," Martin Maki, an American from Minnesota, yelled as he raced at Ardan, lifting him off his feet. "Stop growing man, or you'll be too tall to be an astronaut."

"Aw, he can wash the windows then—without using a ladder," Vic offered. Vic, was one Victor Beaumont III of Strasbourg, France, with all the charm attributed to Frenchmen. He was super fun and brilliant at the same time. Ardan loved the guy but didn't think he wanted to introduce his sister to him. He'd break her heart.

"Yo, bro," Frank Gorman said. "Did you miss us?" Frank was as serious as Vic was fun loving. Frank called Pennsylvania home and had the reserve of the hardworking middle class. Secretly, he possessed a *dry* sense of humor. You had to listen closely, so as not to miss his witticisms. Once you caught on to his style, he was actually the funniest of the whole dang crew.

"What's up?" Ardan replied. "Staying out of trouble?"

"Only 'cause they haven't caught up to me," Marty declared.

It was great to be back. The four of them had been a team last year and had quickly learned to work together. It was as if they'd known each other their entire lives.

"Throw your bags in the room and let's slip over to the food court—see what we can rustle up, ya know." Marty's energy was bursting to be set free. "Looks like a storm brewing. It'll be more fun to be stuck in there where the action is."

"Know what the military calls thunderstorms?" Frank asked.

"I'll bite," Marty said.

"Farts and darts," he shared.

"Only you could come up with that." Vic laughed. "You made that up, didn't you?"

"No kiddin'. And I didn't just make it up. I actually ran across it when I was surfing the internet. You'd be surprised what you can find on the web," he said divulging the bit of trivia to his unbelieving crew.

"And here I was, thinking I missed you guys." Ardan shook his head in disbelief. "C'mon, let's blow this pop stand."

"Yeah, I'm kinda interested in who's coming back this year," Vic said wistfully. "I wonder if that sweet, little thing from Atlanta will be here. Annabella? Cute as a Southern flower she was. But so smart she was a trifle intimidating."

"You mean she didn't fall for your *charm*?" Ardan pointed out.

They all chuckled over remembering his way with the female of the species. You could take a Frenchman out of France, but you could never take the French out of the man.

"Not charm, my good fellow. I'm just naturally a 'nice guy.'" Vic coyly smiled.

"Oh, can it be?" Marty said in disbelief.

"Am I hearing this right? *You* trying to convince *us*, your good buddies, that you aren't trying to work your 'magic' on every girl you meet?" Frank said, adding his two cents to the mix.

"If you play nice, I'll introduce you to one of them," Vic volleyed back.

"Enough already, let's go where the action is so we can see this 'nice guy' practice his moves. We'll judge for ourselves who's the true nice guy," Ardan said as he threw his bag on the bed.

"Maybe when we get back, we can short-sheet a few beds," Marty suggested. "It'll take some of 'em the whole week to figure out how to get into them. Then another week to figure who did it. By then, we'll be gone." He laughed at the thought.

"What are you, ten? I think we can live without the pranks. Let's just focus on the real challenges the instructors throw at us." Ardan loved the crazy nut but wasn't up to TP-ing or any other similar escapade—not this year. This year was important to Ardan. He needed to focus if he was to get his priorities in order. Marty reminded him of Archie—smart, achieving, a do-anything-for-you kinda guy, and a practical joker.

"Na. I think he just got confused. He thought he was registering for Clown College, not Space Academy." Frank laughed. "We'll have our work cut out for us this year—like keeping him reigned in."

⚬ᜃᜃᜃ⚬

"The Quartet" (as the boys had been nicknamed last year, due to the fact they marched to the beat of their own drum) had done so well together they were allowed to team up again. Most activities were, however, included everyone, with a few exceptions. During the special mission was where teamwork came into play, and that was where the foursome felt they had the advantage.

To start this year's program off with a bang, the first item on the agenda was to give the students the opportunity to speak to the astronauts on the space station. While video chatting, they asked about what experiments the astronauts were conducting. Had they run into any problems? How long would they be there? And, Marty wanted to know, how the food was. Last year, the cadets had sampled those same meals and couldn't develop a taste for any of them. Marty hoped there had been some improvement.

"This year, we're putting you on another mission. It's a little offbeat from our traditional form, but we think there's a lot to learn from this technique," the commander said when they got back to the schedule. "But first, you'll need to receive underwater training. Being underwater is a close simulation to working in space. You'll need to employ these skills for your next mission.

"Here's your problem: A panel on the heat shield was damaged while breaking Earth's gravity. Obviously, it has to be repaired if you are to reenter. You'll also be expected to look for any additional problems you might find.

"Your team mission will be to have two of your teammates step outside the specially designed 'space station' and correct the issue. This will be done in two stages. The first trip out is for assessment. As a team, you will formulate the repair plan. This will have to entail every aspect of the job, from tools and parts, to the time needed and most importantly oxygen. Well, it's your challenge. You'll have to figure it out. That's your dilemma this year. 'Houston' will be available to assist you in every way, just as they would in an actual situation. Bear in mind, you are 270 miles away from earth, making one full orbit every hour and a half. You can't call the corner repair service. So, you'll only have the items you came with, and you'll be doing all the work.

"The two 'astronauts' remaining in the craft will monitor the repair team's activities on the screens and maintain standard operations. Here's the fun part. The water team gets to repair what's necessary in *full gear*—especially with the gloves and connection hoses."

The instructor let the mission soak in with the young cadets. The news came with one unified gasp. Then the whispered joking began to fill the room. The commander gave them a few moments before he continued.

"We're not going to put you out there totally unprepared. We have several films to show you actual space walks, as well as footage of water training by our 'crack' astronauts."

A laugh went through the crowd—especially from the teaching staff. The cadets were assured that those who did the water portion would to be certified before being allowed to suit up. There would also be ample training in the pool for everyone. Each team would choose two qualified cadets to continue with the actual repairs. Ardan knew he wanted to be in the water. He loved working with mechanical issues and saw this as an exciting challenge.

"Well, guys," Ardan said that night before lights out. "What do you think? Who wants to do what part of the mission?"

"Me, I work better when I can actually move around unencumbered," Marty said, drawing attention to his larger size. "I'd look like a beached whale out there. I think I'd like the inside computer work—if it's OK."

"Ditto here," Vic chipped in. "I'll be there to push the buttons that perform the magic for you guys. With the dexterity in these fingers, you have no worries. Besides, I don't think these paws of mine would do well with those oversized mitts they give you."

"Well, I'm a water buff. I come from a family of snorkeling and scuba diving. We head for Lake Erie every chance we can. My dad and I even explored a sunken ship that was capsized during one of those vicious lake storms. Water runs through my veins," Frank said, pinching his nose and doing the side-to-side wiggle to the floor.

"Great! I was hoping I could do the water 'sports,'" Ardan joked.

With both Ardan and Frank already trained in scuba diving, they hoped to get a jump on the mission.

"Hey, fellow conspirators," Vic said, "we need some kind of special 'handles' to call ourselves—something snappy, a code unto ourselves."

"Well, I have one for you, *Sweet Cakes*," Frank teased. "Isn't that what all the girls call you? That'd be easy for you to remember, too. Or is it Sweety Pie?"

"C'mon. You wouldn't," Vic protested.

"Oh yes, we would, sweetheart," Ardan laughed. "Sweet Cakes—perfect. Now, how about Wolfman for our northern buddy. Isn't Ely, Minnesota, the wolf capital?" Ardan asked Marty.

"Yes, it is. I'm surprised you knew that. I like the moniker. I'll take it," Marty smiled.

"*And* Goose would work for you, Ardan. Remember last year, you couldn't go near the lake 'cause the geese kept chasing you? Never figured out why they had it in for you. Yep, Goose it is." Frank laughed at the memory of Ardan high-stepping it all the way up the embankment.

"Well now, that leaves our skinny kid from the sticks of Pennsylvania. What would you name a kid like that?" Vic asked.

"That's it. You just said it. Sticks! Skinny—Sticks. Get it?" Marty grinned giving Frank the evil eye."

"Hey, I resemble that remark." Frank feigned displeasure at the suggestion he was "skinny."

"Neato-mosquito, we've settled the biggest obstacle. Now I can get a good night's rest. Goodnight, *girls*." With that, Marty rolled over, turning his back to his friends.

Reveille was an outrageous five o'clock—a.m.

Chapter 61

Houston, We Have a Problem

Technically, after the training, any one of the team could fill in for any of the others. They did, however, stick to their original choices. Goose and Sticks suited up for the plunge. Wolfman and Sweet Cakes headed to the "isolation chamber" of the space capsule.

"I feel like a sloth," Sticks said into his helmet. "Hope we practiced enough with the tools."

"Piece of cake. Let's get to work. To start with, they gave us the heat shield as one problem. We have to be sure we locate that, but let's also see if they threw anything else into the mix. I say we address this in the search pattern we discussed. I'm right side." Ardan was anxious to get underway. The teams would be working under a time constraint for finding the problem(s) and executing the solution(s). They didn't want to be time disqualified this early in the game, so they approached phase one with all seriousness.

"I found the loose heat shield. Mark it as E-14. Doesn't look that bad. I'd say it's doable without total replacement. It's loose but not broken. Don't see anything else that's not nailed down tight," Sticks said.

"I'm looking at a panel in pattern G-4. It appears to be marred. I don't believe the surface has been breached enough to cause a problem, but we'll bring it up to Houston. Still looking," Goose replied.

All in all, the water boys only found those two heat shields in question. The rest of the capsule's structure appeared to be intact. Back at the station, they went over the plans they would employ to correct the issues with the team.

The team then relayed their plan of action to NASA base and were given the OK to proceed.

"I hope we found it all," Sticks said. "I have a weird feeling we've missed something."

"While we're doing these repairs, there's no reason we still can't keep our eyes open for anything else that looks bad," Goose replied into his helmet.

Just minutes into their mission, the impossible became reality. Goose was swept away by a strong, unconventional current in this Olympic-sized pool—a current not unlike an ocean undertow was sucking him away from the craft. He was uncontrollably dangling at the end of his tether when it broke free, leaving him floating in space.

"What ... the," Wolfman said. "I can't find the Goose. I've lost him from the screen! Good grief, man. We've lost him."

"Houston, we have a problem! The Goose is loose!" Sweet Cakes yelled into the mike. He was panicked. Instinct told him he should get to the pool as fast as he could. "We need to warn Sticks! Egad man, we just lost Goose!"

"What? In English, boys. What's going on?" base inquired.

Thoughts were playing wild scenario's in Wolfman's mind. He covered the mike with his hand. "Hey, let's not jump the gun," Wolfman whispered to Sweet Cakes. "What if this is just another problem on our mission? What if the guys are fine out there, but the true problem is here in one of our computers? Hold off on Houston. Just say ... oops, sorry or something. OK? Let's take a minute to think this out. We have to approach this calmly. We're spacemen, remember? Professionals. We don't panic!"

Chapter 62

We Meet Again

Ardan realized something was way off script. He was in free float. His anchor was definitely compromised. *This* was something they had not prepared for—could not prepare for.

In the next instant, Ardan was transported. There was no feeling of speed or g-force—simply a sense of activity, activity out of his control or understanding. As quickly as it started, it was over. In its wake, Ardan was—where?

Everywhere he looked, he saw things—items he never could have envisioned in his world.

"Ardan." He heard the voice first, and then, out of nowhere in particular, an object appeared. "Nice to have you on board."

"Where am I?" Ardan did not think the question unreasonable.

"Your people would say I have kidnapped you, and they would also say that I am an alien. I hope you can accept that I mean you no harm," the person/creature said.

Even in this strange environment, Ardan was not fearful—yet. There was a comfort in the voice coming from the unusual body form. The object was at least seven feet tall; it had two eyes, one mouth, a nose, and hearing articles, along with similar appendages to what humans have. They just looked oddly out of place.

"Why am I here?" Ardan asked.

"Well, I have known of you for quite a while. I've just been waiting for you to grow up. Let me fill you in. Very few humans have the ability to communicate across the barriers of language, space, and time. You and your sister are two of them. You have wondered if anyone else crosses into the fourth dimension. Yes, emphatically, yes. I doubt if you will ever meet any of them or realize you are in their company, but be assured they exist. Like you, they are uncomfortable talking about these episodes. We communicate with some of you in different ways, as each of you are immensely unique. You, Ardan, will be an asset in the realm of preserving the sanctity of our universe. And, it *is our* universe. There are many other entities using the same space. I'm going to show you some of what's out there and how you can play a role in preserving it.

"First, let me give you some good news. I can't guarantee you'll pass your studies at West Point. But believe me, you are in their headlights. Unless something unforeseen happens, you will be accepted. That's one of the reasons I want to personally touch base with you—to let you know you're on the right track," the creature continued. "And, I'd like to suggest studies beneficial to us all as we try to coexist."

"Wow, that's great news. I mean the West Point deal. But I still don't get where you and I fit in. And just how do you know me? You said you've known me for quite a while?" Ardan inquired.

"Remember that video game your neighbor gave you? You were about twelve, I'd say. Well, we hijacked the game. What we wanted was for you to start being aware of the environment and how fragile it can be. We tried to point out the good things and the bad things going on at the various levels."

"And during the last level," Ardan recalled, "you buzzed our spaceship. I do remember that. Ever since then, my sister and I were left wondering if aliens were real or if we were guilty of overactive imaginations," Ardan reflected.

"I hope I can set your mind at ease. We're real. For starters, I'm called Met-trix. I, we prefer to be referred to as galaxy travelers. I am not of this galaxy but of an adjacent one. We'll visit it in just a moment." Met-trix became more human from that point forward. "Are you in?"

"Let's just say, I'm open for learning at this point," Ardan diplomatically replied.

"Fair enough. Let's hit the road, toad. Did I say that right?" He laughed.

Ardan was impressed at Met-trix's trying to make him feel at ease by using earthly jargon.

"Since we're passing Mars, I'll fill you in a little on the mistakes the occupants made. That'll give you a head start at understanding them for when your own planet arrives to explore it in the future," Met-trix said.

"You're right. That's the plan—Mars landing with humans in just a few more years," Ardan replied. "Landings are currently in the robot stage, but what they find will influence future endeavors."

"Well to begin with, the occupants, Martians, were totally resistant to any of the ways they could have implemented to prevent the obvious path they were on—a path, I might add, toward total environmental destruction. Many tried to warn them—to no avail. As a result, they were driven underground. Now, they're living an artificial style of life barely able to venture to the surface.

"When the balance of nature was dramatically altered, Mars could not sustain itself. What you see now is how time has ravished the dry land even more than when it was last occupied. Centuries of decomposition are the direct result of their neglect and misuse.

"Blame can be placed squarely at the feet of the leadership in the various sectors of the planet. They refused to work together. Each entity demanded control, resulting in nothing useful for the planet to succeed. Maybe when Earthlings arrive, enough time will have passed for the Martians to finally listen. And maybe Earthlings will have their eyes opened as well. Let's keep going, Ardan. I can't keep you for too long." Met-trix's heart still bore the heartbreak as he led Ardan away from Mars.

"While we travel, I want you to notice the floating debris. You must develop equipment that will not continue to clutter space. The trash is becoming dangerous. Let me compare it to your oceans. Your people are guilty of using your waters as dumping grounds. Now look. The litter has so contaminated the water that it's affecting the ecosystem. You mistakenly thought that, with so much of Earth being water, trash would somehow disappear into its depths. So now, the plants and fish are paying a heavy price.

"Ardan, you will soon be in a position to have some impact. Take advantage of that. We, the universe, need the cooperation of all who chose to travel within." Met-trix was compassionate as he spoke to Ardan. He knew he had just thrown a heavy burden at the youth. It's nothing one person could change alone, but he hoped Ardan would be able to unite enough people behind him who could.

"Well, this is Zytwill, my new home. My ancestors were originally Martians but left when conditions were getting out of hand. I might add, Earth was a consideration for relocating. But with our obvious physical differences and the troubles Earth was already experiencing way back then, we chose to leave this galaxy completely. Mars—and Earth, too, I might add—were left behind, out of sight but not out of mind." He smiled.

"Out of necessity, we have modified ourselves. On Zytwill, we are each developed for specific abilities to maintain life," Met-trix explained.

"Developed? In what way?" Ardan asked of the unusual terminology.

"I'm a galaxy traveler—an ambassador if you will," he said. "I watch the universe for critical signs of disruption. That's not to say we want domination. No. Our people have made that mistake before. We only want to coexist. Our concern is, however, with the environment of the skies.

"But back to our species. Each of our citizens has been scientifically designed—genetically created—much like in a beehive, where only the queen bee reproduces. Other bees are workers, honey gathers, and so on. We have a similar situation. That's how it is with us. Some of our people are the hosts and will give birth to a specific child, depending on where the need is. As soon as they are weened, those who will be, say, engineers or doctors or carpenters and so on will be cared for by specialty nannies who will continue to raise them to fulfill that particular need. Each of those nannies were also genetically created to train the youth in a preordained occupation. Harsh as that sounds, it's working for us since we had to rebuild a complete society.

"Our looks are slightly different for each vocation. Much of that is simple mathematics. A builder needs more muscles, an engineer more head room for the cerebrum where critical thinking occurs; some professions need better eyes or sense of smell. All appearance variations are subtle to the untrained eye but enough that we can tell the position a citizen holds at a glance."

Ardan felt as if he had left reality. These people were not grotesque as might be expected. Instead they were beautiful in their own right. And happy. Everyone was friendly beyond belief. Each appeared to have found the coveted secret to life.

For as far as Ardan could see, the landscape was comprised of bright, bold colors. The vegetation boasted broad leaves with enormous blossoms. The air was clear and fresh smelling. The buildings were umbrella-like, with pods of apartments hanging from sturdy anchors. The architecture was beyond modernistic; it was downright futuristic—not too unlike a comic book rendition of what the future might look like. So often those authors were ahead of reality. Scientists took time to catch up to the written word in books or portrayed on the silver screen.

Could those authors be like me? Ardan thought. *Can they have traversed time and space? Had they perhaps been space travelers? Had they gotten a glimpse of other universes? Met-trix indicated there were other like Isabel and me.*

"I have to get you back, Ardan. I hope this has been useful to you. I'll be seeing you again. But don't worry; I can be invisible. I would never appear to an unbeliever so your friends will not realize I exist," Met-trix said.

"Well that's a relief. I tend to confuse them enough as it is," Ardan confessed. "All of this is going to take some time to digest. I'm lucky. I have Isabel to confide in. Nothing surprises her."

"Yes, Isabel is another fine specimen—forgive me—a very fine young human. You are absolutely not created in the way my people are," he apologized for the misuse of words. "She'll make her way differently than you. But her abilities will be well utilized. You will be proud of each other for not wasting your unique talents. The time has come. Keep your nose to the grindstone. Did I say that right?" He laughed again.

Met-trix raised his hand in a sign of peace, and Ardan was teleported back to space camp. He became a believer that, perhaps, black holes were mere portals employed to speed universal travel—express elevators, so to speak.

⟨≋⟩

"How ya doing, Goose?" Sticks asked as he rounded the "spaceship."

"Done. She looks good as new. Let's get in and shed these elephant suits," Goose replied.

Once on deck, the water boys were immediately overwhelmed by Wolfman, who couldn't wait to rat out his fellow teammate. "Ol' Sweet Cakes here panicked and yelled for help from 'Houston' before we checked out what the problem was. It's OK though. They didn't understand what he was saying."

"Say, what?" Stick asked, completely caught off guard.

"Ah, what are you talking about?" Goose questioned. "Start from the beginning, will you."

"Well, our screen went blank—the one shadowing you, Goose. It went dead, and ol' Sweet Cakes here panicked—went totally berserk," Wolfman continued or tried to.

"Now, wait a minute," Vic broke in. "In my defense, I had this weird premonition that something dreadful happened to you, Goose. Really. Man, I thought you might have died or something," Sweet Cakes said. "I was really worried."

"That's right. And he panicked! Panicked I tell you. He started yelling like a little girl—'the Goose is loose, the Goose is on the loose!' It was funny. Houston had no idea. Lucky for us, they don't know our code names. I don't think it will count against our time effort. Oh. Oh. That's the other thing. You guys don't know. You see, there *was* another problem, but it wasn't outside the craft. It was right here on one of our screens. Goose, we totally lost you. It took a little tweaking, but we finally figured it out. All's good here. We fixed it in record time," he finished with a sigh of relief. "So, how was it on your end? Anything out of the ordinary?"

"No, not like what you guys had," said Sticks. "Looked pretty routine."

"Yep. Easy-peazy. Nothing out of the ordinary," Goose added.

⚬⚬⚬

"Where did the time go?" Sweet Cakes asked. "This is our last camp, guys."

"Jeez, I'm gonna miss this," Sticks said. "Let's be sure we keep in touch, right?"

"Without a doubt. Let me know if I have to bail any of you out. I know firsthand what troublemakers you guys are," Wolfman mocked. "You can count on me. I'll find any prison you wind up in. Hey, maybe I'll become a lawyer like the family wants. Then I can charge you an outrageous fee."

"I'll keep that in mind," Ardan said. "But seriously, let's vow to keep in touch."

"Indeed. A word to the wise, Sweet Cakes. Stay clear of chasing the skirts, or we'll be attending your wedding and not your college graduation. You'll be the first married. Just saying. It's a simple law of statistics. You can't see that many girls without falling for one of them," Wolfman warned.

"Not me. I just love 'em and leave 'em." Vic laughed.

"Well, I for one hope to attend everyone's college graduation before the wedding invitations go out." Frank echoed Wolfman's warning. "It'll be interesting to see what you guys grow up to be—if you grow up."

"I hate to say this, but it's time. I'll miss my flight it I don't leave now." Ardan was truly finding it hard to separate from the friendship they had achieved in such a short time. Hopefully, their paths would cross again. That thought was the only thing making their goodbye bearable.

Chapter 63

Exchange of Adventures

Isabel was absolutely jumping out of her skin waiting for Ardan's flight to arrive. She had so much to tell him and couldn't wait to share the details.

"Ardan," she yelled from across the terminal. "Over here!"

"Hi. Let me grab my bag," he said.

"I'm so glad Mom and Dad couldn't come. I literally don't think I could have waited to tell you about my trip."

"It's good to see you this excited," Ardan said. Indeed it was uplifting to see her this happy. "I'll drive. Please. You like to talk with your hands. Just sayin'."

"You know me too well." She giggled. "But I don't know where to start. So much has happened."

"Well, why don't you start with Jeff. I'm dying to hear about him," Ardan said.

"Good choice. He's a giant. Really. He's six foot eight. Crazy, huh. And sooo good-looking." Her smile was ear to ear as she rattled on—and on.

"Ooh, Mr. Jolly Green Giant?" He laughed. "And his family? How were they?"

"Is no one off limits with you?" She shook her head at the moniker Ardan had bestowed upon poor Jeff. Moving on, she answered his question. "Remember how nice they were when we met them after the dognapping?" Ardan barely had time to nod his assurance before Isabel jumped ahead. "Well, they were super nice to Audrey and me. I texted you about her. You'd love her. Anyway, the Swansons showed us a super good time. Audrey was extremely impressed."

240

"Sounds like you've made a new best friend," Ardan said.

"Without a doubt. She's already been accepted at the university. She's a year ahead of me. But if I get to go there too, we've made plans to meet up as often as our schedules allow."

"And Jeff? You said he's going to be a vet?" Ardan quired.

"Yes, and he's so dedicated," she cooed. "Oh, I met Bandit again. Jeff said that Bandit was his inspiration. Jeff will finish his last year at the university before I get there. But he'll be interning at a huge veterinarian hospital nearby. He's offered to come help me get started on my studies. Did I mention how good-looking he is? Why did I say that? That's beyond the point." She blushed. "He just wants to be helpful. Isn't that kind?"

"Why, Isabel, I believe you like him," Ardan said.

"I do not! I mean, of course I like him. He's really a kind person," she stated.

"No, my starstruck friend! You are totally crushing over him."

"Stop. It's no such thing. We're just good friends. Now, tell me about you. Did you have a good time? Was it worthwhile?" she asked, trying to get off the Jeff subject.

"I did have fun. The guys I teamed up with last year were all there again. What a bunch of crazies!" Ardan said.

After a thoughtful pause he added, "I had another fourth-dimensional experience. It was so far-out. Remember when we played that video game Mrs. McClain gave us? Remember how strange it got? Well, guess what? The game was all in preparation for our future. The aliens—um, remember being buzzed by an alien spaceship? Well, they were real aliens. I met one of them. His name is Met-trix. He has plans for me. He believes I can influence positive steps as we Earthlings start conquering more of the elements in space exploration. Isabel, he transported me to Mars. There is life on Mars. They have to live underground because of the mess they made of their natural resources. Then he took me to another galaxy where he lives. Bummer, we're almost home. I'll give you the short version until we can get away from the folks," he said. "His relatives escaped Mars and settled on the planet they named Zytwill in a different galaxy. The people there are so unique. They're designer people I guess you could call it."

"Far-out. We always wondered if any of that game was for real. Good thing we destroyed it though," she said as Ardan pulled into the drive.

Their mother was already coming out the front door.

"Well, what say you, my young traveler? Was the trip worth it?" she asked.

"It was wonderful," Ardan said as he gave her a big hug, lifting her off her feet and spinning her around.

"You goofus! Put me down." She laughed. "I made your favorite roast for supper. Dad will be here any minute. I hope you had as good a time as Isabel."

"Well, I didn't go there to play around like Isabel did. I'm the serious one remember," he said, winking at Isabel.

"Fill us in over supper. So glad to have you both home again. Oh, before I forget—Mr. Sawyer called. He's anxious for you to report. They're getting busy and he can use the extra help. I think he might need you flying short junkets. Someone had their appendix out and is still grounded," Mother said.

Dinner together as a family was always comforting. Ardan realized how blessed he was to have caring parents—and Isabel. He was lucky to have her sharing in their unique adventures. Life couldn't get much better than this, he thought as he finished his second helping of roast beef.

The family spent the rest of the evening catching up. It felt good to be home again. Before the twins headed up to bed, Father gave his offspring a hug and, with true passion, reminded them just how much he loved them and especially how much he liked them for the persons they had become.

⚬⚬⚬

"What a dinner! Sure beats 'institution' food," Isabel said when they settled in upstairs. "What did you think of the college food?"

"I try not to think too much about it," Ardan replied. "How come school cafeterias can't figure out how to fix tasty food like the buffet restaurants? Restaurants serve large quantities of people, too. That's just a novice's observance, mind you."

"I'm glad Mom and Dad are getting involved in things for themselves," Isabel remarked on a new observance.

"Hard to believe making all those Halloween outfits for us gave Mom experience for creating costumes at the civic center. She's really quite clever designing clothes for the theater group. They're doing *Fiddler on the Roof* next season. It's one of my favorites. That'll keep her hopping." Ardan was proud of his mother. She was the best volunteer—going way back to her helping as a teacher's aide.

"Funny part is, she's pulling in the whole family. Dad and Grandpa are making some of the props, and Grandma is helping with the costumes," Isabel added. "We'd better lay low before we find ourselves involved, too."

"Did you hear, they've joined a square dance club that meets every month at the Brewsters' farm? That'd be one I'd pay to see." Ardan laughed. "You know we only have one more year before college. As anxious as I am to get on with my life, I hate giving up this part of it. We've been so lucky to have a loving upbringing. I must be crazy not to know my own mind. Shouldn't there be a way to have it all?"

"Mixed emotions. Should I? Shouldn't I? What if I'm wrong? I know what you're saying," Isabel answered with her own indecisions playing tricks. "Life is so complicated."

"Met-trix told me I would definitely get in to West Point. That does give me motivation," he said.

"So what of this space travel thing? You actually left our galaxy?" Isabel asked.

"I did. It was so smooth and fast. I'd say it was more like being teleported. We did slow down around Mars so Met-trix could show me how desolate it had become. He only had stories that were passed down about Mars from when she was in her glory. Just the same, he appeared sad when he spoke of what had become of his ancestors. What's hard to take away from this is how the new Martians chose to rebuild—starting with repopulating their new planet they named Zytwill."

"You indicated they were like 'designer' people? I think that's the word you used," Isabel asked through furrowed brows, not quite getting the concept. "You don't mean in connection with birth, do you? That doesn't seem to apply. Surely you meant like plastic surgery and operations afterward?"

"No, before. Life is all created in a test tube. Each 'person' is genetically designed to fill a specific need—doctor, chemist, engineer, farmer, whatever. They more replace occupations than increase the population. There are nurturing birth mothers; that is their sole purpose." Ardan continued to describe the raising of the individuals to fulfill the planets' needs. "As ridiculous as it sounds, the people have succeeded beyond even our expectations. And they're not robots. They seem happy and content. From what we think of as aliens, his people are really pleasant to look at.

"They live in spectacular buildings. The air is crisp and clean. Since they walk the shorter distances and teleport the farther destinations, they don't have auto emissions polluting the atmosphere. Vegetation is …is … gorgeous—beautiful flowers, succulent vegetables and fruit. Met-trix said they are not 'above stealing ideas' from the life they obverse across the universe. Once on an expedition, he took seeds from our farmers. They cautiously incubate everything foreign for a period of time before introducing it to their atmosphere. During that time, they tweak the genetics to utilize the minerals in their soil. They're extremely careful not to bring in dangerous viruses or small creatures.

"Met-trix liked to hear our children laughing and running around our playgrounds so he incorporated the idea to suit their lifestyles. Far-out! Or more fitting, wild. I don't know if their equipment would pass our safety standards.

"Kiddo, it'd knock your socks off if you ever got the opportunity to see them. Oh, and that's another thing. Met-trix kept trying to use our slang expressions. It was cute of him. He'd smile and ask if he was using words correctly. I liked him a lot."

"Ardan, how do you fit in? They don't want to incorporate you into their solar system do they?" Isabel was concerned to the point of being frightened. "Tell me you're not going to this Zytwill planet to live!"

"No, that wasn't it at all. Met-trix was trying to show me that, if we don't start taking care of what we have here on Earth, we could wind up like Mars. He warned against blowing ourselves up. Met-trix specifically drew attention to the armed satellites already circulating Earth. He did not believe all the countries possessing them have the best intent for the world on a whole. We must learn not only to preserve our environment but also to coexist. Somehow he thinks I might be in a position one day to help. He did say he would contact me again somewhere in the space of time," Ardan explained. "You might be interested in this. He said, your 'talents,' as he put it, would be used in other ways. So, kid, you're not off the hook."

"Thanks. I was hoping we'd outgrow this *talent*. I had an episode myself while at the medical center. I was taken back in time to my hero Florence Nightingale's era. The Crimean War was in full swing. The surgical standards were primeval. I'm so grateful for the advancements we have today. The event did show me that I definitely want to go into medicine—without a doubt. I want to become a general surgeon/ practitioner for a small community. I want to bring big-city techniques to the small villager. I saw how important having proper medical care close at hand is. Those nurses and doctors back in 1853 were real heroes. They had so little to work with.

"I'm tired, Ardan." Reliving those horrors had drained her spirit. "We'll talk more in the morning. Love you, bro."

"You, too, Doc. We'll get through this. We always do." He gave her a reassuring hug. "Love you and like you."

"Ditto," she replied warmed by the familiar phrase.

As Ardan walked to his bedroom window, his steps were not as self-assured as he pretended. The moon and stars were in their proper positions. But what wasn't he seeing? What else was out there?

> Your beauty is beyond compare
> Lost in time and space
> I can but dare
> To step up and take my place.

BOOK TWELVE
Life as Adults

Chapter 64

Dr. Isabel Murphy

Isabel was enjoying a break from the hospital where she'd just finished her internship. Passing her college exams had been a lot of hard work, but it had given her the proud title of doctor. Completing her internship solidified the title.

Under a bright, clear sky, Isabel was driving out to meet Jeff Swanson at his animal clinic. The two had started seeing each other shortly after she'd arrived at the University of Benson Medical her freshman year. He had become her coach and main support throughout those years.

Shortly after her graduation, Jeff proposed. In honesty, reflecting back, she should have expected that. Even more honestly, she should have done all she could to distance herself from him in the very beginning, but that thought was impossible. Isabel had fallen for this tall, lanky humanitarian. He was just too wonderful in every way. Over and over, Isabel tried to justify her reasons for not telling Jeff about her fourth-dimensional experiences. She managed to postpone a marriage commitment until after she'd completed her internship. She was afraid he would be expecting an answer soon. The underlying issue of being honest with Jeff had to be addressed before she could even think of saying yes. Isabel was a smart woman. Deep down, she realized she could never say yes. She had come here today because Jeff wanted to show her his newly acquired land. As excited as he was, she did not want to spoil his special moment by breaking things off just now. But it would have to be soon.

Bandit was there to welcome her the minute she opened the clinic door. Jeff's old sidekick had become the official greeter to all who entered.

Although he was pretty gray, he still had a lot of spunk for a dog his age. A credit to the excellent care he received from his loyal owner.

"Bandit, you're taking my job. Hi, Isabel. Jeff is just wrapping up some paperwork. You can go right back," Barbara, his receptionist said. "Tell Jeff I'm locking up, will you?"

"Of course. Have a good weekend, Barb," she said while heading for Jeff's office.

"Good timing," Jeff said. "I'm done." Jeff drew Isabel close for an affectionate kiss.

How could Isabel give this up? But how would he accept her as this insane woman who thought she moved across the boundaries of time and space?

Jeff was in the process of buying out his partner, Dr. Nathan Richard, who'd started the clinic some forty-years ago. Dr. Richard was the only veterinarian in Park Forest. Now, Jeff was here to take over. Dr. Richard had been the Swanson family veterinarian over the many years with their wide variety of pets. He also was Jeff's mentor having taken the young boy under his wing when Jeff rescued his stolen dog and fought to save Bandit's life. Jeff's passion for humane treatment of animals had started then. It was intensified by the harsh treatment the dognappers had shown to the dogs they'd captured.

The receptionist had already closed the clinic, leaving Bandit patiently waiting to have his day completed as well.

"I'll be back for you in just a few minutes, old boy," Jeff assured his buddy. "I want to show Isabel the farm. You've already seen it. No sense wearing you out."

"Don't worry, Bandit. We'll give you a special treat when we get back," Isabel added.

"I picked up a couple of dirt bikes to get around the farm. You game?" he asked.

"Lead on, McDuff."

⟨✦⟩

Ahead of them was a vast expanse of well over a thousand acres of mixed land usage. As fortune would have it, Jeff had recently inherited the estate when Dr. Richard's brother, James, died. With both brothers being bachelors, they wanted Jeff to have this mostly pristine acreage. The elder brother had only farmed a small portion of the land, leaving the vast majority as God created it. When Jeff had been approached with the prospect of procuring the acreage, he'd expressed his idea of making it an animal sanctuary. Both brothers were highly receptive to his goal. Little did Jeff know at the time, but the man was terminally ill, and the land became the young veterinarian's responsibility sooner than expected.

This left Jeff with some big decisions to make in a short period of time. He wanted the land to be a retirement retreat and not a zoo. Sensibly, that would also free him of many regulations that would have been required for public usage. It would also be more peaceful for its aged and disabled occupants.

Jeff's first goal was to reconstruct the farm to work for the respective animals he planned to house. With so much interest already being shown, Jeff was anxious to get safe lodging in place as quickly as possible.

He could barely contain his excitement in showing The James Richard Animal Sanctuary to Isabel. He marveled at her enthusiasm and the many similar interests they shared. These were the very similarities that had drawn the couple so close so quickly.

"It's breathtaking," she said as they stopped to look at a great pasture that Jeff wanted to fence for aged horses. He described where he wanted to put a barn where the animals could escape inclement weather. Mid-dream of Jeff expressing his thoughts, his phone rang.

"Darn," he said when finished with the call. "That's one of my elderly clients. She's worried about her cat. They're all each other have. It's always critical to her. I have to get back just to calm her. It won't take long," he apologized.

"Can I wait here for you? I'd like to look around a bit," Isabel asked.

"I guess. You'll be OK? Here by yourself?"

"Of course, you silly. Go. The sooner you go, the sooner you can get back." She blew him a kiss and turned to absorb the beauty that was spread out before her.

Chapter 65

Call to Serve

Isabel could almost visualize the various creatures who would be assured a safe life and be cared for by one of the finest, most well-rounded veterinarians in the country. Not that she was biased in any way. Jeff truly was the best.

As she took advantage of the shade offered by one of the many trees lining the field, she felt a presence. It took her off guard. She hadn't heard anyone approach. Yet, someone was there. She straightened. "Hello. Who's there?" she called.

"Isabel. It is you." Quietly, Raugh moved out into the open. "For some time now, I felt you were near."

"Raugh, however are you? And Moof." A rush of joy ran through her. Although she hadn't seen the Bigfoots since she was eleven, apparently neither she nor Raugh had lost their unique ability to communicate through thought transfer.

"Isabel, I need help," Raugh pleaded. "My boy. He's hurt. Your people are so advanced. I hope … maybe you can help?"

"I can try, Raugh. That's the best I can tell you right now. Where is he?" she asked.

"Our cave is not far from here. I'll run ahead. Moof will lead you."

He was right. It wasn't far at all. The Sasquatch forest reserve bordered and even spilled over onto Jeff's land. *Oh no, Jeff,* she thought. She'd be gone when he returned. She'd call him in a minute. First, she wanted to look at the boy.

He was in obvious pain, practically comatose, but regardless of his condition, it frightened the young Sasquatch to see a human in their habitat.

Isabel approached the lad. Visually, she could already see that the boy's tibia was broken in at least one place. The bone had not yet broken through his unusually thick skin, but a jagger edge was prominent just under the surface. A huge puss bag harboring infectious fluid was engulfing the area, adding to the problem.

Soovy, Raugh's life mate, realized something serious was in the making. She demanded to be let in on the verdict.

Raugh explained the problem. Cawe's condition was going to require bringing human's into their world.

Her eyes grew wide and frightened. Looking down at her son, Soovy knew she would risk anything that would save him, but why this? "Do you trust her?" she asked Raugh as she twisted her head toward Isabel.

"Isabel and her brother saved us once before, when we were marooned on their island. I trust her," he replied.

"OK then. I trust *you*, Raugh." Soovy gave her consent. Raugh had shown great leadership and was considered one of the wisest men on the sasquatch council. She put all her trust in his knowledge. "We should do it then."

"Raugh, I know we warned you about interaction with humans, but we're going to have to reach out to my boyfriend. He's a doctor and has a clinic where we can treat your son," she tried to explain. *Doctor, clinic*—the words had no reference in Raugh's world.

Raugh conferred with Moof and Wour while Soovy gave Isabel the once-over. What was there about this human? Why would the trio put such faith in her? Isabel was a little uncomfortable but tried to smile as a way of assurance to the timid woman. She had empathy for Soovy, the mother of the young Bigfoot who would soon be entrusted to the care of humans—a child whose jeopardy was increasing by the minute. Even Isabel was becoming anxious.

"You tell us how this is going to happen, and we'll do it," Raugh said.

"I'm going to step outside where I can get reception for my phone," she said, pulling it out of her pocket. "I'll be right back."

The choice in telling Jeff about her "unique abilities" had just been removed. She and the Sasquatch needed his expertise. She only hoped he would understand.

"Jeff," she began. "I'm going to ask you for a humongous favor. And I'm going to have to ask you to trust me."

"Sounds ominous. What's up?" He wanted to laugh but was worried by the sound of her voice. He never should have left her. He hoped she was all right. "Isabel! What's going on?"

"Well, are you still at the clinic?"

"Yes. I was just about to leave."

"Good. I'd like you to drive your van, the one you converted into an ambulance, to where you left me. I'll explain everything when I see you," she said.

"*What*? Are you all right? Isabel, are you all right?" He was panicked.

"I am. Jeff, I'm perfectly OK. Don't worry. But I need you to do as I ask. It'll be easier if I can tell you face-to-face. Trust me," she begged.

"I'm already on my way!"

⚬⚬⚬

She was waiting for him when he pulled up. Isabel began the difficult task of explaining about not only the Sasquatch but also her unique ability. She was right. He looked at her like she had just gone totally, completely, without question, out-of-her-ever-loving-mind mad.

"This is the real reason I can't marry you. This condition is just so unreal, even I have trouble understanding it. I've hated to think of ever telling you. But now I have no choice. Believe me. I never expected I'd be dragging you into something this strange. But I need your help. I can't do this without you. Will you go with me?" she pleaded.

Jeff's initial shock turned to sadness. The woman he loved and wanted to share in all his dreams had just displayed a side of herself that was beyond comprehension. Where did this insanity come from? Beautiful, sweet Isabel. His love. Dear God. Isabel.

"Let's go. Show me." He thought it would be better to go along with her for now and figure out how he'd handle it along the way.

Jeff was aware of Isabel's anxiety, but he was facing his own emotions, too. His world was collapsing around him. His love had lost her mind. Would she come back? Could she? Would this affliction require hospitalization? Did her parents know? Was this inherited? Egad, he believed he was going insane himself.

"OK, we're here. They're inside the cave. Don't be frightened. They look intimidating, but they won't hurt you." She sounded so earnest. Sweet Isabel. Living this fantasy so intensely. He loved her. He would stand by her no matter how long her recovery would take. He couldn't desert her now. He'd get the best professional help available. His dear, sweet Isabel.

"Do we need flashlights?" His voice quivered as he choked back the decided lump in his throat. Jeff was willing to humor her to the end, even though his legs were trembling as he exited the van.

"No, they have torches that fully light the cavern," she said. "Let's bring the stretcher though."

Jeff was about to call the charade to a halt when Raugh and Wour came around the opening.

He couldn't help himself. Already weak in the knees, he fell backward against the van. "What the ...?" He gasped.

"It's all right. It's OK, Jeff. The first one is Raugh, the father." She reached out to assure him. "Believe me, he's just as worried as you are. I'll introduce you."

Jeff would never take breathing for granted again. He forced himself to inhale before he fainted.

Entering the cave, Jeff had the most godawful feeling that went from his throat to his gut. What had they gotten themselves into? However, as soon as Jeff saw the patient, he became all doctor.

"We absolutely have to get him to the clinic as quickly as we can. This is your patient, Isabel. How do you want to proceed?" he asked with all courtesy due a fellow professional.

"Your experience by far exceeds mine. I'd welcome you to take the lead. I'll assist. The underlying question is the anatomy of a Sasquatch. You've also had more experience from interning at the zoo with its wide variety of species. This is a challenge not taught in school," she lamented. "We're making history—history, I might add, we can never speak of. Oh,

Jeff. I'm not questioning your confidentiality. I guess I'm verbalizing my own frustration. I've had to live with this my whole life."

"That goes without saying. Your secret is safe with me. No sense people thinking both of us are crazy," he said, trying for a laugh, feeble as it was. "OK, Doctor. Let's get him ready for transport. First thing when we get him to the clinic, we'll need an X-ray. Then we'll prep for immediate surgery." Jeff was all business again.

Raugh laid his young son on the stretcher, mindful of the pain the child was already suffering.

"Jeff, hold up. Soovy wants to hold your hand a minute. I think she needs to evaluate you in some way. Is that OK with you?" Isabel asked.

"Of course." Jeff turned to Soovy and took her hands in both of his. In his best nonverbal bedside manner, Jeff hoped his face would assure the worried mother that he would do his very best to care for her son. Looking in her eyes, he saw a mother of great beauty—a mother made more lovely by the concern she held for her young child.

At six foot eight, Jeff was close to the height of the clansmen. Soovy could look him right in the eye. In those unusual blue human eyes that both Jeff and Isabel possessed, she saw a warm, caring person. Turning to Raugh, she nodded for him to take her boy.

***

Raugh rode with his son. He helped Jeff carry the lad through the double doors into the surgical unit. Isabel immediately headed for the scrub tank and donned a clean set of surgical clothes.

"I'll set up the X-ray machine," she told Jeff as he scrubbed. Turning to Raugh, she said, "We're going to give Cawe an injection. This will relax him and relieve some of the pain he feels while we take pictures of his leg. Then we'll put him in a deep sleep for the operation. You're not to worry. I won't have time to keep you updated as we go along, but I need you to stay put—no matter what. As soon as I can, I'll let you know what's happening. You stay here, OK?" she pointed to a double wide bench.

The enormity of the surgical room with all those strange items left Raugh speechless. He had never been inside a human structure before. Did humans actually live like this? Already numbed by the night's events,

Raugh was unable to comprehend much more. He simply obeyed and put his unconditional trust in Isabel.

With the pictures taken, Isabel prepared the site area on Cawe while Jeff examined the X-rays.

Jeff and Isabel consulted on the best method to proceed. They would use permanent screws to hold the break in place and a hard cast. Since they would not be able to keep their unusual patient longer than the weekend, they would have to make "house calls" during the young Bigfoot's recovery. With her internship completed and her own practice not yet open, Isabel was available to administer Cawe's medications and assess his progress.

Other than the unusual thickness of the skin, the operation went without much difficulty. While Cawe was still recovering, the doctors discussed with Raugh what had been done to correct the break and what would be the best way to handle this going forward. For now, they would all stay the weekend in the clinic. A bewildered father indicated he understood.

Bandit had been unusually quiet through this whole process. Jeff and Isabel weren't intimidated by this creature. So, it must be all right? The trusted pet realized this was an emergency by the way the two doctors were bustling around. Over his years at the clinic, he fully understood emergency. He'd witnessed it many times. Still, he placed himself strategically between the doctors and the beast—just in case. Bandit was already familiar with the creatures' scent. He had come across it while moving about the sanctuary. Now, he could tie that scent to a figure that was not exactly human and apparently not hostile.

Jeff was pleased at how well the young Sasquatch responded. While still in some pain, Cawe seemed to find it at least bearable—unlike the stabbing pain he'd come in with. They kept him sedated and comfortable.

Sunday night, under the cover of darkness, Jeff and Isabel returned their friends to their own habitat.

Hovering off to the side, the clan was there to received their fellow comrades. They meticulously observed these odd beings who had once again interacted with Raugh and his group. This had been a long weekend, having been left in the dark without word. Some Bigfoots were still leery of human intervention and questioned this risky behavior. Although this would prove to be a step in the right direction (albeit a baby step) it opened the door for future understanding. Previously, the trio had told the stories of how Isabel and her brother helped them find home after they were shipwrecked. The visual safe return of their comrades eased the tension.

Soovy reached for Jeff's hand and held it for a few tender moments before she went to be with her son. The gesture solidified Jeff's belief that the Sasquatch were very close to being human.

⚬〰〰〰⚬

Back at the clinic, Jeff and Isabel began the process of scrubbing down the unit. They could not risk transferring any foreign elements the Sasquatch might carry into the domestic animal population. They physically had to sterilized everything.

It was dawn before they collapsed into easy chairs for a well-deserved break. A worn-out Jeff raised his tired eyes and looked over at Isabel and simply said, "Now will you marry me?"

Chapter 66

Second Lieutenant Ardan Murphy

Ardan welcomed graduation with a huge sigh of relief. He was ready to apply all this knowledge and training to actual situations. In the audience would be his parents and Isabel, who'd come all the way to America to witness his celebration. The quartet from Space Camp were also intermingled in the overcrowded bleachers, ready to celebrate.

It had only been a week earlier that Isabel had graduated from Benson Medical in Bodenia with a long internship ahead of her. The Murphys could not have been prouder of their children. When they'd brought their babies into this world, they could never have anticipated the lives the twins would chose to lead.

Angela and Mitch Murphy accepted the fact that their offspring would never make St. Delus home again. The lives their children had chosen would take them into a world that was very much larger than the lives of their island-bound parents. But so be it. A parent's job was to prepare their offspring to accept the challenges of adult life—wherever that took them. Undoubtedly, the twins were strong enough to leave the nest and fly off on their own, and Angela and Mitch were strong enough to let them go.

The West Point ceremony was moving. Seeing the hundreds of cadets marching into the arena smartly dressed in their gray uniforms and standing so proudly at attention tugged at everyone's heart. You'd have to be pretty hard not to feel pride in these young people willing to step forward to defend and protect with their very lives.

The band played an array of patriotic tunes, adding to the magnitude of the event. Graduation wasn't just the marking of the end of their formal education; it was more the pride in seeing these young cadets achieve a milestone in their quest to serve humanity. These young men and women represented the best, most prepared officers in the world.

Ardan stood there observing the crowd of well-wishers, and, yes, he *was* proud. He was proud not just of himself, but also of his fellow classmates, who he'd become so attached to in the last four years. West Point was not an easy ride. Everyone struggled. The cadets had supported each other during those tough times when doubt nagged at original goals. They'd celebrated each other's successes. And now, they stood together— army proud.

Although he couldn't pick them out, Ardan knew his family was there, making the day more special. Standing there beside his fellow classmates, he wondered if their paths would cross again. Education never ends in the military. Would he meet them again as they advanced their studies? Would they deploy together?

With the rituals complete, cheers echoed through the arena as the newly commissioned officers threw their military hats into the air. A tremendous roar accompanied the chaotic end to the graduation ceremony.

Angela teared up. She couldn't help herself. Ardan had not only adopted this new way of life, he'd also became one of America's newest citizens. He wanted to be completely committed to this land of opportunity. He truly believed America held the sincerest ideals for the betterment of humankind and had the expertise to share that with others. By making this commitment, Ardan felt he had chosen the right path.

Another round of applause erupted as the young children of the attending families swarmed the field to claim the treasured military caps left behind by the graduates. Perhaps some of these children would become the next generation of cadets. The hats were a little big at this point—time would correct that. For now, the headgear gave the impish youngsters an endearing quality as they posed for pictures with hats that covered half their faces.

⟳⟳⟳

Knowing they would not find each other until after the ceremony, the Murphys had arranged to meet "the quartet" at the Crow's Nest for a celebration dinner. This was about to become a real experience for Mitch and Angela—meeting Ardan's colleagues from Space Camp. They'd heard the milder versions of the foursome's antics. Ardan wondered if they could handle the face-to-face onslaught.

"Goose." Wolfman waved his arm in the air. "We're over here."

"Mom, Dad. I see the fellas—over there by the windows." Ardan beamed. He was the last to graduate. Although they'd attended each other's graduations, distance would probably keep future reunions to a minimum. There's always facetime and twitter, right?

"Guys, these are my parents and my twin, Isabel." Ardan was pleased to acquaint two such important entities in his life with each other. Turning to his family, he continued with the introductions. "The big guy is Martin Maki, an authentic Viking from Minnesota. We call him Wolfman. Sticks, the skinny one, is Frank Gorman from Pennsylvania. He's the brains of the outfit. And last, but not least, is Sweet Cakes. We refer to him as 'our Casanova from France'—Victor Beaumont III. Vic"—Ardan gave his friend a smile—"my sister's already got a fella, so don't get any ideas, just saying."

"If only." Vic laughed. "If only I could have gotten there first. Bonjour, Isabel. I'm not nearly as bad as these guys let on." In the French tradition, he raised her hand for a well-executed kiss.

"You are the charmer—just as Ardan described you." Isabel blushed. "So what are you guys doing these days?"

"I went into law," Marty jumped right in. "Out of necessity. I saw how these guys were messing up their lives and decided I'd better figure a way to bail 'em out. I'm the responsible one." He grinned.

"In a pig's eye." Sticks shook his head. "Truth of the matter, it's a family thing. Everyone in his family's a lawyer. He wouldn't have dared not."

"I even hear they would have disowned him if he didn't follow in the family business," Vic said.

"I beg to differ ol' man. They were hoping he wouldn't so they *could* disown him." Ardan laughed.

"OK. At ease. Now's as good a time as ever, I have a confession of sorts. You guys were right about me. I will be the first to get married. I'm no longer hunting for the right girl. I found her. I know. You warned me. Oh, but, guys, her name's Monique, and there's just something about her. I couldn't let her get away. Hope to see you at the wedding."

"I knew it. Am I good at predicting things or what? Congrats, fella. Aw bummer, now we gotta get you a new title." Marty was all smiles. "Something like, say … Stripes, for our prisoner of love."

"Could it be? Our Casanova off the market? I'll believe it when the ring is securely on your finger," Ardan added.

"If everyone will follow me, your table is ready," the hostess said.

"If I may, charming lady," Vic said as he wove Angela's arm over his own and followed the hostess, weaving in and out of the busy patrons, who were already filling their plates from the amazing array of features displayed on the lavish buffet. Continuing with his grand gestures, Vic pulled out Angela's chair and gave a simple but impressive bow as he seated her at the middle of the table, where she would be the center of attention.

Over a dinner from the seafood buffet, Ardan started to put the pieces together while thinking of the professions they'd each had chosen. Marty was a lawyer with aspirations of becoming a judge—judicial. Vic was going for an advanced degree in investment accounting—finance. Frank was heavy into education and human resources. Running for the senate appeared to be in his future—legislative. Ardan had chosen to serve and protect on and above Earth—law enforcement. Then there was his good friend Archie, who might one day be governor of St. Delus—executive. And never to be forgotten was Isabel. With her interest in the medical field, world health issues could be addressed. Ardan realized he was surrounded by persons who could influence world issues in a positive way. How well would these idealistic graduates move to better the world? He was sure Met-trix was looking over his shoulder.

Words from General Flagstaff, who'd spoken at Ardan's graduation, came to him. "Align yourself with successful, motivated people. They will inspire you to do your best in meeting your own goals. By so doing, you'll find yourself an achiever as well." Ardan's friends would make their mark on the world, however large or small that mark turned out to be. He was sure of it.

Ardan was in the top 5 percent of his class, that enabled him to take classes related to the coveted flight programs as he proceeded with his mechanical engineering degree. Becoming an Army pilot was an honor Ardan would cherish forever. With graduation behind him, Ardan began training on the Valor, a version of the helicopter with the advanced tilt-rotor blades. Although a far cry from being a jet, it could reach speeds of well over three hundred miles per hour, twice the speed and range of its predecessor, and had the capacity of aerial refueling. Four well-trained crewmen could handle the multipurpose craft. The fully armed helicopter was capable of transporting up to fourteen troops, providing accurate firepower to aid ground troops, lifting and delivering heavy pieces of equipment, or quickly medevac wounded. The major difference between the helo pilot and the jet pilot was that the helicopters could not only land practically anywhere but could also get right down at ground level where live action occurs.

Ardan felt privileged when his team was selected to attend the Red Flag program at Nellis Air Base in Nevada. The exercise was geared to train military personnel in true-to-life combat experiences.

Pilots and their support staff came from a variety of allied countries. They trained and worked together as a unit in these simulated battle event. The mission was to complete the objective while flying at low altitude between mountainous terrain so as to avoid radar detection. At the same time, the pilots had to keep their eyes open for an enemy attack from above or even below—all this while flying at top speed. Getting out of the target zone was as tricky as locating the target in the first place. The mental and physical stress was an exhausting preparation for missions they hoped they would never have to experience in real life. Not one soldier ever wished for war; they trained to serve and protect innocent citizens against oppressors. All in all, the program was a valuable training tool designed to save lives.

During the Red Flag training, Ardan (the Goose) piloted one of the "eggbeaters," whose mission was to rescue a downed jet pilot—under enemy fire. The situation was so well orchestrated, the action stimulated their adrenaline, making it seem as if they were in actual combat. When the mission was successfully completed, the team received an excellence in performance award at the graduation dinner.

As the Goose sat in the situation room at the Bagram Air Base in Afghanistan, he realized how important the training he'd received at Nellis would be.

A stern-faced general stood in front of the Special Forces team pointing out the critical mission sites on the wall screen. The "situation" was for the Delta Force team to penetrate enemy territory and rescue three people being detained (polite for captured) by the Taliban—one an American contractor, one a British reporter, and a nun from Belgium. There was no report on the captives' individual physical conditions. Due to the length of time they had each been interned, however, the team had to expect their health might well be impaired. The Taliban was not known for humane treatment of its captives.

The team was briefed with the latest intel—location, guards, and on which side local sympathy lay. Playing on the screen was camera footage from a drone reconnaissance mission, giving them a visual of the town to help identify which house the hostages were in, as well as the major streets surrounding the area. Alternate plans of escape were also covered.

Each captive had been taken separately, but for some reason, over the last few days, they were being assembled in the same location. No chatter indicated an exchange of prisoners or ransom was being demanded, so intel had to consider the worst. Were they to be made some twisted military example? Probably. With the lives of these innocent people in the forefront, people whose only interest was to help give a better life to the citizens of Afghanistan, the International Security Assembly determined it was necessary to put a rescue plan in play—immediately.

The second objective was to provide asylum for the intel provider and his family of four. He was under continued suspicion and feared for his family's lives. Over the past few years, the interpreter had been a valuable asset, assisting in many successful sorties conducted by allied ground forces. Fortunately, his home was on the same side of town as the hostages. He had been alerted and would be ready.

Two choppers would go in, undermanned to accommodate room for the "packages" on return. Goose would fly the Rubber Duck, with Shades in command of the Albatross. They would go in low at the twenty-three hundred hour. Hopefully, most citizens would be asleep, or at least off the streets. The troops were to be let off at the far edge of town and make their way stealthily across the sparsely covered terrain.

In full battle armor, the two special ops teams boarded the Valor crafts and secretly slid away from Bagram Air Base in Afghanistan to the target just barely over the Pakistan border. The trip went quickly. As they approached the target, the good-natured bantering between the men ceased. Historically, joking seemed to be the go-to way of relieving stress. But now, each man focused on the task at hand and his own specific duty in accomplishing it. The helos were equipped with radar-blocking devices, enabling them to come in relatively undetected.

"This is it! Hit the ropes, men!" In a split second, the team propelled themselves down the heavy cables hanging from the craft and regrouped near a profusion of rocks. *Godspeed*, Ardan prayed. The helos flew off to the prearranged location just over the border to await the call for pickup.

"OK, men, from now on—silence. We all know what to do. Lock and load," the major whispered. With a simple hand signal, the two teams set out to rescue these benevolent people.

There were sixteen of them, slipping into town so quietly not even a dog alerted its occupants. Midway, the teams split to accomplish their separate directives.

It appeared the mission would go off like clockwork, as historians like to say. However, the clock spring sprung as soon as A-team breached the front door. An alarm went off alerting the guards. At the same precise moment, B-team strategically broke through the back door.

There was a scramble as guards grabbed for rifles. Shots were fired as one of the insurgents stormed in from a side room. The attempt to defend the complex failed in swift order, and the militants were soon contained. The guards refused to cooperate as to the prisoners whereabouts, professing they didn't understand the language.

Without waiting, assigned soldiers systematically cleared one room at a time.

"Clear."

"Clear," was repeated to coincide with their actions.

"Can't find the Mickies," one yelled. "Running out of tarmac."

"No Mickies!"

They concentrated on looking for false walls or trapdoors in the floor or ceiling.

"Bingo," one whispered as he pointed to the floor.

Verbal commands immediately transformed into a series of hand gestures. The officer indicated for one of the soldiers to raise the door after he threw the carpet aside. Motioning the other three to stand back, he tossed an area rug aside. The assigned soldier lifted the trapdoor. A volley of firepower immediately greeted their effort but not before the first soldier tossed in a stun grenade to disorient the guards. The first soldier vaulted down into the pit, his buddies right behind. Once contained, the single guard willingly gave up the keys to the holding cells.

It took but a moment for the stunned prisoners to realize they were about to be rescued. They had been praying for months, over a year in one case, for this day. They knew they still had to actually get out of wherever they were, but now they were given a chance of survival.

"How ya doin'?" the medic asked each of the prisoners. After a quick assessment, he believed they would be able to transport under their own power. That would make the escape a great deal easier and less dangerous. Each preassigned soldier took control of his charge and began the retreat process.

"Let's get the heck out of here!" the medic said, using language respectful of the presence of a woman—a nun at that.

The empty van parked on the street belonging to the insurgents was already hot-wired and fueled, ready to assist with the hostages' escape. One of the point men waved the van forward, having checked the route beforehand. Right behind the hostages, the team removing the vital computers and documents crammed into the vehicle. Two sharpshooters hung from either side while the entourage moved out.

Fitted with wireless headsets, the Goose and Shades were in constant communications with the forward team. They heard the commotion when the team hit the front door and were airborne immediately—hopefully, retrieval of the team would include hostages.

The whirligigs had been idling in Afghanistan, just across the Pakistan border, since they were not permitted to be in Pakistan without authorization. The urgency of the hostages' rescue overrode protocol. They'd let the diplomats deal with the indiscretion. Orders were orders.

Rendezvous was set for twenty minutes from the time of entry. This time, the helos would be retrieving the ops teams from a large parking lot, which was located much nearer the hostage site. No need for silence now. The mission had aroused other militants in the area, so they were prepared for the team to be coming in hot. Each operative relied on his training to enable a successful completion of the mission.

The van came into view, racing at top speed, taking fire. The Albatross was on the ground with doors flung wide open for a speedy recovery. The Rubber Duck remained airborne providing protective cover. The van slid to a stop, and the crew quickly loaded their liberated hostages into the chopper. The NATO sympathizer and his family were already in tow. Cargo secured; it lifted off.

Goose's crew remained to wait for the foot soldiers carrying the balance of the confiscated loot and picking up two hostile hostages of their own. Not wasting any time, the team arrived in double-time. Within seconds, the well-trained troops began pouring into the craft's cavity. The door gunners on the aircraft provided cover for the men as they each scrambled to safety. A quick spin around allowed the gunners to wipe clean the departure site. The bird was in the air and gone in record time.

"You're hurt, Grease Bag. Let me take a look," a medic said as he looked at his teammate's arm.

"I'm good. Check Stoker first. I think he took a couple. To the leg for sure. That right, Stok?" They were so used to calling each other by their nicknames they barely remembered each other's surnames. "Ol' Rocky here acted like a crutch and hopped him in like they were in some kinda gunnysack race or somethin'."

That's it, guys. Keep it light, the medic thought. *That's as good a medicine as what I'm handing out.*

In the end, "mission accomplished" summed it up well. Goose gave a special thanks to the Man above.

Chapter 67

Building a Sanctuary

Ardan was on leave after his third deployment and was in Park Forest, Bodenia, to attend the wedding of Isabel and Jeff Swanson. The wedding was still weeks away, but Ardan wanted to help with building the sheds and barns in the animal sanctuary that Jeff was struggling to put together. He pulled up to the clinic and made his way through its doors, receiving the official greeting by none other than Bandit himself. Bandit was the conduit that had pulled the twins into the dognapping episode.

"Aw, Bandit. You old fraud. You're just a puppy in gray fur." Ardan playfully rubbed the eager four-flusher behind his ears.

Bandit wiggled excitedly at the special attention.

"I'm guessing you must be Ardan, our Isabel's brother," Barb, the receptionist, said. "Jeff's in his office. Through the double doors; last room on the left. He's waiting. Isabel's back there somewhere, too."

"Thank you, ma'am," Ardan said respectfully.

Bandit followed Ardan like he was some sort of long-lost friend.

The first time Jeff laid eyes on Ardan was awkward. Jeff didn't know how to approach the man he'd first met as a five-year old—the child who, at the time, was there while operating in a parallel universe. How did one bring up such an oddity?

Ardan broached the ticklish situation head-on. "So, Isabel made you a believer, did she?" He laughed. "And I hear you met our friends, the Bigfoots. Do you feel blessed or cursed?"

"Isabel warned me about you. She said you don't beat around the bush," Jeff responded. "Well, I'm of the belief it is a blessing. I've been able to learn a lot from them and their ancient remedies. In return, Isabel and I have helped them make some improvements, too. Win-win."

"I'm anxious to visit them, this time in their habitat. Isabel and I never expected to see them again," Ardan said. "And you. Egad, man, we were just kids. You, you verified our existence in your world. It feels so unreal during those episodes; we've often wondered if it's actual. Could it be fantasy, vivid imagination, or what? Time travel is so strange."

"Hi, Ardan, you're not picking on my man, are you?" Isabel warned as she entered. "Glad you made it."

"Who me? Pick on Ol' Paul Bunyan here? That would be so out of character for me." He laughed. "So, what's up, Doc?"

"You'll never change." She guessed she really wouldn't want him to either. "So, you want to visit our friends? Well, it's an eye-opener. While treating Raugh's son, we've gotten to know them quite well. Cawe is due for his final checkup, so the timing is perfect. I'm really surprised at how well he's responded."

Jeff could feel the closeness the twins held for each other. What a blessing that must have been for them—considering their unique fourth-dimensional experiences. Isabel said he never called her by the same name twice and how much she had grown to love that part of him over the years. He guessed, since he was practically family, he could expect the same.

Ardan stepped back and watched the two, Jeff and Isabel, while they greeted each other. He was happy for Isabel. As teens, they'd each thought the burden of their slipping in and out of the fourth dimension would never allow for them to find a life partner. With Jeff's professional training, Ardan knew he could keep a confidence. Their secret would be safe with him.

"Let's roll, lovebirds," Ardan said. "We're wasting daylight."

⟨∞⟩

Raugh, Moof, and Wour were on alert. Their enhanced sense of smell warned of a human presence. Cautiously, they ferreted out the reason. Should it prove dangerous, they would have time to warn the rest. Things were more complicated since Jeff had started the sanctuary. The Sasquatch were becoming all the more used to humans being around and were more intrigued than ever about their unusual lifestyle. They looked forward to Jeff and Isabel's visits. The two certainly helped bridge the complicated differences between the species. With Jeff trying so hard to communicate with them, he'd won their hearts.

The Bigfoots were delighted to see that it was Jeff's van. Isabel had mentioned that Ardan might come early for the wedding and would want to visit with them. This was what they'd been waiting for.

In their unique way, Ardan and Raugh reunited. Ardan was only six foot one but was not too out of place among the giants. Jeff, at six eight, was a little closer to the massive creatures who stood over seven feet tall. The human difference no longer frightened the Sasquatch. Although the clan trusted the doctors, they were still advised to keep a low profile and to stay away from other humans.

Raugh updated Ardan on the teaching program the trio had begun in the community. The written language Raugh had created was impressive. The children all attended a form of schooling that Raugh had created. Learning had become a morale booster for the Sasquatch as they expanded their abilities to improve their lives. The medical treatment afforded them through Jeff and Isabel would enhance their lifespan immensely. The Bigfoots' future looked to be more promising than ever before.

⚬〰〰〰⚬

As he toured the acreage of Jeff's sanctuary, Ardan ran an idea across Jeff and Isabel.

"I'm here to help you—in any way I can, building barns, fence posts, whatever. But I think you might be able to get these jobs done faster with more help," Ardan said. "I believe that's where the Sasquatch could come in handy."

"Really?" Jeff asked.

"Yes. I think they can be taught. The have fingers, not paws. We know of their dexterity using tools—skinning hides, hunting. I've seen their agility climbing, swinging, jumping. And I'd be here to help translate while they're learning," he said.

"I'm not bragging, but although I can't communicate directly like you can, I've learned to talk things through by demonstrating with my hands.

It's not an exact science, but it works well, to a degree, that is," Jeff said. "You know, I like your idea. What do you think, Isabel? Would this work?"

"I'm already a believer," Isabel said. "I think the idea has merit. First, let's see what Raugh thinks. We have to ensure the tribe's safety above all else, and not just from construction accidents. We need to protect their privacy and their way of life. I wouldn't want to modernize them more than natural progression mandates."

⚬〰〰〰〰⚬

It was fascinating to see the eagerness of the various Sasquatch clans as they tackled the human's projects using human's tools. Their enthusiasm made it fun for everyone, and the manpower made an incredible difference accomplishing the various habitats needed.

The Murphy twins experienced their own reward, with this probably being their last opportunity to work together as a team. Teamwork had been a large part of the twins' lives—a team that was now to be separated as life charted their courses in different directions.

Grandpa Murphy and Uncle Hank used their connections to glean the best prices for the materials, and Mitch Murphy was able to find grant money to fast-forward the project. Jeff had expected the sanctuary's progress to be much slower. He felt it would depend solely on when he was able to set aside a few dollars here and there.

With Isabel's completion of her internship, she was in limbo while the building she was in the process of renting for her clinic was being finalized and refurbished. The free time allowed her to work on the various projects around the sanctuary. With her parents' training, she was as handy building and digging as the rest.

Jeff crowded his patients into a four-day week, giving him extra time to help over the extended weekends. The three and their Sasquatch counterparts completed the compound in record time.

When the remodeling on Isabel's clinic finished, her practice would be just down the street from Jeff's animal clinic. Her practice for human patients would be limited to office visits, compared to Jeff, who was set up for surgeries. Isabel would have to travel to the Freemont Public Hospital to perform her surgeries. Freemont was only eight miles away, so the commute was nominal.

With the biggest renovations on the two fronts nearing completion, they could take time to finalize the wedding plans. Isabel wanted a small, simple wedding. It had always been easier for her to put Ardan in the spotlight. She was more comfortable standing in the wings. This time, the focus was all on her and Jeff. Ardan would be her wingman one last time—as a groomsman to Jeff.

Isabel looked forward to sharing the happiest day of her life with family and the closest of friends. The Bigfoots would get to see pictures. Raugh and Soovy couldn't understand the big deal anyway. *Humans!* they thought. *They are so interesting.*

Chapter 68

Isabel Weds

A very nervous Isabel paced the floor. This was it. Did she know what she was getting into? Did Jeff? *Sweet Jeff. Does he really understand what it will be like marrying me?* Isabel thought.

Earlier, Jeff admitted he was worried about these time travels she had. They had been dangerous in the past. Could it be they might ever become deadly? He felt so helpless. She couldn't predict a crossing over, let alone stop it. If she were to be in one of those moments, it would be happening simultaneously in another dimension without missing a heartbeat in this one. What if she died on an excursion? Would she simply go missing in this life or have a massive heart attack? Knowing how much he worried, would she continue to confide in him? How were they to handle this? Truthfully, Jeff hoped. He always wanted her to feel comfortable enough to confide in him.

Another big problem facing the three was in keeping their parents from comparing the way the youngsters had met during the dognapping incident. Now, with the two families being united through marriage, they would certainly come in contact with each other on countless occasions.

Ardan came up with the idea of combining a couple of events. A month or so after the dognapping the twins finally visited Uncle Hank in Bodinia. While visiting Uncle Hank and his family, the twins had strayed and actually were lost when they'd attended the county fair in Freemont. With a little fast-talking, mixed with some clever inuendo, maybe they could intertwine the dog story and the fair animals. If the three could confuse their parents enough, they might be too embarrassed to keep asking for clarification. It was far-fetched, but they couldn't think of anything else remotely plausible. Double-talking would have to suffice.

Jeff howled. "My life is going to be so wild from this point forward. We'll never have a dull moment." He reached for the warmth of Isabel's hand and to feel her comforting smile. He knew that, no matter what the future held, he always wanted to go through it with Isabel at his side.

◦❈❈❈◦

Isabel was like a giddy teenager when Audrey arrived. Audrey Spencer was her best friend from college and her maid of honor. With Audrey living back in London, their time together was limited to quick visits and Zoom talks.

"Wilikers, tell me everything," Audrey said. "How did he propose? That's a long way down for that lanky hunk to get on one knee. Tell me he didn't fall over. Was it romantic?"

Isabel missed her friend's excited chattering. Audrey tended to explode with enthusiasm.

"Which time?" Isabel laughed. "The first time or the fifth time?"

"You're awful." Audrey laughed. "I knew you were a couple right from that first day you met him at summer camp. You do know what a catch he is, don't you? You're lucky some coldhearted vixen didn't snatch him up while you were trying to make up your mind."

"Yes, I do know he's a catch. I can't imagine a life without him. Now, let's get you to the dressmaker so you can get your gown fitted. My friend Margaret is already there. You'll love her. She should be finished by the time we arrive," Isabel replied. "I don't think it should take more than a simple tuck here or there. Besides, we have to get ready for the rehearsal tonight. I have someone special I want you to meet."

"A handsome bloke of my own, I hope. I'm excited already."

◦❈❈❈◦

The minister was going through his routine of the proper entry sequence for the wedding party. Isabel nervously eyed Jeff's parents going over to her mother. Hopefully, they were only exchanging niceties. *Stop*

274

it, she told herself. *Don't borrow trouble. Enjoy this special time. If they get into how we all met, well, we'll scramble it all up later.*

Isabel always looked forward to the company of Dean, Jeff's brother. Dean was Jeff's best man and a real cutup—perfect for Audrey, her maid-of-honor. Ardan was a groomsman. To round out the wedding party, Isabel chose Margaret (nee Wallis) McNabb as her bridesmaid. That was it—sweet and simple.

Margaret and Archie had been grade school sweethearts. They'd married four years ago and already had two children. This was the first time they'd taken a trip without the youngsters, and they suffered twinges of missing their little ones. Her parents, on the other hand, were thrilled with the opportunity to watch their grandbabies for more than the occasional weekend sleepover.

After the rehearsal dinner when the old folk turned in, the younger members of the bridal party slipped away for some continued celebrating. Between Archie and Dean, the evening didn't have a chance of being boring. Isabel was right. Audrey and Dean hit it off even better than expected—that is if exchanging phone numbers, sitting next to each other (closely), and engaging in secret glances meant anything.

Ardan was relieved to see his sister this happy, and Isabel was in seventh heaven. If she were any happier, she knew she'd explode. In two days, she'd be Mrs. Jeffery Swanson.

⟨∭⟩

Angela Murphy finished connecting the row of satin buttons down the back of her daughter's wedding dress. Isabel had chosen a simple off-the-shoulder satin gown with an empire waist and slightly flared skirt. Her fingertip veil was edged in Chantilly lace. Completing her attire, she wore the single strand of pearls that Jeff had given her as a wedding gift. Isabel had straightened her hair and pulled it to the top of her head in a bouffant style, allowing wisps of soft curls to trail down the sides of her beaming face.

"You are so beautiful," Angela said, holding back tears.

"Now, now, Mum," Audrey squeezed her. "Lordy, don't think of this as losing a daughter but as gaining an extra room for sewing those theater costumes." She took Angela by the hands and whirled her around under her raised arm. "This is a day for merriment."

"Indeed it is," Margaret added laughingly. "I was beginning to think you'd be stuck with her. Good thing Jeff took pity on her."

"Oh, now, Margaret"—Angela pretended to be offended—"if we'd gotten too desperate, we'd have auctioned her off on eBay."

"Hello. I'm still here," Isabel protested. "In the room. Hearing every word."

There was a knock on the door. "Are you ready? Can I come in?" Mitch Murphy was there to escort his treasure down the aisle.

This was just as hard on him as it was on Angela—seeing his little girl leave their home. Should he laugh or cry? His own marriage brought him such happiness; he couldn't deny his daughter the same. Mitch knew this was just a fleeting selfish moment of not wanting to give her up. Jeff Swanson was a great guy. And both he and Angela loved Jeff already. They were happy for Isabel. As parents, they couldn't have chosen a better match. This was perfect.

The processional music started. Jeff was nervously waiting at the other end of the aisle with Dean and Ardan at his side. Amid oohs and aahs, Margaret and Audrey slowly glided their way past the rows of well-wishers. Resplendent in their teal gowns with a simple, cascading ruffle crossing from the left shoulder and down their right hip, they glowed.

Dean couldn't take his eyes off Audrey. He was fascinated by the English beauty who was Isabel's best friend. He wondered why they hadn't run into each other sooner. Jeff was smitten with Isabel from the time she and Audrey attended summer camp. The three of them hung out regularly. Although Dean attended a different college, he was home often enough. Funny they'd never met. He'd heard about Audrey from his parents and from Jeff and Isabel. But why hadn't their paths ever crossed? Oh, the years he'd missed. Now Audrey was a continent away.

The music changed. Strains of the wedding march filled the chapel as the guests began to rise. With his face beaming with pride, Mitch looked over at his daughter. "I couldn't love you more than at this very moment. But even more, I'm proud of the woman you have become. Love you and like you, sweetheart." He drew a deep breath and squeezed her hand.

Then there she was—Jeff's long-awaited love—standing beside her father, the sun filtering around her. Slowly, she approached, one carefully placed step at a time. Their eyes met and held for just one tender moment. This was perfect. They were already bound together in heart and soul, and now, before God and everyone, they would declare their love.

The reception was filled with greetings of newly introduced guests. This was a second cousin, an uncle by friendship, or a favorite aunt. It would be near impossible to comprehend all the names. Thank goodness for pictures. Everything was moving so quickly. Isabel was afraid she would not remember each and every precious moment without the physical portrayal.

Chapter 69

Looking to the Future

Ardan was relieved in ways he wasn't expecting. He'd always tried to protect Isabel, whether at home or on one of their visits into a parallel universe. He knew Isabel was more than capable of taking care of herself. She'd proved that time and again. Maybe it was male chauvinism that he hated for her to be alone. Having Isabel married to Jeff made him as happy as it made her. His teammate had a new wingman at her side.

For Ardan, he was soon due back at the army base. But first, he wanted to make a special stop to visit with Mr. Sawyer, his old boss from the Barshire Airport. He owed so much to this man, who'd encouraged him every step of the way. His having learned to fly while still a teen was entirely due to this man's efforts. Keeping Mr. Sawyer informed of his future was almost like keeping his own father updated.

"Hey, hey. The kid's back in town," Mr. Sawyer said. "I hear you've picked up some 'fruit salad' for your chest."

"Na, that's just window decoration," Ardan replied modestly.

"Sure. Saving lives never played a part in it."

"Training and instinct," Ardan said.

"Ever had to ditch?"

"No. Never," Ardan replied. "And you? You ever have to hit the silks?"

"Once. Went down in Nam. Got lucky though. Our guys picked me up first," Sawyer said. "I appreciate the risks you helo pilots take. Saved my life. So how do you think your chances are on getting into the astronaut program? Still interested?" Mr. Sawyer changed the subject.

Neither wanted to get in depth about their experiences on the front. Soldiers rarely do.

"Indeed I am. You never know. Every time the program opens up for new applications, I'm the first one to apply," Ardan said. "You'd think the review board would accept me just to get rid of my pushing them all the time. You know, pass me on, let the other guys deal with me kinda thing. I doubt I can ever stop trying. The space program is so in my blood."

"If it's meant to be, it'll happen. Now don't go thinking that's the only thing you're suited for. I hear you've made quite a mark for yourself on those fancy whirligigs the army has. I'd give my eyetooth to ride on one of those new Valor copters. Love the tilt-rotor blade concept," Mr. Sawyer said wistfully.

"You ever get to the states and are near me, I'd sure try to pull a few strings to get you up there." Ardan smiled.

He couldn't tell his mentor that he'd be shipping out again. His unit was scheduled for another tour abroad. This time, he would get to experience the unique culture of Iraq. Although he had always believed the culture was similar to that of Afghanistan, he was advised that there were some strong differences. Ardan saw his role as being a peacemaker for the oppressed societies in the Middle East, protecting those who couldn't protect themselves against powerful mercenaries who fought for more and more control. The hatefulness of the aggressors imposing their twisted will on their own kinship was not even reasonable. He'd secretly reached out to Met-trix for insight. How do you bring extremes to the peace table? So far Met-Trix was being elusive.

As Ardan walked away, Mr. Sawyer couldn't help but have pride in the tall, young man he had grown to be. You could tell Ardan was military simply by the way he held himself—and by the respectful way he addressed people. This simple island of St. Delus had produced another citizen the islanders could point to with pride.

⟨⟩

After a short honeymoon, Isabel busied herself setting up her practice. The building was larger than she needed, but while Audrey was there for the wedding, she indicated she might be interested it opening up a rehabilitation therapy center in the other half. The talk continued as they Skyped.

"Might your setting up your practice next to mine have anything to do with a certain young man?" Isabel teased. "Someone who looks a wee bit like my Jeff? Just for comparison sake, of course."

"Isabel! You know me better than that. I'm all business. Park Forest needs a good physical therapist." She giggled, giving herself away. "He is cute, isn't he? He says he's coming to London so we can spend a little time together. Isabel, he wants to meet my parents. Can this be happening? This fast? It's so funny, and yet I feel like I've known him all my life."

"Yes, it happens, and he's a good man. What I know of Dean is that he's a man of great integrity," Isabel assured her. "Now that he's met you, I think he doesn't want you to get away. There are certain things Dean takes very seriously. He's not always the cutup he portrays when people first meet him. Frankly, I believe he's crazy about you. How about you? What's your heart saying?"

"Isabel, my heart jumps at the very thought of him. I can't have a clear thought without his face appearing. I must be going insane." Audrey smiled. Nodding, she added, "He's my Mr. Right."

The girls were already close. The possibility of being related was icing on the cake. Isabel couldn't be more pleased. This was a gift—her best friend and new brother-in-law finding they couldn't live without each other. Life couldn't get much better.

That Audrey would consider moving to Park Forest was a double blessing. Dean's parents had fallen in love with Audrey years ago when the girls were first invited to dinner. If the lovers decided to make it official, his parents were on board with the sweet girl from London who had come for an authentic Bodenian meal those many years ago. It was still a mystery to Dean, who couldn't understand how the whole family knew of this treasure, that he was just now finding her.

Dean had his degree in agriculture and talked of purchasing a farm to put his knowledge to use. He was especially interested in tackling environmental issues.

Jeff, Isabel, and Ardan had previously discussed drawing Dean into their confidence regarding the Sasquatch. With his veterinary practice, Jeff would not be able to farm the land. He wanted to partner with Dean and have him take over that part of the operation.

The idea of continuing to use the Bigfoots for the chores of maintaining the sanctuary was becoming more of a possibility with the Bigfoots' increased interest. Dean would be immensely useful in training them to farm. Enough food could be grown to maintain the animals and the Sasquatch, with a sizeable amount for marketing. The income would help maintain the sanctuary.

With the sanctuary far enough away from human traffic, the secrecy of the Bigfoots' existence could remain safe. Through the wellness trips Isabel and Jeff made to the Sasquatch habitat, Raugh, Moof, and Wour had learned a sign language of sorts in order to work with Jeff. With practice and patience, they were sure this would work.

Helping in the sanctuary was a desire Raugh had expressed earlier. He marveled at the humans' ability to transform a situation for the greater good and wanted to learn these abilities for the betterment of his kind as well. Raugh hoped, by accepting a few of the modern human ways, he would help extend the lives of the Bigfoots. Their lifespan was still far less than that of their counterparts, the humans.

Before they could approach Dean, it was becoming obvious Audrey would have to be a part of that confidence. They would never want to be a part of a husband keeping secrets from his wife. But involving yet another human came with risks. That would be just one more human who might inadvertently slip up in natural conversation and mention the existence of the Sasquatch. Would the need outweigh the risk?

⟨∞⟩

When Ardan came back from his fourth deployment, he was greeted with a letter handed to him by the base commander:

> You have been accepted into the Space Program. You are required to report to NASA Space Center in Houston, Texas by 5 November 2024.

The rest was a blur, while Ardan tried to get past the first phrase—*you have been accepted.* He threw his head back and howled. Totally unprofessional. Completely understandable. Ardan's boyhood dream was about to be fulfilled.

⊙〰〰〰〰⊙

Author's note: Again I can't predict the future. But from what I have currently found out, Ardan did make at trip to the International Space Station and is assisting in the planning and design for a manned spaceship headed to Mars. By using the information, the 2021 Rover (named Perseverance) gathered in that Mars mission, and with Ardan's knowledge of previous Martian life, the first manned trip should be much more fruitful. He will have to suggest they search for life underground in a clever way so as not to tip his hand and reveal details that would suggest his own extracurricular travels. Met-trix reconnected with Ardan to assist in the details of working with the Martians. It will be interesting to learn of the outcome—providing it is not top secret.

Audrey and Dean married and both supported the Sasquatch endeavors at the sanctuary. The sanctuary is filling with a variety of aging pets and retired exotic animals. The Sasquatch are learning to speak English with the help of Audrey. As a part of her training in helping human stroke patients recover their speaking ability, she has modified the technique to the vocal cords of the Sasquatch. That is one of the most remarkable aspects of the sanctuary's purpose. Fortunately however, the secret of these amazing creatures' existence is still kept from the rest of the world.

Jeff and Isabel have successful clinics, and Isabel is pregnant with twins. I'd like to say Isabel and Ardan have outgrown their fourth-dimensional travels, but they have not.

Ishkabibble, Mergatroid, and Bandit lived out their lives as ambassadors in Jeff's clinic.

Archie has worked his way up in the political arena on St. Delus Island and will become its governor at some point.

It has been fun to share these unusual experiences with you. Due to my advanced age, I probably won't be writing any additional stories about them. As imaginative readers, I hope you will finish the characters' lives as you see fit.

Thank you for letting the unusual twins into your reading adventures.

Love you and like you!

Carol L. Doose

Printed in the United States
by Baker & Taylor Publisher Services